The yellowbacks... classics of popular fiction

The yellowjackets or yellowbacks were a great series of bestselling adventure and crime thrillers that had its origins in the mid to late 19th century following on from the 'penny dreadfuls'. They virtually began the mass market revolution of the early 20th century with a clear standard format and imprint/series livery (what would today be called branding). Hodder & Stoughton published the yellowjackets in two main series with series run dates of: 1923-1939 and later 1949-1957.

As the tagline ('where thrillers really began') on the back cover implies, the imprint and series focused on thrillers that were the bestsellers of their time. This current reissue or retro revival if you will, brings back many of these masterpieces, now classics in their own way and extends it further by including key titles from that period that were either great crime or thriller or even general commercial fiction (including sub-genres of noir, horror, gothic, romance, westerns, etc.) influences of their time. There are some perennial favourites and many rarities either lost or not easily available being revived in the current series. Writers and characters ranged from adventure heroes like Bulldog Drummond, Allan Quatermain, Richard Hannay or the Saint through thriller grandmasters Edgar Wallace and E. Phillips Oppenheim, crime and mystery maestros like Patricia Wentworth, GK Chesterton, Agatha Christie and the Detection club, to western and swashbucklers like Zane Grey, Max Brand, Captain Blood and even romance or general fiction classics like Hermina Black, Denise Robins, Marie Corelli or Stella Morton. These were books that had storytelling at their heart and always entertained.

The yellowbacks had both hardback (with varying design elements) and paperback (which built the series look) versions with the latter still carrying the imprint 'yellowjacket'. The current reissues pay tribute to both and use an amalgam of elements from both editions while retaining the complete yellow (or 'mustard-plaster') livery with the author's name in blue beveled type with a 'simulated emboss' effect and a white outer 'outline', and the book title in black. These reissues retain the distinctive size of the original mass market paperback and follow the three main category variations—the thrillers (crime, westerns, mystery, adventure) had blue lettering for the author's name, while Romance and softer general fiction had red; and other categories like humour had green.

For more detail and a full list of titles visit https://www.hachetteindia.com/home/yellowbacks

THE MEMOIRS OF SOLAR PONS

THE MEMOIRS OF SOLAR PONS

August William Derleth (February 24, 1909 – July 4, 1971) was an American writer and anthologist. Though best remembered as the first book publisher of the writings of H. P. Lovecraft, and for his own contributions to the Cthulhu Mythos and the cosmic horror genre, as well as his founding of the publisher Arkham House (which did much to bring supernatural fiction into print in hardcover in the US that had only been readily available in the UK), Derleth was a leading American regional writer of his day, as well as prolific in several other genres, including historical fiction, poetry, detective fiction, science fiction, and biography. Derleth wrote more than 150 short stories and more than 100 books during his lifetime.

THE MEMOIRS OF SOLAR PONS

August Derleth

HODDER AND STOUGHTON
YELLOW JACKET

hachette
INDIA

The Memoirs of Solar Pons

First published in book form in 1951 by Mycroft & Moran

(Registered Name: Hachette Book Publishing India Pvt. Ltd.)
An Hachette UK Company www.hachetteindia.com

1

The texts in these editions in most cases have been reprinted as is, with minimal editorial changes and by and large no bowdlerizing for political correctness; though in some editions, a few words and phrases considered archaic, or those considered offensive now, along with archaic punctuation may have been modified in places to make the text more accessible to today's readers. The narratives, language, beliefs, social mores and/or cultural depictions, in these volumes are a reflection of their times and must be viewed as such. They may also contain certain cultural, racial and gender prejudices and stereotypes that may be outdated or clearly wrong then and wrong today; but their removal would be tantamount to claiming these prejudices never existed. The Publisher does not endorse or support those depictions or stereotypes; and these books have been made available for a discerning audience that will read it for entertainment value and a chronicle/record of popular fiction of past times.

Cover design by Priya Singh adapted from the original classic yellowjacket by Hodder & Stoughton.

Cover illustration by Ishan Trivedi.

Series note: Some of the books in the series (unless otherwise credited) may have cover or inside illustrations from the original yellowbacks or early editions, and while full restoration has been attempted, some images may be grainy or faded due to the condition of the original material. The end notes or bonus material or blurb details may have been sourced from the public domain or free use publications such as Wikipedia and attribution is hereby made also allowing similar free use reproduction from here. Sources requiring further specific attribution may write in and further detailing and/or corrections shall be made in subsequent printings/editions.

Reprint specifications may be subject to change including but not limited to finishes, paper, colour sections.

ISBN: 978-93-5731-182-3

Hachette Book Publishing India Pvt. Ltd.
4th & 5th Floors, Corporate Centre,
Plot No. 94, Sector 44, Gurugram - 122 003, India

Typeset in Electra LT STD 10/12.5 pt by Manipal Technologies Limited

Printed and bound in India by Manipal Technologies Limited

MIX
Paper from responsible sources
FSC www.fsc.org
FSC™ C043100

CONTENTS

AUGUST DERLETH
The Memoirs of Solar Pons
UTPATEL
With a foreword by ELLERY QUEEN

Foreword

NO SOPHOMORE CURSE
BY DAVID MARCUM

They say that an author has a lifetime to write his first book, and just a year or so to come up with the second. This sometimes leads to what is called "the sophomore curse", as the second book isn't always as successful or well-done as the first. This isn't true in the case of August Derleth's second collection of Solar Pons tales, *The Memoirs*.

After writing and publishing his first Solar Pons stories while a college student in the late 1920's and early 1930's, Derleth didn't produce any more of them until 1944, when one of his Pons tales was included in Ellery Queen's *The Misadventures of Sherlock Holmes*. Upon encouragement by several noted Sherlockians, Derleth then edited some of his old Pons stories, wrote some new ones, and published *In Re: Sherlock Holmes* the next year. He was promptly challenged by the Conan Doyle Estate, who resented anyone setting a single foot into their self-defined Sherlock Holmes boundaries. They wished for the first Pons book to be withdrawn. Derleth ignored them.

Having published a whole book about Pons, Derleth found that he'd been bitten by the bug. He'd written quite a bit after those initial 1920's Pons stories, having published dozens of novels both before and after the 1945 publication of *In Re: Sherlock Holmes*. Through the late 1940's and early 1950's, he wrote a steady number of new Pons adventures, a few appearing in magazines, but most being held back for inclusion in this book. It was first published in 1951, and consisted of eleven stories. This number was chosen to reflect the eleven stories in the published version of *The Memoirs of Sherlock Holmes.* (Sherlockians know that there were originally twelve Holmes stories in *The Return*, but one of them – "The Cardboard Box" – was originally suppressed for its supposedly shocking content and then published years later.)

There was no sophomore curse with this collection. Many feel that this is Derleth's strongest Pons offering. Here we have "The Perfect Husband", with one of the earliest of the references to Sherlock Holmes that crop up in the Pons stories. "Ricoletti of the Club Foot" has the double distinction of introducing Pons's brother Bancroft, as well as being one of several that address some of Sherlock Holmes's "Untold Cases". "The Six Silver Spiders" has some very Holmes-like workmanship.

"The Circular Room" has an interesting history. Originally written as a Sherlock Holmes story, it first appeared that way in *The Baker Street Journal* (Vol. I, No. 3, 1946 – I'm the proud owner of an original copy.) It was revised as a Pons tale for this book. As a die-hard Pons and Holmes chronologicist, I'm still torn as to which chronology it should be placed. (For comparison purposes, the original Holmes version is included in Volume 8 of this new edition of *The Complete Solar Pons,* entitled *The Apocrypha of Solar Pons.*)

"The Proper Comma" is the first of several Pons stories where some of the other London Consulting Detectives are mentioned. This one refers to Dr. John Thorndyke, one of my particular favorites, who works with his friend and biographer Dr. Jervis out of 5A Kings Bench Walk, across town from Pons and Parker's digs at 7B Praed Street. (I've long been fascinated by this era, when so many great detectives were working in London after Holmes's retirement to Sussex – Thorndyke, Hercule Poirot, and Lord Peter Wimsey, to list just a few. Thorndyke's mention here isn't the first time he'll be referenced, and Poirot, among others, will show up too, although somewhat disguised.)

This book is full of possibilities for the Ponsian Chronologicist. There are some contradictions presented – which were shamefully smoothed away in a previous edition! (See below). This edition, taken from the original Mycroft & Moran texts, helps to reaffirm Derleth's initial intent.

For those meeting him for the first time, Pons is very much like Holmes. He solves crimes by using ratiocination and deduction. He plays the violin, smokes pipes, and lounges around his rooms in dressing gowns, as well as occasionally conducting chemical experiments there. His brother, Bancroft Pons, is an important fixture in the British Government, rather like Sherlock Holmes's brother, Mycroft. His landlady is Mrs. Johnson, and his closest contact at Scotland Yard is Inspector Jamison. And his friend and biographer, in the mold of Dr. John H. Watson, is Dr. Lyndon Parker.

While most of Holmes' Canonically-recorded adventures stretch from the 1870's until his retirement to Sussex in 1903, Pons operates in the post-World War I-era, with his cases extending from when he and Dr. Parker meet in 1919, after Parker has returned to England following his war service, to 1939, just before the beginning of World War II. Pons had also served in the War, in cryptography, and when the two meet, Parker is disillusioned at the England to which he has returned. However, this is quickly subsumed as the doctor's interest in his new flatmate and friend grows when he joins Pons on a series of cases that he later records.

For too long, the Solar Pons adventures have been too difficult to obtain. Fortunately, these new editions will change that. Here's how that came about.

In the late 1970's, I had been a Sherlockian for just a few years, having found Mr. Holmes in 1975. Those were the early days of the Sherlockian Golden Age that began with the publication of Nicholas Meyer's *The Seven-Per-Cent Solution* in 1974, and has continued to the present. Meyer reminded people that there were *other* manuscripts by Dr. Watson out there, still waiting to be found – hidden in attics, filed away in libraries, or suppressed by paranoid individuals for a plethora of reasons. These began to be discovered, one by one. Meyer himself subsequently published the amazing *The West End Horror* (1976), along with an explanation as to how the appearance of the first book had led to the second. Other Sherlockian adventures continued to surface – *Hellbirds* by Austin Mitchelson and Nicholas Utechin (1976), *Sherlock Holmes and the Golden Bird* by Frank Thomas (1979), and *Enter the Lion* by Sean Hodel and Michael Wright (1979), to name just a very few. The Great Sherlockian Tapestry, after consisting of mainly just sixty main fibers for so long, was about to get much heavier.

And around that time, someone with great wisdom realized that Solar Pons should be a part of that.

Pinnacle Books began reprinting the Pons adventures in late 1974, just months after the July publication date of *The Seven-Per-Cent Solution.* In the world of book publication, at least in those days when things took forever, Pinnacle certainly didn't jump on the bandwagon at the last minute to get the books immediately into print, after seeing how popular both *The Seven-Per-Cent Solution* and Sherlock Holmes were. Rather, the re-publication of the Pons books must have been planned for quite a while, and it was just their great good luck that their Pons editions appeared right around the same time as Meyer's *The Seven-Per-Cent Solution.* Planning and setup would have required a great deal of effort, as would designing the distinctive "Solar Pons" logo that they would use on both their Pons books, and later on Sherlock Holmes books by Frank Thomas. And most of all, they would have needed time to solicit the wonderful cover paintings of Solar Pons and Dr. Parker.

It was these paintings that drew me into the world of Solar Pons.

Living in a small town in eastern Tennessee, finding things related to Sherlock Holmes in the latter 1970's was difficult. My hometown had both a new and used bookstore, and I regularly scoured them looking for new titles. Strangely, several of my most treasured Sherlockian books from these years were found – not in the bookstores – but on rotating paperback racks at a local drugstore. However, it was at the new bookstore, a few weeks before my fourteenth birthday, that I happened to notice seven books lined up in a row, all featuring a man wearing an Inverness and a deerstalker.

I grabbed them, thinking I'd found a Holmesian motherlode. Instead, I saw that they were about... *Solar Pons?*

I had a limited amount of Sherlockian research material then, and I don't recall if I found anything about Mr. Pons to explain why he dressed like Sherlock Holmes. (I had quite forgotten then, although it came back to me later, that I'd first read a Pons story back in 1973 – before I'd ever truly encountered Sherlock Holmes. That story, "The Grice-Paterson Curse", was contained in an Alfred Hitchcock children's mystery anthology, and I credit how much I enjoyed it then with shaping my brain to be so appreciative when I first read about Holmes a couple of years later, in 1975. That one is still my favorite Pons story to this day.)

Those seven books haunted me, and I somehow managed to hint strongly enough to my parents about it that they ended up being birthday gifts a few weeks later – along with some other cool Holmes books. And so I started reading the Pontine Canon, as it's called – the first of countless times that I've been through it. (It's strange what the brain records. I vividly remember reading and re-reading those books frequently in an Algebra class throughout that year – particularly one story on one certain day, "The Man With the Broken Face". I was lost and behind for a lot of that year in that class, and instead of trying to catch up, I'd pull out a Pons book, which felt much more comfortable. The teacher, who later went on to be beloved and award-winning for some reason that escapes me, knew what I was doing and did nothing to pull me back. Pfui on her! But I did like reading about Pons.)

As time went on, I discovered additional Pinnacle paperbacks, featuring new Pons stories by British horror author Basil Copper. It was great to have more Pons adventures, but his weren't quite the same. Around the time I started college, I discovered that Copper had edited a complete *Omnibus* of the original Pons stories, and it was the first grown-up purchase that I made with my first real paycheck. (Many thanks to Otto Penzler and The Mysterious Bookshop!) I was thrilled to see that the stories had been arranged in chronological order, which appealed to me. (That kind of thing still does.) Little did I realize then that Copper's editing had been so controversial within the Pons community.

For it turned out that Copper had taken it upon himself to make a number of unjustified changes. For instance, he altered a lot of Derleth's spellings in the *Omnibus* edition from American to British, causing some people to become rather upset. I wasn't too vexed by that, however, as I was there for the stories.

Copper continued to write new Pons stories of his own, published in various editions. I snapped those up, too, very happy to have new visits to 7B Praed Street. Over the years, I noted with some curiosity that Copper's books came to take on a certain implied and vague aspect – just a whiff, just a tinge – that Pons was *his* and not Derleth's.

Meanwhile, the Battered Silicon Dispatch Box published several "lost" Pons items, and also a new and massive set of the complete stories, *The Original Text Solar Pons* (2000), restoring Derleth's original intentions. It was in this book that I read Peter Ruber's extensive essay explaining Copper's changes in greater depth, and the reaction to them within the Ponsian community. However, Ruber didn't mention what I found to be Copper's even more egregious sin. But first a little background...

Over the years, there have been various editions of the Pons books – the originals published by Derleth's Mycroft & Moran imprint, the Pinnacle paperbacks, the Copper *Omnibus*, and the Battered Silicon Dispatch Box *Original Text Omnibus*. (There has also been an incomplete set of a few titles from British publisher Robson Books, Ltd.) Only a few thousand of the original Mycroft & Moran books were ever printed, and for decades, Pons was only known to a loyal group of Sherlockian enthusiasts by way of these very limited volumes. The Pinnacle books made Pons available to a whole generation of 1970's Sherlockians – such as me – that would have never had a chance to meet him otherwise if he'd only remained in the hard-to-find original editions.

As time has passed, however, even these Pinnacle books have become rare and quite expensive. For modern readers who have heard of Pons and are interested in learning more about him, or for those of us who are Pons enthusiasts who wish to introduce him to the larger world, it's been quite difficult, as all editions of his adventures are now quite rare and expensive, unless one is stumbled upon by accident. The Mycroft & Moran books can be purchased online, usually for a substantial investment of money, and the Copper and Battered Silicon Dispatch Box *Omnibi* were always expensive and hard to come by, and now it's only worse. Finally, with these new publications, the Solar

Pons books will be available for everyone in easily found and affordable editions. With this, it's hoped that a new wave of Pons interest will spread, particularly within the Sherlockian community which will so appreciate him.

In 2014, my friend and Pons Scholar Bob Byrne floated the idea of having an issue of his online journal, *The Solar Pons Gazette*, contain new Pons stories. Having already written some Sherlock Holmes adventures, I was intrigued, and sat down and wrote a Pons tale – possibly almost as fast as Derleth had written his first Pons story in 1928. It was so much fun that I quickly wrote two more. After that, I pestered Bob for a while, saying that he should explore having the stories published in a real book. (I choose real books every time – none of those ephemeral e-blip books that can disappear in a blink for me!) When that didn't happen, I became more ambitious. Bob put me in touch with Tracy Heron of The August Derleth Society, and he in turn told me how to reach Danielle Hackett, August Derleth's granddaughter. I made my case to be allowed to write a new collection of Pons stories, as authorized by the Estate, and amazingly, I received permission. I introduced Danielle (in this modern email way of meeting people) to Derick Belanger, and then set about writing some more stories, enough to make a whole book. Amazingly, the first new authorized Pons book in decades, *The Papers of Solar Pons*, was published in 2017.

But that started me thinking...

Realizing that this new book had the possibility to reawaken interest in Pons, or spread the word to those who didn't know about him, I wondered if the original volumes could be reprinted. After all, interest in Sherlock Holmes around the world is at an all-time high, getting the word out by way of the internet has never been easier, and shifts in the publishing paradigm mean that the old ways of grinding through the process for several years before a book appears no longer apply.

The Derleth Estate was very happy with the plan. Now came the hard part.

Being fully aware of the controversy surrounding Copper's *Omnibus* edition, it was evident that that new editions had to be from Derleth's original Mycroft & Moran volumes – for after all, he had edited and approved those himself. Thankfully, modern technology allows for these books to be converted to electronic files with only a moderate amount of pain and toil.

I had several friends, upon hearing of this project, who very graciously offered to help me to "re-type" the original books. I can assure you that, if these books had needed to be re-typed from scratch, there would have been no new editions – at least not as provided by me. Instead, I took a copy of each of the original Mycroft & Moran Pons books, of which I am a very happy and proud owner, and scanned them, converting them all into electronic files. So far so good – that only took several hours of standing at a copy machine, flipping the pages of the books one at a time, and hitting the green button. (And sometimes re-doing it if a scanned page had a gremlin or two.)

After that, I used a text conversion software to turn the scans into a Word document. That raw text then had to be converted into another, more easily fixed, Word document. Then came the actual fixing. Early on, it was decided to try and make the new editions look as much like the originals as possible. Therefore, many inconsistent things that niggled me as an editor-type remain in the finished product, because they were that way in the originals. For instance, Derleth's punctuation improved quite a bit from his early books to the latter – but it was very tempting to start fixing his punctuation in the earlier books. If you see something that looks not-quite-right, chances are it was that way in the original books.

There were times that a letter or a note, as quoted in a story, would be indented, while on other occasions it would simply be a part of the paragraph. I wanted to set up all of those letters and notes in a consistent way throughout the various books, but instead I kept them as they had appeared in the original editions, no matter how much the style varied from story to story. Finally, some of the racial stereotyping from those stories would not be written that way today. However, these are historical documents of sorts, and as such, they are presented as written, with the understanding that times have changed, and hopefully we have a greater awareness now than before.

Since the early 1980's, whenever I've re-read the Pons stories – and I've done so many times – it's been by way of the Copper *Omnibus* editions. I enjoyed having them all in one place in two matching handsome and heavy books, and I was very pleased that they were rearranged for reading in chronological order. The fixing of British-versus-American spelling didn't bother me a bit. This time, as part of the process to prepare the converted-to-text files, I was reading the stories as they had originally appeared, in the order that they had been published in the original volumes. I hadn't done it that way for years. The conversion process captures everything, and that means some items do have to be corrected. For instance, when setting up for printing, original books from the old days often *split* words at the end of a line with hyphens, whereas modern computer programs *wrap* the text, allowing for hyphens to be ignored. When converting the text of the original books, the program picked up every one of those end-of-line hyphens and split words, and they all had to be found and removed. Likewise, the text-conversion program ignores words that are italicized in the original, and these each have to be relocated and re-italicized. (However, in some cases, Derleth himself was inconsistent, italicizing a word, such as a book title or the name of a ship, at one point in a story, and not at a later point. That had to be verified too.)

I have long been a chronologicist, organizing all of the thousands of traditional Sherlock Holmes stories that I've collected and read into a massive Holmes Chronology, breaking various adventures (book, story, chapter, and paragraph) down into year, month, day, and even hour to form a *complete* life of Holmes, from birth to death, covering both the Holmes Canon and traditional pastiches. It was inevitable that I would do the same with Pons. For several decades, I've had a satisfying Pons Chronology as well, based on research by various individuals, and largely on Copper's arrangement of the stories within his *Omnibus* – with a few disagreements. By re-reading the original stories in their original form, for the first time in years, I realized that, in addition to changing spelling, Copper had committed – as referred to earlier – a far bigger sin.

I discovered as I re-read the original stories for this project that a number of them weren't matching up with my long-established Pons Chronology, based a great deal upon Copper's arrangement in his *Omnibus*. Some of the stories from the originals would give a specific date that would be a whole decade different from where I had placed the story in my own chronology. A quick check against Copper's *Omnibus* revealed that he had actually changed these dates in his revisions, sometimes shifting from the 1920's to the 1930's, a whole decade, in order to place the story where he thought that it ought to go. Worse, he sometimes eliminated a whole sentence from an original story if it contradicted his placement of that story within his *Omnibus*.

As a chronologist, I was horrified and sickened. This affront wasn't mentioned in Ruber's 2000 essay explaining why Ponsians were irritated with Copper. I can't believe that this wasn't noticed before.

There has always been ample material for the chronologist with the Pons books, even without these changes. Granted, the original versions, as written, open up a lot of problems and contradictions about when various stories occur that Copper smoothed out – apparently without anyone noticing. For this reason, and many others, I'm very glad and proud that the original Solar Pons adventures, as originally published by Derleth, are being presented here in these new volumes for a new generation.

Join me as we go to 7B Praed Street. *"The game is afoot!"*

David Marcum
"The Obrisset Snuffbox", PSI
(excerpted from the Belanger edition reissues)

A COLLECTION OF ATYPICAL ADVENTURES

> *"When I look over my notes on the problems which commanded the attention of my astute friend, Solar Pons, during 1922, I find myself faced with some difficulty in the selection of a typical adventure."*
>
> – Dr. Parker, "The Adventure of the Proper Comma"

Dr. Parker must have had much trouble throughout the career of Solar Pons finding a typical adventure. The collection, *The Memoirs of Solar Pons,* contains eleven adventures, none of which could be called typical, and all of which are some of the finest stories scribed by Mr. August Derleth. It is not surprising that out of the Solar Pons books, many experts (myself included) consider this collection to be the very best.

While *In Re: Sherlock Holmes* introduced us to the Solar Pons character and his ensemble cast, it is in *The Memoirs* where the characters come across as fully fleshed and fun. We also see a writer of mysteries hone his craft, improve in his storytelling, and add his own Derlethian flair to the narratives.

This is seen in the creepiness which seeps into the tales of this collection, a sign Derleth was impacted as much by Lovecraft as he was by Doyle in these tales. Many of the adventures in this collection deal with the question of sanity. Take for instance "The Adventure of the Circular Room", where the architecture of a house may provide clues as to the mental state of Pons's client, or "The Adventure of the Ricoletti of the Club Foot", in which a guard believes that he has seen a monster occupying an office chair. There is also "The Adventure of the Tottenham Werewolf", where a man suffers from lycanthropy and believes himself to be a wolf when the moon is full in the sky. Whether or not he takes his belief to the level of ripping out the throats of his fellow countrymen is a puzzle Pons must solve.

Lovecraft fans will also enjoy the "The Adventure of the Six Silver Spiders", which involves the sale of some rare occult books, including the *Necronomicon*. And there is plenty for Holmes fans to enjoy as well including "The Adventure of the Ricoletti of the Club Foot", an untold tale from the Holmesian canon, here solved by Pons. You also get "The Adventure of the Lost Locomotive", which is not quite a retelling of Doyle's apocryphal tale, "The Lost Special", but it is most certainly influenced by that story which may or may not involve Sherlock Holmes. (That's a debate for another day.)

Whether you're a fan of Doyle, Lovecraft, or you just enjoy great reads, you will not be disappointed by *The Memoirs of Solar Pons*. Enjoy!

Sincerely,

Derrick Belanger
April 2018

The Memoirs of Solar Pons

INTRODUCTION BY ELLERY QUEEN

(From the 1951 Mycroft & Moran Edition)

Dear Reader:

It is common knowledge by now that in the world of fiction the name "Ellery Queen" stands for two people: the detective-character who at the time of this writing is the protagonist of twenty-five novels, one novelette, thirty-nine short stories, and hundreds of radio plays; and the detective-author who created all these adventures and misadventures. It is equally common knowledge that in the world of real life the name "Ellery Queen" also stands for two people: Frederic Dannay and Manfred B. Lee, first cousins on their mothers' side, who have been collaborating, through thick and thin, come hell and highwater, for lo these past twenty-two years. So, in all ways, the name "Ellery Queen" is merely a coinage of the brain – a figment of our united imaginations.

Now, one of the questions we are asked most often is: Where in the world did you get the name Ellery Queen? And most of the time we answer: out of the blue. And that's about as accurate an answer as we can give. The name was invented while we were plotting and writing our first collaborative story. All we remember now is that we strove to fashion a name which possessed – or so we hoped – a marvelous mnemonic quality. Did we succeed? We must conclude that we did – for we have been told by a great many people all over the world that the name Ellery Queen, once read, seen, or heard, has never faded from their memories.

But always behind the known is the unknown: it is not common knowledge that we once experimented with two trial-balloons before we hit upon that euphonious arrangement of sounds which is now irrevocably our joint pseudonym; and these two trial-flights of fancy were, to all intents and purposes, the first forms of our present fictional name. The only record of these earlier fumblings is written on the front flyleaf of a first edition of THE GREAT DETECTIVE STORIES, edited by Willard Huntington Wright (S. S. Van Dine), and published in 1927, the year before we actually began our first novel, THE ROMAN HAT MYSTERY. This book was a birthday gift from Dannay to Lee, and the donor inscribed it as follows:

Jan. 11, 1928

To Manny,

Let's touch glasses to the eventual (and successful) realization of "James Griffen," "Wilbur See," or their successors –

Dan

Their successors, of course, were "Ellery Queen" and "Drury Lane" (first published under the author's name of "Barnaby Ross") – and we must confess that we are deeply grateful now for whatever circumstances of twenty-two years ago led to the collapse, demise, or jettisoning of such unmnemonic character-names as "James Griffen" and "Wilbur See"! Although who knows what might have resulted from so curious a concoction as "Wilbur See"...

How many other detectives of fiction have gone through a similar evolution of nomenclature? Perhaps most of them.

Surely one of the greatest of them all – the one almost universally considered The Master – had an infinitely more interesting trial-and-error period. Yes, the name of Sherlock Holmes, which seems so inevitable today, passed through various metamorphoses, was shuffled and reshuffled, before it crystallized into that peculiarly magical and satisfying combination of syllables which is now accepted as a permanent part of the English language.

The name Sherlock Holmes did not come to Sir Arthur Conan Doyle's mind in a lightning flash of inspiration. Sir Arthur had to labor over it. His first choice, according to H. Douglas Thomson on Page 139 of his MASTERS OF MYSTERY (1931), was Sherrington Hope. But it is Vincent Starrett's opinion that in this statement Mr. Thomson merely trusted to his memory and that his memory failed him. Vincent Starrett himself, relying neither on memory nor theory, claims the first form to have been Sherrinford Holmes, and substantiates this claim with a reproduction in THE PRIVATE LIFE OF SHERLOCK HOLMES (1933) of a page from Conan Doyle's old notebook. On this page "Sherrinford Holmes" can be clearly deciphered in his creator's own handwriting.

On the other hand, in A. Conan Doyle's autobiography, MEMORIES AND ADVENTURES (1924), Sir Arthur made the statement: "First it was Sherringford Holmes; then it was Sherlock Holmes." Note the additional "g" in the first name; this is unsupported by the notebook page and must be interpreted as a quirk of Doyle's memory, similar to Mr. Thomson's. For it is difficult to ignore the probability that in claiming Sherrington Hope to have been the first form, Mr. Thomson garbled Doyle's own statement about Sherrin(g) ford Holmes with Jefferson Hope, *the name of the murderer* in A STUDY IN SCARLET, the very first Holmes story. The truth is, despite the existence of Conan Doyle's notebook, we have no proof that even the notebook entry represents Doyle's earliest thinking. Some matters are irretrievably lost in the mists of memory, and perhaps it is better that way: the mysteries of origin sometimes remain more provocative if never completely disclosed.

As to the ultimate form – Sherlock Holmes – it has been said that Doyle chose the surname "Holmes" because of his great admiration for Oliver Wendell Holmes, the American essayist, poet, and physician, who, by the way, was a famous devotee of detective fiction; and "Sherlock" because Doyle once made thirty runs against a bowler of that name and thereafter had a kindly feeling for it. Both theories are apocryphal, though eagerly embraced by aficionados. It is significant that Doyle himself revealed no details whatever in his autobiography as to how the final form evolved.

To think of Sherlock Holmes by any other name is now, to quote Vincent Starrett again, paradoxically unthinkable; yet there have been more alternate names invented for Sherlock Holmes than for any other character in the entire history of literature. Indeed, Sherlock Holmes has a host of aliases – his name, literally, is legion.

The reason for this multiplicity of variants is simple: more has been written *about* Sherlock Holmes than about any other character in fiction, and more has been written about Holmes *by others* than by Doyle himself. The numerous pastiches, parodies, and burlesques of Sherlock Holmes have given birth to a whole mythogenesis of reasonable and unreasonable facsimiles, both of the character and the name. As a general rule, the writers of pastiches have retained the sacred and inviolate form – Sherlock Holmes – and rightfully, because a pastiche is a serious and sincere imitation in the exact manner of the original. But writers of parodies and burlesques, which are humorous or satirical take-offs, have had no such reverent scruples. They usually strive for the weirdest possible distortions, and it must be admitted that many highly ingenious travesties of the name have been conceived. Fortunately or unfortunately, depending on how much of a purist one is, the name Sherlock Holmes is peculiarly susceptible to the twistings and misshapenings of burlesque-minded idolators.

Here is a list, in alphabetical order, of Sherlock Holmes's appellative disguises. We do not pretend it is complete – there may be many variants we have overlooked or do not know about; and we have omitted listing all parodies and pastiches in which the detective's name is used in its pristine Doylesque state, without distortion of any kind. But the compilation which follows is the only definitive directory now in print, and as such may have its canonical and conanical uses:

Sherlock Abodes

In *Publishers Take Notice*, by Bob Higgins. "The Wisconsin Octopus" (Madison, Wisconsin, January 1946). Other detective names parodied: Ellery Presidentswife, Perry Bricklayer, Sam Shovel, Nero Coyote.

Fetlock Bones

In *The Pekinese of the Basketvilles*, a radio play broadcast April 9, 1944 by CBS, with Fred Allen in the role of Fetlock Bones, the brother-in-law of Sherlock Holmes. Watson's name: Dr. Potson.

Thinlock Bones

In *The Adventure of the Table Foot*, by Zero (Allan Ramsay). "The Bohemian" (London, January 1894). Watson's name: Whatsoname.

Warlock Bones

In *The Adventure of the Diamond Necklace*, by George F. Forrest. MISFITS: A BOOK OF PARODIES (Oxford, 1905). Watson's name: Goswell.

Sherlock Cohen

In *Cohen the Detective*, a radio play broadcast July 11, 1943 by WJZ (New York). Watson's name: Wasserman.

Oilock Combs

In *More Adventures of Oilock Combs: The Succored Beauty*, by William B. Kahn. "The Smart Set" (New York, circa 1905). Watson's name: Spotson.

Herlock Domes

A character in the October 1944 issue of "Supersnipe Comics."

Fu-erh-mo-hsi

The name sometimes used for Sherlock Holmes by Chinese detective-story writers. He is invariably treated as a great popular hero who wages deadly combat with ghosts, fox-women, tiger-men, and other supernatural horrors so dear to the heart of the Chinese people.

The Great Detective

In *Maddened by Mystery; or, The Defective Detective*, by Stephen Leacock. NONSENSE NOVELS (London and New York, 1911).

Also in five parodies by Richard Mallett, which appeared in "Punch" (London, 1934, 1935). Never collected in book form.

The Great Detective

In *An Irreducible Detective Story*, by Stephen Leacock. FURTHER FOOLISHNESS (New York, 1916; London, 1917).

H-LM-S

In *The Adventure of the Stolen Doormat*, by Allen Upward. THE WONDERFUL CAREER OF EBENEZER LOBB (London, 1900).

Hawgshaw

A take-off on Hawkshaw (see below) – in other words, a parody of a parody. Hawgshaw is, of course, a pig, and he and his Watson, called "Cully," have appeared in Walt Kelly's comic strip, Pogo.

Hawkshaw

Famous in a series of paperbacks, on the stage, and in a comic strip drawn by Gus Mager in the late 1910s and early 1920s; the comic-strip Dr. Watson was called "Colonel." All the American versions of Hawkshaw were undoubtedly patterned after Sherlock Holmes, but the original Hawkshaw had his origin in E. L. A. Brisebarre's and Eugene Nus's two-part police drama, LA ROUTE A MLLUN and LE RETOUR DE BREST (circa 1862, a quarter of a century before the birth of Sherlock Holmes), and in Tom Taylor's adaptation in English, known as THE TICKET-OF-LEAVE MAN (1863).

Picklock Holes

In eight parodies which first appeared in "Punch" (London, 1893, 1894), signed by "Cunnin Toil"; collected in book form as THE ADVENTURES OF PICKLOCK HOLES (London, 1901), by R. C. Lehmann.

Hemlock Holmes

In THE ADVENTURE OF THE ELEVEN CUFF-BUTTONS (New York, 1918), by James Francis Thierry. Hemlock Holmes triumphs over Inspector Letstrayed.

Loufock Holmes

In *Les Aventures de Loufock Holmes* (circa 1895), by Cami. Mentioned in Regis Messac's LE "DETECTIVE NOVEL" ET L'IN-FLUENCE DE LA PENSkE SCIENTIFIQUE (Paris, 1929).

Raffles Holmes

In nine "remarkable adventures" by John Kendrick Bangs. R. HOLMES & Co. (New York, 1906).

Sherloc Holmes

In two books by "Detective," printed in Armenian. ABDUL HAMID AND SHERLOC HOLMES (Constantinople, 1911) and EN-VER, TALEAT, JEMAL AND SHERLOC HOLMES (Constantinople, 1920).

Sherlock Holmes, Jr.

The hero of a color-comic series which appeared in the Sunday supplements of many American newspapers between 1911 and 1914, drawn by Sidney Smith, creator of *The Gumps*.

Sherlok Holmes

In LA CAPTURA DE RAFFLES, 0 EL TRIUNFO DE SHERLOK HOLMES (Barcelona, 1912), a five-act melodrama, by Luis Milla and G. X. Roura. First presented at the Teatro Moderno, Barcelona, Spain, November 29, 1908.

Shirley Holmes

In THE ADVENTURE OF THE QUEEN BEE, by Frederic Arnold Kummer and Basil Mitchell, based on the London stage play, THE HOLMESES OF BAKER STREET, by Basil Mitchell. The prose version appeared as a four-part serial in "Mystery" (New York, July, August, September, October, 1933) but has never been published in book form.

Also in *The Canterbury Cathedral Murder*, by Frederic Arnold Kummer and Basil Mitchell. "Mystery" (New York, December, 1933). Shirley Holmes is the only feminine facsimile of the great Sherlock. Watson's name: Joan Watson.

Sir Sherlock Holmes

In four adventures by Cornelis Veth. DE ALLERLAATSTE AVONTUREN VAN SIR SHERLOCK HOLMES (Leiden, Netherlands, 1912).

F. H. A. Homes

A character in a radio play broadcast May 6, 1943, as part of the Rudy Vallee show, with Basil Rathbone in the ratiocinative role.

Padlock Homes

A series-character in "Speed Comics." Watson's name: Dr. Watsis.

Sherlock Homes

In 1949 The City Planning Commission of Grants Pass, Oregon, approved realtor G. C. Sherlock's request to name his new building development Sherlock Homes. The main street was christened Watson Drive.

Shylock Homes

In eight parodies which were syndicated in U. S. newspapers in 1903, under the general title of *Shylock Homes: His Posthumous Memoirs*, by John Kendrick Bangs. Never collected in book form.

Purlock Hone

In *Our Mr. Smith*, part of the Introduction to THE REVELATIONS OF INSPECTOR MORGAN, by

Oswald Crawfurd. Appears only in the U. S. edition (New York, 1907).

Sheerluck Hums

A series of burlesques by Larry Yust, son of Walter Yust, editor of the ENCYCLOPIEDIA BRITANNICA. Young Yust began writing these "adventures" when he was 11 years old; he is now about 17. They appeared in his own privately-printed journal, "Hullabaloo" (Winnetka, Illinois).

Shamrock Jolnes

In *The Sleuths* and *The Adventures of Shamrock Jolnes*, by O. Henry (William Sydney Porter). SIXES AND SEVENS (Garden City, New York, 1911). The first separate edition of THE SLEUTHS is now one of the scarcest of all O. Henry titles. The book is 2 1/8 inches wide, 2 7/8 inches high, and 1/16 of an inch thick; it was issued in 1914 as one of "The World's Best Short Stories now presented with Egyptienne 'Straights' Cigarettes, Piccadilly Little Cigars, and Sovereign Cigarettes – One Story accompanying each package." Watson's name: Whatsup.

Also in *The Detective Detector*, by O. Henry. WAIFS AND STRAYS (Garden City, New York, 1917).

Hamhock Jones

The dog-protagonist of a still unpublished series of short stories, by Nelson Bridwell. Some of the tales are *A Study in Starlet*, *The Sign of the Bear*, and *A Sandal in Virginia*. Watson's name: Dr. Possum.

Hemlock Jones

In *The Stolen Cigar Case*, by (Francis) Bret Harte. CONDENSED NOVELS: SECOND SERIES (London and Boston, 1902).

Neckyoke Jones

The title of a column in "The American Cattle Producers" (Denver, Colorado).

Pharaoh Jones

The name by which Sherlock Holmes is disguised in A. Conan Doyle's *The Disappearance of Lady Frances Carfax*. CHALLENGE TO THE READER (New York, 1938), edited by Ellery Queen.

Sherlock Jones, Jr.

A character who has appeared in television, with Jimmy Savo in the role.

Sherlaw Kombs

In *Detective Stories Gone Wrong: The Adventures of Sherlaw Kombs*, signed by the pseudonym, Luke Sharp. "The Idler Magazine" (London and New York, May 1892). Retitled *The Great Pegram Mystery*, and included in THE FACE AND THE MASK (London, 1894; New York, 1895), by Robert Barr. Watson's name: Whatson.

Sherlock Monk

A series-character in the comic magazine called "Funny Animals."

Mr. Mycroft

Sherlock Holmes's alias in three detective novels by H. F. Heard. A TASTE FOR HONEY (New York, 1941). REPLY PAID (New York, 1942). THE NOTCHED HAIRPIN (New York, 1949).

Sheerluck Ohms

In no less than twenty parodies by Thomas B. Dowdall, which appeared in "The Anaconda Wire" (New York, July, 1946 through May 1950). The variant names, for both Holmes and Watson, are particularly clever considering their significance in a house organ published by Anaconda Wire & Cable Co. Watson's name: Dr. Watts Ion. Ohms's "arch-adversary" is Professor Morey Vasive.

Sherlock Ol-mes

The protagonist in numerous pulp-pastiches written by anonymous hacks, published in Barcelona, Spain, and distributed throughout the Spanish-language countries of the world. There are at least two series of MEMORIAS INTIMAS, the first containing 76 different titles, the second 74.

Solar Pons

In twelve adventures by August Derleth. "IN RE: SHERLOCK HOLMES" THE ADVENTURES OF SOLAR PONS (Sauk City, Wisconsin, 1945). Watson's name: Dr. Lyndon Parker.

Also in a second series of eleven stories, one of which won a special prize for the best Sherlockiana in "Ellery Queen's Mystery Magazine's" 1949 Contest, and appeared in EQMM, October 1950. THE MEMOIRS OF SOLAR PONS (Sauk City, Wisconsin, 1951).

Murdock Rose

A passing reference in The Vanishing Diamonds, by M. McDonnell Bodkin. PAUL BECK, THE RULE OF THUMB DETECTIVE (London, 1898).

Sherbet Scones

In Chapters IV and V (The Food Mystery Story) in Hugh Lofting's GUB GUB'S BOOK. (New York, 1932).

Holmlock Shears

In *Holmlock Shears Arrives Too Late*, by Maurice Leblanc. THE EXPLOITS OF ARSENE LUPIN (New York, 1907); titled in England THE SEVEN OF HEARTS (London, 1908). In U. S. reprints, titled ARSÈNE LUPIN, GENTLEMAN-BURGLAR (Chicago, 1910), the name Holmlock Shears was changed to Sherlock Holmes. The French first edition is titled ARSÈNE LUPIN, GENTLEMAN-CAMBRIOLEUR (Paris, 1907) and in this book the name is probably Herlock Sholmes.

Herlock Sholmès
Herlock Sholmes

In ARSÈNE LUPIN CONTRE HERLOCK SHOLMÈS (Paris, 1908), by Maurice Leblanc. First published in England as THE FAIR-HAIRED LADY (London, 1909), with the detective's name reverting to Holmlock Shears; reissued as ARSÈNE LUPIN VERSUS HOLMLOCK SHEARS (London, 1909); reissued again as THE ARREST OF ARSÈNE LUPIN (London, 1911). Published in the U. S. as THE BLONDE LADY (New York, 1910), with the detective named Holmlock Shears; reissued as ARSÈNE LUPIN VERSUS HERLOCK SHOLMES (Chicago, 1910); reissued again as THE CASE OF THE GOLDEN BLONDE (New York, 1946), with the detective's name changed again, this time back to Sherlock Holmes.

Also in L'AUGUILLE CREUSE (Paris, 1909), by Maurice Leblanc, with the detective named Herlock Sholmès. Published as THE HOLLOW NEEDLE (New York, 1910; London, 1911), with the detective's name reverting to Holmlock Shears.

Only a Mastermind like Sherlock Holmes himself could avoid becoming bibliographically confused by the interlocking appearances of Herlock Sholmès, Holmlock Shears, and Herlock Sholmes!

Kerlock Shomes

In *The Theft of the World's Rarest Stamp*, by E. Tudor Gross. "Stamps" (New York, September 11, 1943). Watson's name: Dr. Warsaw.

Also in *The Mystery of the 10-20-Thirt*, by E. Tudor Gross. SHERLOCKIAN STUDIES, edited by Robert A. Cutter (Jackson Heights, New York, 1947).

Herlock Soames

In *The Arsène Lepine-Herlock Soames Affair*, by S. Beach Chester. DÌNERS À DEUX: MEMOIRS OF A MAÌTRE D'HÔTEL (London, 1912). Watson's name: Dr. Watts.

Sheerluck Soames

A reference in *Automata*, by S. Fowler Wright. THE NEW GODS LEAD (London, 1932).

Sherlock Watson

In *Sherlock Watson's Last Call*, by A. F. Arnold. "The Amateur Mart" (March 1935).

Sweet are the uses of diversity – even in Sherlockian nomenclature; and one of the sweetest is August Derleth's invention of the name Solar Pons...

Unlike Conan Doyle, August Derleth did not have to twist and turn, reflect and reject, to find the perfect name for his Sherlockian scion. "There was never an alternate," Mr. Derleth confesses. "I wanted a name which, like Sherlock Holmes, had three syllables; I also wanted it to suggest, if possible, the nature of the calling." At the time the christening occurred, August was studying Latin at the University of Wisconsin. Instinctively he had hoped to retain the original initials – S. H. – but when he hit on the Latin word *pons* (meaning bridge), it struck him at once as a particularly felicitous one-syllable surname. Was not the Master the bridge between darkness and light? And that very question suggested the required two-syllable first name – Solar – the bridge of light.

Once he had evolved this classical combination – which, like all inspirations, had taken only a matter of split-seconds – August realized that the names Sherlock Holmes and Solar Pons had still another point in common. In the 1890s the name Sherlock was decidedly unusual, even in England; and surely Solar was equally out of the ordinary.

So, the die was cast. Solar Pons satisfied his creator on three counts: the number and distribution of the syllables, the inner meaning, and the similar *outré* quality. Mr. Derleth accepted Solar Pons as *le nom juste* without even troubling to seek further.

Now, meet Solar Pons, the Pride of Praed Street, in his favorite habitat – *fin de siecle* London. Join him and his ever faithful Dr. Lyndon Parker in their amazing mysteries, in their plots and counterplots, in their clashing climaxes. The gasogene, the Persian slipper, the coal scuttle full of cigars – these and other props of beloved memory are not visible, though perhaps they linger off-stage. The Master too is not visible – that is, to the naked eye. But you will feel his dynamic presence when once again you are confronted with a client "after our own heart," when once again you are smoking a "three-pipe problem," again groping your way through the "yellow fog," again hailing a "smart" hansom and flying through the ghastly, gaslit streets, again chilling to the eternal chase, again clutching at elusive clues, again trembling on the threshold of truth – "the truth that is better than indefinite doubt," the truth whose mother is imagination –

Yes, dear reader, but turn a page, and again – *the game is afoot*!

Ellery Queen

FOREWORD BY LUTHER NORRIS

To the 1975 Pinnacle Paperback Edition

One does not have to be a mystery buff to recognize that in the annals of detective lore none has been so widely imitated (and so widely abused) as the master of them all, Mr. Sherlock Holmes. This growing parade of pastiche detectives includes such outlandish names as Sherlock Abodes, Thinlock Bones, Shamrock Jones, Sheerluck Ohms, Picklock Holes, and Fu-erh-hsi (the honorable or obviously dishonorable Chinese interpretation). Anyone worth his deerstalker will, however, probably agree that perhaps the best and most widely read is Solar Pons.

August Derleth once told me that "Pons and Holmes are as alike as two peas in a pod." This may be true to some extent but it is the *difference* between Pons and Holmes that commands attention – plus the fact that the Pons stories stand up on their own merit. The very name itself, Solar Pons, shows the desire of the late Wisconsin author to show individuality. Again, the true spirit of the Holmes canon is maintained in the Pontical tales.

Holmes, as we know, is an accomplished violinist, often interrupting an investigation to attend a concert or play his violin. Among the varied "interests" of Solar Pons we find that he has an "addiction to good music of all kinds" indicating that he is apparently an auditor rather than a true performer or musicologist. Even his friend and associate, Dr. Parker, states that he has occasion to complain about Pons' "infernal scratching on the violin."

In Solar Pons we find a widely traveled man with headquarters not only in Praed Street, London, but also in Paris, Vienna, Prague, Rome, Chicago, and New York (possibly in a small, street off Madison Avenue). Sherlock Holmes, as we know, does most of his sleuthing in England and occasionally in Scotland and France and his headquarters are located only in London. This can probably be explained by the difference in times in which the two famous detectives worked and lived. Holmes is a resident of Victorian England, while Pons does his ferreting in the early twentieth century. Since Pons worked a few decades later than Holmes, he has the advantage of better transportation (if you can believe your local travel agent) and this accounts for his widely distributed residence.

It would also seem that in order to maintain seven offices and travel to and from them Solar Pons must, from sheer necessity, charge higher fees than Holmes. We can assume from the rather grubby appearance of Praed Street in comparison with Baker Street that Pons does not maintain quarters in the high-rent districts of the cities mentioned. Reimbursement for just his expenses, as in the case of Holmes, would hardly allow him to make ends meet or pass out a handful of guineas to his Irregulars instead of a shilling as Holmes does.

Another striking difference between the two detectives exists in their attitudes toward their colleagues, Drs. Watson and Parker. While Holmes and Pons both find a source of amusement in their colleagues' poor attempts at deduction, Pons is at times a little too critical of his old companion, Dr. Parker, whereas Holmes is very understanding. Pons, though, seems to have a keener sense of humor, referring to Holmes (with a twinkle in his eye) as his "illustrious predecessor" and telling Parker that he (Pons) can now retire to Sussex to keep bees since Parker has learned his methods so well. As the Agent,

Derleth, like Pons, often displayed a sly sense of humor by passing out calling cards engraved with the detective's name, London address, and private telephone number.

What August Derleth probably considered when he made comparisons between the two detectives was the very similarity of the stories themselves. A client seeks, the detective helps, the detective examines the scene of the crime, the detective investigates and, finally, the detective exposes the criminal and brings the culprit to book. Ratiocination, eh what! But though the blueprints (or should I say footprints) are the same, here again Derleth differs from Doyle. Pons has some cases, such as "The Adventure of the Blind Clairaudient," which contain a note of the supernatural while Holmes has no cases which are not "down to earth." The two written in collaboration with Mack Reynolds, "The Adventure of the Snitch in Time" and "The Adventure of the Ball Nostradamus," both of which appear in *The Science-Fictional Sherlock Holmes*, are certainly far from being down to earth and provide delightful reading for the green cheese set.

Both Holmes and Pons are authors of many monographs. Those written by Holmes deal, for the most part, with subjects related to his detective work. In the case of Solar Pons, however, we find more varied interests. "An Inquiry Into The Nan-Natal-Rains of Ponapae" and "An Examination of the Cthulhu Cult And Others" are two examples, for instance, that show that Pons has more varied interests than Holmes. Holmes, as we know, has little concern for topics not related to his "little problems."

Sir Arthur Conan Doyle, of course, was a frequent visitor to the United States, while August Derleth never set forth in London or England. This no doubt accounts for the Americanisms that occur in the stories, although my old friend, Michael Harrison, did check many of the manuscripts before they appeared in print. Like Doyle, however, Derleth grew weary at times of his role as the agent, thinking that it deterred him from more serious work. As he once said, "I can promise to do no more."

Although there are many differences between Pons and Holmes, there are also many similarities which help to show that Pons was born of Holmes. Both of the detectives had friends in the medical profession with whom they share quarters in London and who record their cases; both have brothers who possess the knack of pure deduction even better than they themselves, but because Mycroft Holmes and Bancroft Pons are not energetic enough to investigate for themselves, work for the Crown. Their methods are certainly much the same and they both have their own little band of street urchins who help them carry out their inquiries – Holmes the Baker Street Irregulars and Pons the Praed Street Irregulars.

Until now *The Memoirs of Solar Pons* has been the most difficult book in the Pontine canon to obtain – and the most sought after. Now, for a mere fraction of what the original Mycroft & Moran first edition would cost (if you can find it!), you can enjoy what I consider along with the late Vincent Starrett to be the finest collection of Solar Pons stories ever written. Ah, how I envy the new reader who has yet to meet Solar Pons of Praed Street.

Yes, the game's *always* afoot.

Luther Norris
Lord Warden of the Pontine Marsh
Praed Street Irregulars

I

THE ADVENTURE OF THE CIRCULAR ROOM

It was a wild, windy night in April of a year in the early twenties when the diabolic affair of the circular room was brought to the attention of Solar Pons. I had been engaged in compiling my notes from which these narratives of my friend's experiences are fashioned in an effort to elucidate his extraordinary methods, and this task had taken all the leisure moments of that day, for my medical practise had not yet grown to such a degree that I had no free time during the afternoon. Pons was at work on his since-published commentary, designed as a companion piece for Dr. Hans Cross's remarkable *Criminal Investigation*. He had just put his notes aside, and had reached for his violin upon the mantel, when he heard the sound of hoofbeats on the road beyond our lodgings in Praed Street.

"Who could be seeking our lodgings on such a night as this?" I asked, hoping I had correctly interpreted the slowing-up of the hoofbeats.

Pons had already stepped to the window and drawn aside the curtain, to look down to where the street-lamp shone before the building.

"A young woman of great determination, to dare such weather. Wind and rain, Parker – Oh, to be in England now that April's here! – But she is coming up the steps, and her brougham waits."

Our bell pealed insistently.

Pons stood with his head cocked a little to one side, listening. He had permitted the curtain to fall back over the window, and stood with his hands in the pockets of his dressing-gown. "Ah, Mrs. Johnson has not yet gone to bed. She has not long since put on her bedroom slippers and her robe. There she is at the door."

In a moment Mrs. Johnson's heavy footsteps came creaking up the stairs, followed by lighter steps, which, however, came with no less assurance. Mrs. Johnson knocked on our door, tried it, and opened it apologetically.

"A young lady to see you, Mr. Pons."

"Show her in, by all means, Mrs. Johnson."

Mrs. Johnson stepped back, and there walked into our quarters a firm-eyed young woman whose dark hair was molded severely about her head under a small toque of an inexpensive fur. She paused just past the threshold, her waterproof thrown back over her shoulders.

"Do sit down, Miss...?"

"Manahan."

"Miss Manahan. I trust nothing has happened to your patient?"

"So do I." She gasped. Then she smiled, and her rather severe face broke out into most attractive features. "I have heard of your methods, Mr. Pons. That is why I came to you."

"It is evident that you are a trained nurse, for your cuffs show under your jacket, and there is a small iodine stain on your finger, though there is no wound there. You have come to consult me about your patient?"

Miss Manahan sat down, having given me her waterproof to hang up. She clasped her hands, bit her lip, and looked faintly uneasy.

"I do hope I am not doing the wrong thing, Mr. Pons, but I have such a strong feeling about this that I could not put it off any longer."

"I assure you, I have every respect for a woman's intuition."

"Thank you. You make me feel more right about coming here, though I am sure I do not know what Mr. and Mrs. Davies would think if they knew."

"They need not know. But pray let us hear your story, Miss Manahan."

Thus urged, our attractive visitor composed herself, sat thinking for a moment as if to choose a point of departure, and then began. "Mr. Pons, I have been out of work for some time, and quite by accident I chanced upon an advertisement in the *Telegraph* a fortnight ago. I have it here." She took it from a little bag she carried in her pocket, and handed it to Pons, who spread it on the table so that I, too, could read it.

> "Wanted: A capable young woman with professional nursing knowledge to serve as companion for elderly lady. Applicant should be prepared against distressing circumstances. Good remuneration. Please apply to Mr. Wellman Davies, in care of this paper."

Pons handed it back without a word.

"I made application, and three days later I received a letter asking me to call at a house in Richmond, just out of London along the upper reaches of the Thames. I found the house to be of recent construction, very pleasant and rather modern, set on the shore of the river in commodious surroundings, and occupied by Mr. and Mrs. Wellman Davies, who had in their care Mr. Davies' elderly aunt, a Mrs. Lydia Thornton, who had only recently been released from an institution for mental health, and was still in an uncertain state to the extent of needing a companion with some knowledge of professional nursing.

"Mrs. Thornton proved to be a genteel lady approaching sixty years of age. She had been confined, she confided, for seven years, during which time her nephew had very kindly managed her affairs, and finally, when her condition had improved, she had been released, so that she might come to live in the house the Davies had built for her with funds which the executor of her late husband's estate allowed them at her request. My patient was very unsure of herself, still; following her husband's death, she had gone through a mental breakdown not uncommon to people of middle age; she was difficult at night, but by day, generally, she was so normal that it was hard to believe in her mental state."

"It is often so," I put in.

"Yes, and I soon discovered that she was the victim of alarming hallucinations. She was convinced, for instance, that her late husband called to her to come to him. She heard his voice in the night, and told me about it quite matter-of-factly, as if it were nothing at all strange. That, I believe, is common enough in such cases."

"Is it, Parker?" Pons looked at me.

"Yes, indeed. The woman has plainly come to accept it as part of her existence."

"Pray go on, Miss Manahan. I fancy you have something more to tell us."

"The hallucination which seems to me the strangest of the lot is one which so profoundly disturbs my patient that I fear for her mind, and I am sure she will eventually need to return to confinement. I discovered it on the second morning after I came, though I was not wholly unprepared for it; both Mr. and Mrs. Davies had very considerately and delicately told me that Mrs. Thornton might 'break out' at any time, and I must not be too distressed or alarmed, for her 'seizures' did not last long. Nevertheless, I was alarmed at Mrs. Thornton's initial 'seizure.'

"I occupy the adjoining room to Mrs. Thornton's, which is a lovely, circular room at one corner of the house, constructed to afford a view of the grounds, the summerhouse and the Thames there. On the morning in question, I had not yet risen, when I heard my patient scream; then my door was flung open, and she came into my room wide-eyed with fear, and trembling, laboring under the amazing hallucination that her room had been changed, that she was being preyed upon by outside forces – for she had gone to sleep with her bed facing the windows, as usual, and had awakened to find herself and her bed facing my room.

"I persuaded her to return to her room with me, and we found it just as I had last seen it when I left her on the previous night. I thought this a most amazing hallucination, and I found it recurrent – sometimes nightly for a while, and then not occurring for two or three days at a time. I could understand her auditory hallucination about her dead husband's calling to her, since I could believe in the psychological basis for this; but the more I considered this hallucination of hers about her room, the more puzzled I became.

"At the same time, I began to be aware of something strange in the house. I cannot describe it, Mr. Pons, but it was an impression that grew upon me. I cannot understand it, either, for I have been very well treated, not only by my patient, but also by Mr. and Mrs. Davies and their single servant, a woman who comes by the day from the vicinity. As my patient's hallucination persisted, my own impression about the strangeness of the house grew, and several times I found myself being regarded with something akin to alarm by Mr. Davies, who looked away when I saw him looking at me. This has been going on for approximately a fortnight; I am unable to put my finger on anything wrong, Mr. Pons, yet I know there is something wrong there."

She was still, expecting Pons' questions. Pons sat touching the lobe of one ear with his long, bony fingers for a few moments in silence; then he asked whether our client had correlated any facts in the matter. "Did the occurrence of your patient's outbreaks or 'seizures', as you call them, coincide with any household event apart from them?"

"I think not. It is only that on the day before her first seizure, she was visited by her sister-in-law, who said something which upset her very badly; In the early dawn of the next day she had her first outbreak."

"Ah! Has her sister-in-law visited her since then?"

"Three times, Mr. Pons."

"And afterward?"

"She had those outbreaks."

"According to your narrative, however, she also had such outbreaks on mornings which did not follow visits by her sister-in-law."

"Yes, Mr. Pons."

"Neither Mr. nor Mrs. Davies offered any explanation of these seizures?"

"No, Mr. Pons. They were very much distressed by them, and hoped that I would not mind too much, for they had looked forward to bringing Mrs. Thornton back to a normal existence, and wanted, at all costs, to avoid the necessity of sending their aunt back to the asylum."

"Do you know what form her insanity took?"

"I believe it was manic depression which came as a result of her husband's sudden and rather shocking death; this took place during her delayed climacteric. The situation is not uncommon."

Pons flashed a glance at me.

"Yes, that is right. Those years are very difficult, and any untoward shock may bring about disastrous mental breakdowns."

Pons touched his fingertips together in a characteristic gesture, and closed his eyes. "With what does Mrs. Thornton occupy herself during the day?"

"She reads, or I read to her. She plays solitaire; sometimes I play with her. Once or twice she has evinced a desire to play chess, but she always tires and is unable to finish a game."

"How does she strike you as a chess player?"

Miss Manahan was somewhat startled by the abruptness of Pons' question. "She is not a good player."

"I fancy that is in part due to her mental instability, wouldn't you say so, Parker?"

I agreed.

Pons' eyes flashed open and fixed upon Miss Manahan in a long, keen stare. "Have you yourself sought any explanation of why your patient should labor under the extraordinary delusion that her room and bed, as well as her own person, are at the mercy of malefic forces?"

"No, Mr. Pons, I have been unable to do so. My knowledge of mental cases is limited."

"What would you say of this, Parker?" asked Pons.

"It is highly unusual. In most such cases there is usually a well-hidden source for all hallucinations and illusions, and once it is discovered and exposed to the patient, the cure is often forthcoming. Mrs. Thornton's illusion is most extraordinary."

"Surely, Miss Manahan, you have your patient's case history from the institution where she was confined?"

"Certainly, Mr. Pons."

"You have studied it?"

"Of course."

"Very well. What then of her previous record?"

"In what respect?"

"Manifestly in regard to the particular hallucination to which you refer."

"There was no previous record of its occurrence."

"Ha!" exclaimed Pons, sitting upright in his chair and regarding Miss Manahan with that peculiarly benevolent expression which he always bestowed upon his clients when his interest was aroused. "Surely even insanity has a pattern, Miss Manahan?"

"There are many kinds, Mr. Pons."

"Yes, yes – but you yourself have grave doubts, is it not so?"

"Yes, it is. But, Mr. Pons, Mrs. Thornton is very convincing in her agitation. She struggles so hard not to believe in her hallucination, and each time we return to the room to find it as it was before, she breaks down in tears; that sorrow is genuine, Mr. Pons, and it is most terribly distressing. I am appalled by it; I was impelled to come here by it. I cannot understand what is happening; I admit that I have had little experience with mental cases – but, Mr Pons, if ever I saw a woman who is fighting very bravely and very hard to escape her mental prison, that woman is my patient. I admire her very much, I admire her courage, and it is heartbreaking to endure her horror and terror and her final grief, as each time she is brought to face the room unchanged in every respect."

"You have come here on your own account, then?"

"Entirely. I want so to help her, if I can, and if somehow her sister-in-law is responsible for the pattern of events, so I want to know what to do to prevent my patient's being dreadfully upset."

"What do you suggest?"

"Mr. Pons, it is Thursday, my day off. Tomorrow night Mr. and Mrs. Davies are leaving to visit some relatives in Edinburgh. If it is possible, could you come out to the house at 23 Linley Road and yourself speak to Mrs. Thornton?"

"At what time are your employers leaving?"

"They are planning to take the seven o'clock from Euston."

"Very well. We shall be at the house at approximately that hour, or as soon thereafter as possible."

Miss Manahan rose. "Thank you, Mr. Pons."

I brought her waterproof, helped her into it, and showed her to the door.

Pons was sitting in an attitude of deep contemplation when I returned.

"What did you think of the young lady, Parker?"

"Most capable and conscientious."

"With spirit, imagination, and levelheadedness, moreover. Miss Manahan clearly suspects a nasty business, and I have no doubt she is correct. Is that not a most curious hallucination of Mrs. Thornton's?"

"I have never had any clinical experience with anything even remotely similar."

Pons chuckled. "Allowing for the fact that your clinical experience is somewhat limited, I fancy that states the case well enough. What explanation could you, as a medical man, have to offer?"

"I have not seen the patient, Pons."

"Come, come – do not stand on ceremony. I am not asking you to prescribe."

"Well, then, I should say that some sudden dislocation in time or space could account for it."

"If, for instance, the sister-in-law had imparted to the patient a piece of very shocking information?"

"Possibly."

Pons closed his eyes. "And what did you make of her dead husband's voice calling to her?"

"Very common in such cases. The relation between the shock of his death and her initial collapse is very clear."

"Dear me! How insistent we all are upon simplifying even the most remote aspects of human experience! It has been well said that perhaps it is we who are insane, and the so-called insane who are sane. What a proposition! – eh, Parker? And yet, how dreadfully logical! The case of Mrs. Thornton fascinates me out of all proportion to its importance, for its evidence of the depths of depravity and despair of which the human mind is capable."

"'Depravity' is not the word."

"I beg your pardon, Parker. Let us just settle on 'decay,' then. I fear poor Mrs. Thornton is close to the brink, and our client is rightfully loath to see the poor lady go over it again. Would that more young ladies in the nursing profession were possessed of such conscience!"

The house in Richmond was indeed an attractive one, viewed as we saw it in the early twilight of the following evening. It was a building of one storey, low and rambling, with a quaint round corner crowned by a colorful turret; clearly it had been built by someone of imagination with a good sense of harmony, for even its color scheme in white and blue was pleasing to the eye. It was set, moreover, on a gentle slope toward the Thames, in spacious grounds which had been landscaped, and the summer- or tea-house Miss Manahan had described was placed in the midst of a scant grove half way between the house and the river.

Mrs. Thornton was plainly the most genteel of ladies. She was dressed in a white dress, with a few frills, and wore a velvet band about her neck to support a cameo. Her eyes were bird-like, and her appearance elfin. Pons and I were introduced to her as friends of Miss Manahan's, and the old lady seemed quite pleased to meet someone new.

For a little while Pons talked generalities in his most garrulous vein. Both Miss Manahan and Mrs. Thornton easily fell into his mood, and it was with something of a grave change in manner that Pons introduced the subject of the late Mr. Thornton.

"I understand you have lost your husband, Mrs. Thornton?"

She seemed somewhat startled, but responded readily enough. "Yes, that was eight years ago – no, nine it is now, I think. It was sudden."

"Quite a shock to you?"

"Yes, a severe shock." She smiled. "It took me some time to get over it. I am afraid we poor women are not as strong mentally as we are physically."

It was Miss Manahan who next undertook to change the subject, by making mention of her patient's sister-in-law. "I am afraid Miss Lavinia is not very kind," said Mrs. Thornton hesitantly. "If she could only know Wellman and Pauline as I know them."

"They are very kind to you, Mrs. Thornton?"

"If it had not been for them, I would still be – I would be in the asylum." She said this bravely, though with obvious effort. "When it seemed that I was improving my condition, Wellman was notified, and he would not rest until he had secured my release. He had my authority to build this little house for me, and we are all living here very cozily together. I do not know where I should be without Wellman; he has always managed my affairs, and it is distressing that my sister-in-law should say the things she does." She looked toward the window suddenly and, with an expression of dismay, cried out, "Oh, it is coming up fog!"

"We'll draw the curtains, never mind, Mrs. Thornton," said Miss Manahan reassuringly. Then she turned to Pons and asked casually whether he would like to see the house before Mrs. Thornton retired.

"If Mrs. Thornton would not mind."

"By no means, Mr. Pons. I am quite proud of it. I worked over every detail of it with Wellman when it was under construction, and it is almost like my own creation! Do you go, too, Dr. Parker; I can keep quite well by myself for so short a time!"

Thus urged, I followed Pons, whose interest, of course, was Mrs. Thornton's bedroom, the spacious chamber in the rounded corner of the house. This was, as Miss Manahan had said, a singularly attractive room, with a small bed set almost in the center, and facing toward the windows which opened upon the lawns sloping toward the river. A dressing-table stood over against the wall to the left, and to the right, immediately next to the door leading into Miss Manahan's room, stood a little case filled with books. A comfortable rocking-chair of recent manufacture, a little table, and several other chairs were distributed about the room, into which opened three doors – one to a bath jointly shared by Mrs. Thornton and Mr. and Mrs. Davies, on the left, one to Miss Manahan's room, and one into the hall that ran along the building there, separating the bedrooms from the drawing-room, dining-room, and kitchen on the side of the house facing the road.

Pons stood for a few moments in silence, gazing about the room. "This is the way the room has always been?"

"Yes, Mr. Pons."

"And when Mrs. Thornton has her seizures?"

"She describes it in various ways. She says she has awakened to find herself facing the door to the hall, with the bookcase over against the windows; or again, facing the Davies' room, with the dressing-table against the windows."

"You have never observed anything which might give her cause or reason for such hallucinations?"

"No, Mr. Pons."

"Have the Davies offered any explanation?"

"Yes. They felt that perhaps the fact that the room was unusual in that it was circular was at the bottom of her hallucination, and they offered to exchange rooms with her; but she would not hear of it."

"Ah! Why not?"

"Because she felt she must fight this out by herself."

Pons looked at me with a strange gleam in his eyes. "Surely that is remarkable insanity, is it not, Parker?"

"Most remarkable."

He smiled and began to move around the room; he looked casually at the dressing-table, the bookcase; he examined the windows and opened the door to the bath, muttering to himself as he went along. "Hm! Bath in pale green. Very neat... They have certainly given her the best view of the river," adding over his shoulder to Miss Manahan, "You will have to draw the curtains all the way, for the fog is growing thicker every minute. I can hardly make out the summerhouse." Then he got down on his knees and examined the bed and the floor, crawling around in a manner which puzzled and amused our client, for he was careless, as always, of his clothing, and he picked up all manner of lint, hairs, and the like, for only a few small rugs were laid on the floor, and the rest of it was bare, though not highly polished. He was occupied at this for some time before he rose to his feet, dusted himself, and confessed himself finished.

"There are only two bedrooms besides this, and two baths?" he asked.

"Yes, Mr. Pons."

"A drawing-room, a kitchen, a dining-room – and what else?'

"A little room for storage, and two closets, with a pantry. That is all."

"No basement?"

"Only a small cellar for fruit directly under the kitchen."

"Ah, well, I shall just look around."

So he did, much to my amazement, even descending into the small, square concrete cellar under the kitchen. When he came up again he looked extremely thoughtful and somewhat perplexed.

"We can return to Mrs. Thornton now," he said.

Upon our return, darkness having fallen, Mrs. Thornton bade us goodnight and retired to her room, accompanied by Miss Manahan. Pons lit his pipe and sat with his long legs stretched out before him, looking quizzically over at me with his keen eyes.

"Did not Mrs. Thornton strike you as a most unusual mental case?"

"Indeed she did."

"I watched you with some interest, Parker. The expressions of your features are informative. I submit you did not believe Mrs. Thornton at all deranged."

"Well, it is true her entire manner is that of one who has recovered from a mental lapse."

"Is it not, indeed! I fancy very few patients would have the courage to speak so openly and frankly of their troubles."

"Oh, some of them do nothing else."

"Ah, yes, the hypochondriacs. But you did not think Mrs. Thornton one."

"No."

"You felt that her conduct was inconsistent with her seizures? Come, is it not so?"

"Well, yes, I admit I did. But of course, the trouble with such mental cases is that the patient always seems perfectly normal, and it is difficult to tell which is the real psyche, to put it in those terms – the woman we saw or the woman she is overnight. I thought her comments about the sister-in-law most indicative."

"That it was Miss Lavinia Thornton who was at the bottom of her trouble?"

"I think there can be no doubt of it. I believe we should pay the lady a call and hear what she has to say."

"Oh, I fancy we can avoid doing so," said Pons with assurance. "I know what the lady has to say."

"Surely you have not seen her already?"

"I have had no occasion to do so. Mrs. Thornton told us," He left me to puzzle this out for myself, and went back into reflective silence, puffing at his pipe from time to time, and crossing and re-crossing his legs. He got up presently and suggested that, in view of Miss Manahan's present occupation, we might just walk about the grounds a bit.

We left the house and found that the fog had indeed grown thick. It was evident, however, that Pons wished to see the summerhouse before we returned to our lodgings, for it was directly there that he walked, with an uncanny instinct for its direction from the house. It was, like the house, of wood. but with a little stone terrace around it, and a stone flow it was not locked – indeed, it seemed to have no lock – and Pons made his way inside. Like most structures of its kind, it was obviously designed chiefly for use at lawn or garden parties, or for reposing on a summer's day, made up, as it was, of a single large room, with quaint, rustic benches and a table to match. Pons used his lantern to examine the walls and floor.

"Are those not large stone blocks, Parker?" he inquired thoughtfully.

"Yes. Though I have seen larger."

"It is a substantial floor."

I agreed that it was.

"Hm! It does not seem to you that there is anything noteworthy about it?"

"Nothing beyond the fact that it is a very workmanlike job. If ever I decide to leave Praed Street, I shall have to look up Mr. Davies' builder."

"Well, there is surely no time like the present. Perhaps Miss Manahan can find it out for us."

We returned to the house, where we found our client awaiting us amid some wonderment as to where we had gone. Pons explained that we had walked on the grounds, and then asked whether Mrs. Thornton had gone to sleep.

"Not yet, Mr. Pons."

"Ah! Would you be so good as to ask her two questions for me? Whether, if she knows the name of the builder of this house, she might be kind enough to let my friend Parker here have it? And whether her late husband's executor can easily be reached by telephone?"

Miss Manahan looked at him somewhat strangely, but immediately departed to do as he requested. She came back in a few moments with both questions answered; the builder lived in London, not very far, as it turned out, from Praed Street; and, as for the executor, he was no longer active, since her husband's estate had naturally now been turned over to her, and her nephew was taking care of it for her.

"Now there is just one more thing," said Pons. He produced from his pocket a piece of ordinary chalk. "After your patient has gone to sleep, let us just try an experiment. Take this chalk and draw a small line down any portion of the wall, across the narrow molding between wall and floor, and out onto the floor, constructing a line of approximately a foot in length, as inconspicuously as possible."

She took the chalk with an absurd expression of bafflement on her attractive features. "I am afraid your methods are quite beyond me, Mr. Pons."

"Oh, there is nothing at all mysterious about my methods, Miss Manahan, believe me. They are all too simple. We have been proceeding all along on the theory that Mrs. Thornton's tale is a fabrication born of hallucination out of her mental condition. Let us just now proceed from the opposite pole. Mrs. Thornton's tale is either true or not true; that is simple logic.

We shall have to discover the answer to the riddle ourselves, for plainly she cannot help us."

I could not help adding a question of my own. "Would it not be appropriate to learn whether or not Mrs. Thornton's sister-in-law has visited her recently?"

Miss Manahan responded at once. "It is strange that you should ask, Doctor. Miss Lavinia called this morning."

"Ah, and I fancy the result of her call was the same as before?" put in Pons.

"Yes. Mrs. Thornton was left much distressed."

"Well, I daresay we can do no more here. How long, by the way, are Mr. and Mrs. Davies planning to be gone?"

"They expect to return Sunday night."

"Capital! That will give us every opportunity of solving this little mystery. I trust your night will not be too difficult a one, Miss Manahan, but if any trouble should arise, pray do not hesitate to call on us, no matter what the hour. In any case, I hope you will send us a wire in the morning and inform us how Mrs. Thornton spent the night."

"I will do so, Mr. Pons."

We bade our client good night and made our way back to the nearest conveyance into the city. Pons was singularly silent, with a foreboding frown on his forehead, and he walked hunched up, his chin sunk into the folds of his coat.

"What do you make of it?" I asked.

"A devilish business, Parker. It goes against my grain."

"Ah, you have a theory, then?"

"On the contrary, I have the solution."

"Impossible!" I cried. "I have been with you every moment."

"Ah, yes, physically. Nothing is ever impossible with quite your vehemence, my dear fellow."

More than that he would not say.

In the morning Miss Manahan, instead of using the telegraph, came to see us in person.

She had a sorry tale to tell, for Mrs. Thornton had suffered a most difficult night. It had begun, as on other occasions, with the conviction that she heard her husband's voice calling to her, but last night there was an additional note in that the poor distraught lady had fancied her husband had begged her to leave this earthly plane and join him, and this had kept her awake for more than an hour at approximately midnight. In the early hours, everything had gone as usual: Mrs. Thornton had come into Miss Manahan's room crying that "they" had changed things again, "they" were after her, as always. When they had returned, the room had been just as it should be.

I listened attentively to Miss Manahan's recital, and when she had finished I could not prevent myself from identifying the poor woman's type of delusion. "Paranoidal delusions," I said, shaking my head. "I'm afraid it is all up with her. She will get progressively worse."

"And the chalk mark, Miss Manahan?"

"I believe it was just as I made it."

Pons chuckled delightedly. "Aha! I detect a note of hesitation in your voice, Miss Manahan. Come, come – what is it?"

"Well," she laughed nervously. "I'm afraid I am beginning to have hallucinations, too, Mr. Pons. I did think the mark was a little off kilter, but I guess I must have drawn it crookedly; I did it in a hurry, and did not want to wake my patient; but when I first saw it this morning, I did get somewhat of a surprise."

"Ah, no doubt. I fancy we shall be over in your direction tonight, Miss Manahan. Can you put us up?"

"Why – I think so."

"Expect us then. We shall arrive directly after dinner." He turned to me when she had left. "It is as I thought, Parker. We shall have to lose no time putting an end to this diabolic game."

Fog rose again, as on the previous night, when we set out for Richmond, and Pons made no secret of his elation, saying that he preferred not to be seen in the vicinity of 23 Linley Road, and generally acting in a most mysterious manner, which he said nothing whatever to explain. Nor did he volunteer any explanation to Miss Manahan; he asked at once to see her patient, the gentle Mrs. Thornton, and when the old lady came, he sat down next to her, took one of her frail hands in his, and spoke most cajolingly.

"Do you know, Mrs. Thornton, I have become most interested in your trouble. Unlike Miss Manahan, I am beginning to believe that your room actually is changed, just as you described it to Miss Manahan to be."

I thought that this blunt approach might be harmful to the patient, and was hard pressed to interfere; but I knew better, and Mrs. Thornton's reaction was one of bewildered interest, as if at first she had not understood that Miss Manahan had spoken to us of her hallucinations, and secondly, as if she were pleasantly surprised to discover someone who did not dismiss her hallucinations for what they were.

"Will you give Dr. Parker and me an opportunity to look into the matter?"

"Why, certainly, Mr. Pons." She looked hesitantly at Miss Manahan, and was reassured by the young woman's confident smile.

"Then for tonight only I want you to share Miss Manahan's room, and permit Dr. Parker and myself to occupy your own. I assure you we shall look into the matter with fairness and impartiality."

For only a moment the old lady hesitated. Then she began to tremble, biting her lip, her emotions aroused. "I am afraid – I – it's no use. It is nothing anyone else sees, or hears – nothing. Oh, Mr. Pons, if only you could!"

"Let us just see," replied Pons calmly. "Surely there is no harm in trying."

In the end, Mrs. Thornton gave in. Thereupon, Pons and I retired at once to the patient's room, though not before adjuring both the ladies to carry on for the remainder of the evening as if they were quite alone in the house.

Once in the room, Pons drew the curtains and turned up the light. He took a magnifying glass from his pocket, found the chalk mark Miss Manahan had made, and came to his knees to examine it.

"Ah, our Miss Manahan is not perfect in observation. Look here, Parker."

I took the glass and held it over the angle of the chalk line. "I submit that Miss Manahan could not have drawn that line in such a fashion. There is a clear, if fractional break, between the wall and the floor. Or let us say, rather, between the edge of the molding and the floor."

"Yes, that is all very true," I conceded, "but what is the explanation?"

"Ah, it is the obvious one, surely." He pocketed his glass, took out his penknife, opened it, and slipped its blade beneath the molding; he moved it freely about. "Does not that suggest anything to you?"

"The molding appears to be attached to the wall rather than the floor."

"Ah, well, that is very often done." He moved along the wall five feet and again passed his knife-blade between the molding and the floor. "I fancy that is the rule." He got up. "Hm! Now let us see. We shall not go to bed, of course, but let us rig up some sort of dummy to occupy Mrs. Thornton's place. I fancy we shall want to be out of sight of that bathroom door, for, unless I am greatly mistaken, it plays its own small part in this mystery."

I looked at the door. "I am in the woods, Pons. How can you possibly make such an assertion?" I strode over, opened the door, and looked into the bathroom.

Pons observed me with manifest patience. "Let us say that you make yourself comfortable on the floor behind the door as it opens. I myself will find a place behind the bed." As he spoke, he began to arrange Mrs. Thornton's bed with a roll of blanket and a pillow to simulate someone sleeping there. Having finished this, he turned out the light, crossed to the windows, and threw up the shades, together with the central window, which was the largest; this, despite the fog, he opened half way. In the adjoining room, meanwhile, the ladies were preparing for bed.

"Now, then, Parker – not a sound. Whatever you hear, say nothing; whatever happens, do nothing until I give you the word."

"If you would give me a hint, Pons..."

"We shall see devil's work tonight, Parker, unless I am much mistaken."

He said no more; so I composed myself to snatch as much sleep as possible.

Some two hours passed in absolute silence, when there came to my ears the faint sound of a whispered voice. It seemed to rise from somewhere in my immediate vicinity, and, as I listened, it increased in volume.

"Lydia! Lydia!" it cried. "Come to me. Come over. All is pain where you are. Only here will it end in joy again. Lydia! Lydia!"

A man's voice – or was it a man's voice? It had a hollow, funeral sound, and I felt my skin prickle, as if something of the fog flowing into the room through the open window had penetrated my flesh. It was horrible, it was grotesque, it was damnable.

Then I heard Pons stir, and in a moment he raised his own voice in a remarkable quavering cry that might have been Mrs. Thornton herself replying "Frank? Frank? Where are you, Frank?"

"Come over to me, Lydia. Come. It does not matter how you do it, only come. We can be happy again over here." Then the voice faded as it had come, diminishing altogether in a last whispered, "Lydia!" urgent and compelling.

Pons waited a few moments before coming quietly to my side and whispering into my ear. "I fancy that is somewhat more than an auditory illusion, is it not, Parker?"

"Good God! I begin to understand!" I answered. "It is damnable. But why – why?"

"Wait yet a little. It is far from over."

In two hours time, everything happened as before, I had dozed off and was awakened by the voice calling once again. This time Pons did not come to my side, though a low clucking sound he made after the voice had ceased assured me he had heard.

Then all was silence again, and so it remained until dawn.

It was then that I became conscious of a tremor in the floor of the room where I sat. I was about to call out to Pons when his cluck of warning stopped me. And then the entire floor began to move, slowly, almost imperceptibly. I had hardly time to assimilate this before Pons' urgent whisper reached me. "Keep behind the bathroom door." I crept backward along that weirdly moving floor, revolving slowly, soundlessly, until the dressing-table was indeed before the windows lining the east wall of that room, and the bookcase over before one door. There was now light enough in the room to see it as Mrs. Thornton must have seen it, and it took no imagination to understand how horrified and terrified the poor, stricken lady must have been at this sight, and how much more to come back into the room and find it as it should be.

As soon as the movement stopped, Pons twitched the folded blanket and pillow from the bed, gave vent to a low sobbing moan, and, hastening across the floor to the door leading into Miss Manahan's room, he opened it and slammed it shut. This accomplished, he raced silently around the room to where I crouched, one hand warningly grasping my shoulder.

On the instant, the door to the bathroom was cautiously opened, someone looked into the room, and then immediately the door was drawn noiselessly shut once more.

"So!" whispered Pons. "That is dastardly work indeed, Parker. And one alone could not do it, no!" He peered around one edge of the window nearest us. "Ha! There is the signal. Come along."

He darted to the open window, crawled out, dropped to the ground, and ran off into the now rising fog. I followed close upon his heels. Without hesitation, he ran to the summerhouse and entered it.

The rustic table had been moved aside, and in the center of the floor gaped an opening through which light flowed upward. Pons walked cat-like to the edge of the opening and looked down. I peered over his shoulder.

There below was an extraordinary sight. A man was bent at some kind of great instrument, whose shafts passed into a tunnel leading in the direction of the house we had just left, and before him, attached in some fashion to the machine at which he worked with such quiet persistence, was a perfect miniature, walls and floor, of the room we had just quitted, and, as he worked, the miniature floor slowly shifted its position, righting itself.

"Good morning, Mr. Wellman Davies," said Pons in a scornful voice. "I fancy you will have no further occasion to carry on your devil's work."

At the sound of Pons' voice, Davies whipped around. His hand reached out for a spanner which lay nearby, but Pons' hand was quicker; he showed his revolver, and Davies, a short, benevolent-looking man with pale grey eyes and a clipped moustache, whose nose showed signs of eyeglasses having been worn, hesitated, and glared at us in baffled rage.

"Come up, come up, Mr. Davies. We have yet to take your wife. How did you find your friends in Scotland?"

"In reality," said Pons in the brougham on our way back to Praed Street through the first morning sun to penetrate the night's dense yellow fog, "the problem offered of no other solution. Indeed, Mrs. Thornton, poor unsuspecting soul, told us all herself. What had Miss Lavinia, her sister-in-law, to say that would upset her? Why, could it be other than criticism of, and warnings about Mr. and Mrs. Davies? Surely not, for Mrs. Thornton said, you remember, 'If she could only know Wellman and Pauline as I know them.' Alas! poor woman!

"The fundamental problem was, of course, that of the circular room. Either it was changed, as Mrs. Thornton said, or it was not. Miss Manahan and Mrs. Thornton herself were convinced that it could be nothing but an hallucination. On the contrary, I proceeded from the assumption that something was wrong with that room, and I sought for evidence that it was so. Obviously, the walls were fixed, but the floor did not seem to be. When the space between the molding along the wall at the floor and the floor itself was manifest, it was clear that in some fashion the floor was constructed on a large turntable. I thought there might be a clue in the basement; but there was no basement beyond that concrete walled cellar. Hence I sought the summerhouse, and it was immediately apparent to my eye that the large stone blocks concealed a trapdoor. The assumption was obvious that that diabolic business was carried on from there. An accomplice was clearly indicated, and who else but Mrs. Davies? It was she who made sure that Mrs. Thornton had fled her room, and signalled her husband in the summerhouse so that he could return the room to its normal appearance, which he was enabled to do by means of that small-scale model geared to the original.

"It was Davies, of course, who imitated her dead husband's voice from the bathroom. Obviously, they did not go to Scotland, but crept back to the house to carry on their fell game, and the reason for that blind seemed inherent in Miss Manahan's story; she told us, you will remember, that Mr. Davies had begun to look at her with apprehension, as if he feared she might leave them; it was just the opposite; he realized that Miss Manahan was not obtuse, and might begin to suspect their involvement in the matter; so he and his wife absented themselves, for this purpose of establishing to Miss Manahan's knowledge that things occurred in their absence, never dreaming that Miss Manahan had already consulted us.

"And the motive for this horrible plot to drive that poor lady into hopeless insanity was surely obvious, too; Davies had had control of his aunt's money, and he did not want to relinquish that control. She was wealthy; he was not. He had already squandered some of her money on this house, and if he could succeed in so breaking down the poor lady's mental health that she could be confined once more, or in driving her to suicide by that bogus haunting of her with her husband's voice, his squandering might never be uncovered, and he would remain permanently in control of her late husband's estate, for it had been placed in her hands, and she had given it over to Davies to manage. A callous, diabolic business long premeditated. I shall see to it that Mr. and Mrs. Wellman Davies get their just deserts."

II

THE ADVENTURE OF THE PERFECT HUSBAND

"Any street in London is capable of offering an adventure in human travail," observed Solar Pons from the window at which he stood looking down into Praed Street. "It is extraordinary what a gamut of emotions the human face is capable of expressing."

"Whom do you see, Pons?" I asked.

"A prospective client, I fancy. A woman in her middle thirties, obviously in a quandary, and quite agitated. Having come this far, she is no longer so certain that she wants to go all the way. She may have chosen unwisely; her trouble would appear to be marital, if I can be permitted a long shot."

I came up beside him and looked down.

"Come, what do you say, Parker? You know my methods."

A well-dressed woman walked up past the entrance to Number Seven, turned several doors away, and walked back, once again passing the entrance, and, as before, glancing uncertainly at it. She appeared to be wringing her hands from time to time and was, clearly, as Pons had said, in her middle thirties.

"A woman of more than modest means, though not necessarily wealthy," I ventured.

A brief smile appeared on Pons' thin, eager face. "Elementary, my dear Parker. Would you not also say that she has not been too long married? Say – within three years?"

"Next you will be telling me she is having trouble with her mother-in-law who insists on spending five days of each week at her home," I said, not without asperity.

"No, I daresay she could handle her mother-in-law or her husband in any ordinary difficulty," replied Pons tranquilly. "Her marital trouble is of some less common kind. Surely the ring she removes from her finger from time to time, clenching it in her fist, only to replace it, can be none other than her wedding ring? And if she has reached her middle thirties without the need of a private inquiry into her husband's affairs, she would not be so agitated if she had been long married." He paused, leaning forward until his high brow almost touched the pane. "Ah! She has made up her mind. She is coming in."

In a few moments Mrs. Johnson ushered our visitor into our quarters.

With but a fleeting glance in my direction, she introduced herself immediately to Pons. "Mr. Solar Pons? I am Mrs. Lucy Kearton."

"My dear lady, I trust your little difficulty with your husband has not progressed to so serious a stage that you find it necessary to resume your maiden name."

"Forgive me, Mr. Pons. But I am so upset, and I have an embarrassing habit of falling back upon my Christian name. I have not been married long enough to lose the habit. It's Mrs. Robin Kearton."

Pons smiled and introduced me, assuring our visitor that she could speak freely before me. I observed that she was no sooner seated than she once again began to twist the wedding ring on her finger.

"It is odd that you should mention my husband, Mr. Pons. It is about him I came to see you. I hesitated for hours, but

I knew I must see someone who might be able to help me. You must understand, Mr. Pons, that until this time I could not in truth have uttered the most inconsequential criticism of my husband's conduct toward me. We have been married now slightly over two years, and in all honesty I must admit that he has been a perfect husband. Last night however, an extraordinary thing occurred, and I cannot quite yet credit my senses."

"Pray compose yourself, Mrs. Kearton. If I can help you, be assured I will do so. I think I should say, however, that I am not in the habit of looking into marital difficulties."

She gazed at him for a moment in manifest distress, her lower lip drawn in and caught by her teeth. "Oh, but this isn't what you might think, Mr. Pons. I am not looking for evidence for a divorce; I wouldn't dream of divorcing Robin. You see, as I told you, Robin has been a perfect husband. I wanted for nothing; he has always been as attentive to me as he was before our marriage, when first I met him almost two and a half years ago.

"Ever since our marriage, he has been punctual at all times. He is employed as an associate editor of the *Beekeeper's Journal*, with offices in Bouverie Street, and I could be sure enough of his return from the office to set the clock by him. Last night, however, he telephoned from the office that he would be detained over the supper hour. I could not guess what might be the cause of this change in his custom, but I did not ask, and he did not offer an explanation. After he had rung off, however, it occurred to me that his voice sounded strained – it seemed to me in retrospect the voice of a man who was gravely disturbed but was trying his best to prevent anyone's noticing it. Mr. Pons, the more I thought of it, the more upset I grew. Finally, I called a cab and drove around to the office.

"But before I reached it, I saw my husband walking down a street with another woman. I was so astounded that I could hardly believe what I saw; so I had the driver go around and let me off in advance of where he walked, so that I could walk toward him and assure myself that it was not, after all, he. I had plenty of time in which to examine both of them carefully as they approached me; the woman was a complete stranger to me – very dark of complexion, almost swarthy, with black hair and something of gold or imitation gold in her ears. She seemed somewhat foreign, and had mean eyes, I thought. She walked with a swagger. The man, of course, was Robin. In view of my knowledge of Robin, I could not be mistaken; I would have been quite willing to believe that I had made a mistake, but the fact is, Robin has a very noticeable wen on his left ear, and while there might be some amazing coincidence be two people who looked enough alike to be mistaken for each other, it is surely beyond the bounds even of coincidence that both should possess such a distinguishing mark.

"Mr. Pons, I put myself directly in his path. I was not angry, but I admit I was bewildered and hurt. I expected him to be embarrassed, to stop and offer some explanation. But judge if you can, my utter astonishment to have him give me a little shove and say, 'Please watch your step, Madam.' That was all.

"I was literally rooted to the spot. I could not have spoken to save my life. I looked after him, open-mouthed, I do not doubt, until he was out of sight; by the time I thought of calling a cab and following him, it was too late; they had vanished, and besides, it was beginning twilight and a fog was coming over. So I went home and waited for him.

"But he did not come until long after midnight, and I had gone to bed by that time. I tried to talk to him at once, but all he said was, 'Please, Lucy, I'm very tired, very tired.' And indeed, he sounded very tired; so, feeling confident that he would explain in the morning, I lay waiting for dawn, while he slept. This morning I asked him right out for an explanation. Mr. Pons, he denied everything. He said I must have mistaken someone else for him, that I could not have seen him where I said I saw him – in short, he treated me with a kind of severe stiffness which was utterly unlike him. Mr. Pons, I am convinced that only the most serious kind of trouble would induce my husband to deny me. He does not know I have consulted you, and I do not wish him to know, lest he think I doubt him. But I must know, so that if necessity arises I can help him."

Pons sat for what seemed a long time with his chin sunk to his breast and a frown furrowing his brow. Presently, without looking up, he asked, "Mr. Kearton has always been employed in the offices of the *Beekeeper's Journal*?"

"Ever since I knew him, Mr. Pons."

"And before that?"

"I understand he was in colonial service."

"Where?"

"Stationed in Calcutta. He returned to London about three years ago."

"A man of continent habits, I take it?"

"Yes, Mr. Pons."

"Very well, Mrs. Kearton. I shall look into the matter."

After she had taken her leave, Pons turned a quizzical eye on me. "What do you make of it, Parker?"

"Clearly a case of mistaken identity."

"What a pity you were not a police officer, Parker! You have a distressing tendency to fall back upon the easiest solution, which is always to reject the premise. No, I think we have in Mrs. Kearton a woman of intelligence, discrimination, and determination. Such a woman is not likely to make an error in a matter which is one of such manifestly vital concern to her. We must assume then, that her story is true in every particular."

"Well, then, it is the old story – a triangle."

"Surely a most singular one, if so," said Pons. "Indeed, I might almost suggest that it is too unusual to be quite probable. Here is a man of the most regular habits who is suddenly found with a woman his wife does not know, and who not only by no sign betrays his wife's identity to the other woman, but denies completely all that has taken place. We can take Mrs. Kearton's word for it that her husband is in most respects a model husband; his actions of last night and this morning, then, are profoundly out of character. Why?"

"I defer to your judgment."

"I submit that Mr. Kearton is acting to protect one of the ladies."

"Elementary," I said. "Why not both?"

"I think if you will re-examine the facts, Parker, you will discover that this is no common triangle. Mr. Kearton is acting in what he conceives to be the best interests of his home."

"Indeed, and why should he not?" I demanded. "It would be in any case the indicated course of action."

Pons chuckled. "I think we might sound out Mr. Robin Kearton." He took out his watch and looked at it. "It is just past the lunch hour, and I daresay he will be at his desk by the time we reach the offices of the *Beekeeper's Journal*. However, it would be as well if I undertook a few minor transformations, since it might give Mr. Kearton a touch of unease were he to see me in my customary garb; it is almost too much to expect that an associate editor of the *Beekeeper's Journal*, who would certainly be familiar with my illustrious prototype's famed monograph on bees, would not be likely to detect a slight resemblance. Let me see – a Homburg in place of the fore-and-aft, pince-nez, perhaps an ascot. Come, this will do."

We descended to the street, where Pons hailed a cab and gave the Bouverie Street address. Pons rode in thoughtful silence, his eyes half closed, his lean face in repose. His chin was sunk in the familiar attitude, touching his breast, which was the sign of his preoccupation with the problem of the moment. I had no hope that Mrs. Kearton's problem was other than the customary unpleasant triangle.

The offices of the *Beekeeper's Journal* were a compact suite of rooms on the second storey of a modern building. Pons had no sooner stepped across the threshold than he became a fusty bee enthusiast. He inquired after Mr. Robin Kearton, and we shortly found ourselves ushered into a small cubicle of an office, which was occupied by a man of about forty years of age.

He had got up at our entrance and stood, I saw, somewhat shorter than Pons, almost by a head, which made him of medium height. He was neatly dressed, but his cravat was askew, and his hair dishevelled. He was not ill-favored in looks, with sharp grey eyes, a thin-lipped mouth, and a Roman nose. He seemed somewhat nervous.

"What can I do for you, gentlemen?" he inquired in a rasping voice.

Pons introduced himself as a beekeeper, and me as his neighbor. He went on to say that he was in search of an article entitled, *The Role of the Queen in the Swarm*; he was under the impression that it had been published in the *Beekeeper's Journal*, but could not find it. A friend had mentioned Mr. Kearton's name – perhaps Mr. Kearton could help.

"I'm afraid you have come in vain, sir," replied Kearton. "No such article has appeared in our periodical at any time during the past four years."

Pons affected disappointment. "I shall have to look elsewhere, then. I am sorry to have troubled you."

"Not at all, sir. If we can be of service, do not hesitate to call on us."

Though he spoke earnestly, it was patent that Kearton was not anxious to detain us. Thanking him, Pons made his way from the building; in every gesture and mannerism, he was the picture of what he pretended to represent. Once outside, he did not call a cab, but set out on foot, his expression one of cogent thought. He did not speak until several minutes and several doors had been passed.

"What did you make of him, Parker?" he asked at last.

"He appeared to be somewhat agitated and preoccupied," I ventured.

"Yes, yes – so much was immediately apparent. And to such a degree that he seemed unable to remember that the article about which I made inquiry was published in the *Journal* seven months ago. What else?"

"I fear that nothing else of significance was evident to me."

"Indeed! For my part, I thought it obvious that he has not always been employed in this kind of position. His hands indicated that they had at one time been quite severely calloused. Yet he was presumably in 'colonial service,' according to his wife. Surely that is ambiguous, is it not? One hardly conceives that someone in 'colonial service' should be doing menial work. More likely he was employed in some capacity other than that which his wife assumes him to have been; we are not told that these were his words. Very well. He was employed in Calcutta at some occupation rougher than his present one. A man of some sensibilities, so much is clear. His return to London is followed by his courtship of and marriage to the lady who is now his wife. She maintains that he has been a 'perfect husband,' to use her own words. Now, then, either she is right or she is not."

"She could have been deceived."

"You think him a man who could readily deceive his wife?"

"A woman in love," I said, "and later in life, at that..."

Pons smiled. "Have you ever tried to deceive a woman for any length of time, Parker? I daresay you would not find it so easy as to justify your glib assumption. No, I think Mrs. Kearton has basis for her statement. He was in every respect a perfect husband; yet he did something last night which was grotesquely out of character. We are left to assume that if he reflects for her the same feelings she reflects for him, he was compelled to take the course he did in order to protect her from some knowledge he believed must be inimical to her or to both of them."

"A past robbery, perhaps – or murder?"

"Dear me!" exclaimed Pons, smiling wryly. "Those are harsh words, Parker. I should hardly have thought him capable of either. No, I fancy it is something a little more complicated. I should like at the moment to have a look at Mr. Kearton's bank account, and particularly his withdrawals of the past forty-eight hours."

"Blackmail!" I exclaimed.

"Ah, you are astute, Parker. We shall see. However, since that seems out of my ken for the present, I shall doubtless have to content myself with an examination of the past week's ship registry."

With this enigmatic statement he was silent. Presently he tired of walking, summoned a cab, and we were driven back to Number Seven, Praed Street, where Pons immediately lost himself in a careful examination of the ship registry of the *Journal of Commerce*.

Next morning, when I rose, I found that Pons had preceded me. He sat at the breakfast table studying the *Daily Mail*, his breakfast half eaten and the dishes pushed aside. His ascetic face was intense, he fingered the lobe of his left ear, as he customarily did when preoccupied, and he did not look up at my entrance. Yet he had noticed me.

"Ah, good morning, Parker. Just step round and take a look at this, will you?"

I did so. Looking over his shoulder, I found myself gazing upon a photograph of what appeared to be the head of a sleeping woman, flanked by an artist's conception of the woman awake. The caption read: *Unidentified Woman Found Slain in Thames! Is She Lilli Morrison?*

"An interesting face, not so?" pursued Pons.

I agreed. "Black hair, swarthy – a half breed, perhaps?"

"I believe so."

"Those are foreign earrings, too. Gold bands or bars – or imitation."

"Exactly," said Pons, chuckling. "Now pray cast your memory back to yesterday morning's visitor, Parker."

"Mrs. Kearton?"

"Allow me to recall her words to you. When she described the woman with whom she saw her husband she said – 'very dark of complexion, almost swarthy, with black hair and something gold or imitation gold in her ears. She seemed somewhat foreign...'"

"It would be more than a coincidence," I protested.

"No, no, not at all," answered Pons at once. "It is the natural sequence of events. It is she. I have had Mrs. Kearton on the telephone; she has identified her. I should add that she and her husband saw the picture almost simultaneously."

"Aha! And she watched his reaction!"

"You are leaping ahead of the story. She did. There was no reaction. But she observed, as he set out for the office, that his step seemed considerably lighter and that he had relinquished somewhat the burden which he had carried secretly since the day before yesterday." He pushed the paper away from him and got up, beginning to take off his dressing-gown. "I fancy another visit to Mr. Kearton is in order as soon as you have had breakfast – and if I am not mistaken, here is Mrs. Johnson now with your eggs and bacon."

Even as he spoke the pleasant, homely face of our landlady appeared in the doorway, followed by her plump person. She greeted me, as usual, and eyed with grave disapproval the remains of Pons' breakfast, while depositing my own before me. But, wise woman that she was, she made no protest, save for the sigh with which she gathered up the dishes and took her departure while I fell to with a hearty appetite.

Pons once more assumed the guise of the inquiring beekeeper of yesterday, and, so apparelled, he sallied forth. "Unless I am much in error," he said in the cab which carried us to Bouverie Street, "we shall find Mr. Kearton a man of somewhat altered mien from the gentleman we encountered yesterday."

In this, Pons was not mistaken. The man into whose presence we were ushered this morning was an entirely different individual from the somewhat agitated and unkempt man of yesterday. He was immaculate in dress, his hair was combed, and the moment we appeared on the threshold, he leaped to his feet and advanced upon Pons with an extremely apologetic manner.

"My dear sir – I am glad to see you back," he said without preamble. "I fear I did you a grave disservice yesterday when I told you that we had published no such article as *The Role of the Queen in the Swarm*. We did indeed publish it, and within the year."

"I have it, Mr. Kearton, thank you," said Pons. "This morning, however, I have a slightly different problem."

"I am at your service, sir."

"It is something I am most desirous of knowing, if you can remember."

A faint frown appeared on Kearton's forehead, but he did not interrupt.

"This morning," said Pons, with the same dignified and fusty air, "I want to know if at any time on the evening before last, you observed anyone following you and the lady who was in your company at that time."

The effect on Robin Kearton was instantaneous. He had seated himself, but now he half rose from his chair, his lower jaw dropped, and the color drained from his face. This reaction, however, lasted but a moment. He pressed his lips firmly together once more, sat down slowly and eyed Pons with intent interest.

"You have the advantage of me, sir," he said finally.

"I confess I am more accustomed to a deerstalker and Inverness than to pince-nez and ascot, Mr. Kearton."

"Mr. Solar Pons!" cried Kearton.

"It is I who am at your service, Mr. Kearton. How did you pay the woman – in currency or by cheque?"

"I gave her a cheque."

"Sizeable, no doubt?"

"Two hundred pounds. Yet not as large as it would have been had she known that I had married again."

"Your first wife, then. You were not divorced?"

"Mr. Pons, I thought her dead. She left me two years before I left Calcutta. A year later I received a note by the hand of the man with whom she had run away. He wrote that she had died in Ahmedabad, and returned an inscribed watch-fob which was my property. I do not know whether she had managed to deceive him by some means or whether she had been believed dead. My life with her was somewhat worse than hell."

"So I would have assumed."

"Enough so to make me appreciate Lucy. I wanted to spare her."

"I think, though, that there is now no longer any danger to your marriage from your first wife. I should lose no time, therefore, in telling Mrs. Kearton everything without a moment's further delay. You paid the woman by cheque. I submit that in all probability she had not cashed it by the time of her death. If the cheque was found on her, the metropolitan police will shortly be around to ask you some questions. It seems inevitable that your relationship with her will be uncovered in good time. Quite possibly, before many days have passed, you will be arrested for her murder. Mrs. Kearton, therefore, should be forewarned."

"Great Scott!" exclaimed Kearton in alarm.

"Let me remind you – I asked you previously whether or not you were followed when you were with your first wife."

"Of course. Lilli had someone keep an eye on us. A brute of a fellow with a scarred lip and a dark moustache. I took him for a sailor or a dock-worker, as I, myself once was. She would hardly trust me, knowing what she meant to threaten."

Pons got up. "Very good, Mr. Kearton. Let us not detain you longer."

"I am going straight to Lucy and tell her everything. But if I may ask, Mr. Pons – how does it happen – " A light broke in upon him. "I see! I see it all – Mr. Pons, it was Lucy! Lucy came to you!"

"You are blessed with a most devoted wife, Mr. Kearton. She merits your trust."

"Indeed, I know she does!" cried Kearton, reaching for his hat.

"Now, then," said Pons, once we had returned to Praed Street, "I shall have to devote a little time to a more onerous kind of inquiry, and in somewhat less reputable attire."

So saying, he began to rummage about for the most disreputable old clothing he could find. I watched him in silence for a few moments. He looked up, his eyes twinkling, and added, "I daresay it would take a hell of living with a she-cat to turn a man into a perfect husband, eh, Parker?"

"If the woman was what he suggests she was, I can't blame him," I said. "But he ought to have made sure he got his cheque back."

Pons laughed heartily, while he divested himself of his clothes. "What a wonderful trust of your fellowmen you betray, Parker! Between you, you and Inspector Jamison will have him in irons by nightfall!"

When Pons returned that evening, he was silent as to where he had been. Nevertheless, it was evident that he had been in Limehouse or Wapping, or some area close to the Thames and the sea, for there was about him an indefinable odor of water which is never quite dissipated for some hours after leaving the seashore, a kind of moisture which permeates clothing and thus heightens the natural smells of cloth.

He changed clothes and made himself comfortable in his dressing-gown and slippers. He assured Mrs. Johnson, who made anxious inquiry, that he wanted no meal; he had eaten and was content. She went back downstairs, lamenting that he was determined to starve himself, that he grew thinner every day – which assuredly he did not – and that some day she would find him emaciated in his bed.

Pons' amusement at this proprietary concern of our landlady was cut short by a sudden assault on our front door, the rattle of footsteps on the stairs, and the unceremonious entry of Mrs. Robin Kearton, pale, dishevelled, and tearful.

"Oh, Mr. Pons," she cried, "forgive me – but they have taken Robin away."

"Do sit down, Mrs. Kearton, and dispel your alarm. Have they arrested him?"

"No – not yet. They've detained him for questioning."

"And the detaining officer?"

"An Inspector Jamison. Is it possible – do you know him?" she asked hopefully.

"My dear lady, I assure you Mr. Kearton is in no danger. May I ask – has he explained the circumstances to you?"

"He has told me all about the wretched woman. But he did not kill her, Mr. Pons, I swear he did not. I would know, if he had."

I looked at her with pity. Nor did Pons say anything further to her. He looked at me and suggested that I telephone Inspector Jamison and tell him that he might learn something to his advantage if he would step around to Number Seven. "You might add that it concerns the murder of Lilli Morrison. That will fetch him."

In less than a quarter of an hour Inspector Jamison made his appearance – bluff and hearty as ever, his carefully trimmed moustache fairly bristling with suspicion, which was heightened at sight of Mrs. Kearton, who sat now, pale but composed, at some distance from the fireplace, where Pons himself waited upon Jamison.

"Pray draw up a chair, Jamison," said Pons. "Will you have a cup of tea? We have just been having some fine Darjeeling, Mrs. Kearton, Parker, and I. No? You know Mrs. Kearton, of course."

"I have the pleasure of her acquaintance," said Jamison, not without a faint trace of embarrassment.

Mrs. Kearton nodded politely, but did not trust herself to speak. She sat with her hands clenched tightly in her lap. "I'm afraid, Pons, this time you're a little late," began Jamison.

"Dear me," murmured Pons imperturbably, "do not say so. I hope you have not given out anything in the nature of a statement in the Lilli Morrison matter?"

"Not yet."

"Ah, how wise to be cautious!"

"Pons, it is absolutely wide open, cut and dried," said Jamison. "I'm sorry, Mrs. Kearton."

"Of course it is," agreed Pons. "But it is not cut quite the way you have cut it. Kearton did not murder Lilli Morrison. I concede that it was he who had the obvious motive, certainly; who would deny it? Not he, I venture to guess. But not even he would be so muddled as to allow her to retain the cheque by which you traced him. No, the murderer of Lilli Morrison is a man named Amos Sakrisan, a half-breed, like herself, first mate of the *Prince of Hyderabad*, scheduled to set out from the East India Docks tomorrow morning. He is a dark man with a moustache, black and unkempt, a scar on his lower lip at one corner of his mouth, and he walks with a slight limp. He is excitable and dangerous. He carries a knife and will not hesitate to use it just as he did on Lilli Morrison when he found out she had no intention of coming back to the ship which brought her here.

"You see, Robin Kearton was not the only man Lilli Morrison ran away from. He was only the first. Once back in London, she found Kearton, who thought her dead. I daresay it was simple enough to do so, since his name is listed in the telephone book at his office as well as his home. She telephoned his office, where she correctly assumed he would be. She meant to blackmail him and had no intention of returning to Sakrisan, who had brought her from India as his wife. Kearton, now married, knew that the pressure she could bring upon him if she found out how happily married he was would be unbearable, took every means to keep her from discovering his marital status, even to the extent of cutting his wife dead when he met her face to face while he was in the woman's company. Kearton saw the man who murdered Lilli Morrison in fury and jealousy, but he assumed it was some creature of hers, guarding her, to keep her from any possible harm Kearton might do her."

Pons turned to Mrs. Kearton. "I am sure, Mrs. Kearton, though Inspector Jamison has no time to lose, he can find it possible to see you home so that you will be there when your husband returns. I understand that perfect husbands are an increasing rarity in our time."

Jamison came to his feet with alacrity. "I am in your debt, Pons." He turned to Mrs. Kearton, somewhat awkwardly, and offered her his arm. "If I may, Madam?"

A month after the successful prosecution and conviction of Amos Sakrisan, Pons received an exquisitely carved plaque, showing a pair of doves in the traditional billing pose, surmounted by a queen bee and the initial "K."

III

THE ADVENTURE OF THE BROKEN CHESSMAN

In June of the same year in which Solar Pons examined into the singular affair of the Black Narcissus, he was sitting one evening, engaged in the compilation of his voluminous scrapbook of British crimes and criminological data, and talking desultorily of the events which passed under his eye.

"The majority of crimes are remarkably unimaginative," he a said. "A body found in a little-traveled lane – a corpse in boudoir – murder during robbery. Here, for instance," he read, "'Lodger Found Dead. Mrs. Ottilia Baker, 37 Woburn Place, this morning discovered the body of a lodger dead in his room. The unfortunate man's head had been battered in, and his room had been ransacked. Mrs. Baker identified her lodger as Landon Hall. Relatives are asked to communicate with Scotland Yard.' Surely nothing could be more prosaic?" He paused thoughtfully, his hand going to the lobe of his left ear. "And yet," he went on, "'Landon Hall' is almost certainly an assumed name. One can infer as much not only by its sound but also by the patent indication that his landlady knows so little about him and his origins that 'relatives are asked to communicate with Scotland Yard.'"

"I suppose there are thousands of people who drop out of sight only to assume new identities and begin life over in some other place," I ventured.

"Elementary," murmured Pons. "It is their motives which are of primary interest."

He put the clipping away and went on to others. From time to time he read sentences from the dispatches, making brief comments on them. Ostensibly, the matter of Mrs. Ottilia Baker's murdered lodger had been forgotten. Yet it was destined to be brought again to our attention, and that before the evening was done.

It was at eight o'clock that the doorbell jangled. Pons was at the moment near the window; he drew aside the curtain and looked down into Praed Street.

"Ah, we are about to have a visitor of some importance," he observed. "It may well be an invitation to another of those little adventures which you are so fond of chronicling, Parker."

He returned from the window in time to greet the tall, cloaked individual Mrs. Johnson admitted to our quarters. He came into the room somewhat diffidently, inclined his head slightly, and looked toward Pons.

"Mr. Solar Pons?"

"I am at your service," answered Pons, and placed a chair for our visitor, whose voice, I could not help noticing, had a distinctly foreign accent.

Of our visitor's face, I could see very little, for his long black cloak successfully covered his chin, and his eyes were hidden by smoked glasses, attached to what appeared to be an expensive black cord which, followed downward, disappeared into the folds of his cloak at the neck. His hands were gloved, and he carried a walking stick, which was of ebony with an ivory handle. His lips were thin and firm, his nose was sharply aquiline. His hair was jet black, and the bushy eyebrows projecting above the rims of his glasses were black, too.

"It will be necessary that my identity remain a secret, Mr. Pons; it would not be politic for my connection with the matter in question to become known."

Pons seated himself to face our visitor and inquired, without a flicker of mischief, "What is the matter in question, M. Parenin?"

Our visitor started slightly, but betrayed himself by no other sign. "Ah, you know me."

"I submit that as long as the ensign on your motor remains unaltered, any attempt at personal concealment is foredoomed to failure. The ensign suggests the Russian consul," replied Pons. "But I daresay the matter you have come to see me about is not connected with your official status or with the official business of the government you represent."

"Not directly, Mr. Pons. That is to say, not as yet. I may at any moment receive orders from Leningrad to proceed in the matter, but thus far I am acting solely on my own initiative."

"Pray let us consider the problem, M. Parenin."

"You may have read of a Mrs. Ottilia Baker's discovering a murdered lodger at her establishment at 37 Woburn Place this morning," began Parenin crisply.

"I remember doing so. A gentleman named Landon Hall; obviously, I thought, an assumed name."

"It was not Landon Hall who was found dead, however," continued Parenin. "A description subsequently published in the metropolitan papers was called to my attention by my secretary. I recognized the victim at once as one of Russia's secret agents – a certain man, notoriously known for his shrewdness and bestiality, as well as the disturbing degree of his success in the zealous prosecution of his assignments. You will be familiar with his name, Mr. Pons – it is Pyotor Propov."

"Indeed!" exclaimed Pons. "At one time of the terrible Inner Circle; the same man who shot the aged Prince Casimir in 1918, who assassinated the children of Madame Kolosov, who decapitated the Grand Duchess Yolande – among other outrages."

"Your information is correct, Mr. Pons. It was he whose body Mrs. Baker discovered in Landon Hall's room this morning. My secretary has viewed the body; there is no question about his identity."

"I have little inclination to apprehend his murderer," said Pons dryly.

Our visitor smiled. "It was not my intention to ask you to do so. It is because I desire the opposite end that I have wished my identity kept secret. Mr. Pons, I would wish you to do all in your power to so confuse the official police that they will not suspect the identity of the actual murderer!"

Pons looked his surprise and delight. "Dear me, M. Parenin! What an extraordinary request!"

"I confide in you that I never had any love for Propov or his methods; I am not alone in my convictions," our visitor assured Pons. "Believe me, sir, I could mention many names closely associated with our government."

Pons rested his chin briefly on his clasped hands. "I can understand your abhorrence of Propov's methods," he said presently. "But, in view of the unusual nature of your request, I am sure you will allow me some time to consider it, M. Parenin. I do not think that I could with conceivable justice block the investigation. I should be forced on my honor to give the police such assistance as I can, though manifestly I need not do so in so direct a fashion that they have only to act to complete the matter. We shall have to learn who is in charge from the Yard."

"An Inspector Jamison," replied our visitor at once.

"Ah, our old friend, Jamison." Pons smiled. "I am curious to know what he makes of the problem. I fear, though, that the official police will have had ample time to muddle up the scene."

"On the contrary," interposed the Russian consul. "I have used the influence of the consulate to have everything kept as it was found until you arrived on the scene."

"Capital!" exclaimed Pons. "We will run over without delay."

Our ride to number 37 Woburn Place was painstakingly slow, for the consul's chauffeur found it necessary to drive with caution in the thick yellow fog which had settled over London. Traffic was halted for some time at Charing Cross Road junction by extremely heavy traffic pouring down Tottenham Court Road from North London. Moreover, travel along New Oxford Street and Holborn was little better. Yet, in a relatively short time, we came to a stop before a three-story building which loomed up darkly in the fog.

Pons and I left the car without the consul.

M. Parenin leaned from the machine. "It would not do for me to be seen here, Mr. Pons, but I shall be found at any time at the consulate. I shall be happy to call on you if you wish and to do whatever I can to assist your inquiry."

A constable called out from the entrance to the lodging-house; at this, M. Parenin gave a curt order to his chauffeur; the car started up and was quickly swallowed by the close-pressing fog. The constable came part way down to the street, barring the way.

"No admittance," he announced flatly. But at this moment the light from his torch found Pons' face. "Oh, it's Mr. Pons. And Dr. Parker. Excuse me, sir. Just follow me, Mr. Pons. Inspector Jamison's inside."

The torch went out and the constable moved away from us to throw open the outer door. At the sound of our entrance, a constable looked from a room at the far end of a long hall, his head framed in the light streaming through the open doorway. He withdrew, and gave place to Inspector Jamison, whose rotund form was readily recognizable as he stepped out into the hall to confront us.

"My word, Pons!" he exclaimed. "I never thought to encounter you at the scene of so ordinary a crime."

"However intentioned, you flatter me," said Pons with a thin smile. "Yet it hardly strikes me that the discovery of an unknown victim of murder in a room let to someone else is entirely commonplace."

Jamison shrugged and stepped aside, his chubby face with its carefully kept moustache turned now toward the contents of the room. "Take a look around, Pons. We'd like to have the body moved; the Foreign Office ordered us to disturb nothing until you had seen the place."

The first object to attract Pons' attention was, of course, the corpse of the victim, almost in the center of the room, the body slumped upon a small table from a large armchair. The head and shoulders had fallen forward to a chessboard on the table and lay grotesquely amid a scattered group of overturned chessmen. In falling forward, the victim's arm must have swept half the table clear, for chessmen were flung over the floor to the left. The right arm supported the victim's head, and in his right hand a chessman was still tightly clenched. Quite evidently the murdered man had been struck down from behind; next to the chair on the floor lay the heavy candelabrum already designated by Scotland Yard as the instrument of death.

The victim, I saw after but a little examination, was not too well dressed; yet there were some indications that his dress was casual rather by deliberation than of necessity. He was extremely obese, and his large, flabby hands with the puffy face beneath the bushy black beard which covered the lower half of it, testified to indulgent living. He was far from an attractive man; he would easily have repelled many people in life.

Pons, however, paid scant attention to the body. He seemed more concerned with traces of the former occupant of the room than with the victim's appearance. The room itself was indeed in a state of disorder, as the accounts in the press stated;

it gave every evidence of having been hastily gone through in a determined search. Drawers stood half open, clothes lay on the floor of the open closet at the far end of the room, books and papers were tumbled indiscriminately from the shelves and stands along the walls.

"Has anything been taken from Propov's pockets?" asked Pons.

Jamison nodded and pointed silently to a chair opposite the victim. There lay two objects: an ordinary sandbag and a peculiar metal seal. Pons examined one after the other with his customary care.

"The sandbag is Propov's trademark," said Jamison. "The seal seems to be that of some secret organization."

"The Inner Circle," suggested Pons with an oblique smile.

"I wondered about that," assented Jamison, "but I'm not sure the organization's still in existence. The Yard's had no definite word of the Circle's work of late; neither has British Intelligence. We can assume that the Circle has either been suppressed or that it's gone underground."

"The design in the seal is crudely stamped in and suggests the Soviet government," said Pons, handing the seal to Jamison. "The Inner Circle has probably been absorbed into the OGPU."

Pons now walked attentively about the room, examining drawers and books on the shelves, pausing before one shelf of books for some time. He invaded the clothes-closet and the adjoining lavatory. He returned at last and stood with Jamison gazing at the body.

"Undoubtedly the Yard has evolved a theory," said Pons.

"Nothing definite, no," answered Jamison. "It's my idea this man Propov came here to do away with Mrs. Baker's lodger, but something went wrong and the tables were turned. I don't entirely eliminate the possibility of a third person's concern, of course."

"You have a description of the man who called himself Landon Hall?"

"As far as it goes, yes. Mrs. Baker's statement isn't particularly helpful. A man of medium height, with a small pointed beard – "

"Yet someone shaved in the bathroom not less than twenty-four hours ago," interposed Pons.

"He might have shaved himself," agreed Jamison. "That would be the logical thing to do if he killed Propov and hoped to escape."

"Clean-shaven, then. A man who walked with a limp, and probably had a left leg of cork – you too certainly noticed the smooth left boots of each pair in the closet."

Jamison nodded casually.

"A man of some wealth," Pons went on, "for only a wealthy man would afford a single private printing of a Russian translation of Brillat-Savarin's *Physiology of Taste*, with an inlaid original plate by Augustus John. A highly cultured man; he has books in seven different languages. And I daresay a pronounced aesthete, for he owns such books as Huysman's *A Rebours* and *La Bas*, Machen's *Hill of Dreams*, Pater's *Marius*, Ruskin's *Stones of Venice*, and others expounding aesthetic doctrines. Finally, he was either of the Russian nobility or in a position to receive their books, for many of his volumes are marked with the Romanoff coat of arms."

Jamison looked at Pons a little askance.

"Of course, you noticed that the man wore his hair rather long, and that he was of middle age or past, as the long grey and black hairs on the great coat in the closet tell us. And you will doubtless have seen that Hall was of a highly nervous temperament, and that he wore a monocle?"

"You have the better of me, Pons," said Jamison with admirable patience. "One would think you know the man."

"I fancy I do," said Pons quietly.

Jamison looked the amazement he felt. "Oh, come now, Pons! You don't expect me to believe that?"

Pons smiled enigmatically.

"But if you do, of course, your inferences about his appearance are elementary," continued Jamison. "His nervous temperament, for instance."

"In the second drawer of that bureau beyond the table you'll find an eyeglass on a cord; the cord is badly frayed along a section covered by the movement of the clip on it," answered Pons. "I submit that nervous people who wear glasses consistently play with the clips on their cords, twirl them, and otherwise occupy their hands. But these matters are, as you say, elementary. You were beginning to tell me your concept of what took place here, assuming that Propov came here to do away with Hall."

"Yes." Jamison would have gone on, but Pons once again interrupted him.

"And then softened sufficiently to sit down for a game of chess with him?"

Jamison was momentarily disconcerted. "Perhaps. The tenant Hall may not have known Propov."

"I rather think he did. As a matter of fact, an old picture of Propov, clipped from a newspaper, lies between the pages of one of the books on the top shelf of the rack across from the table. A book with a bright red binding," Pons went on, as Constable Jones went over to examine the books on the top shelf.

The picture was shortly laid down before Jamison, who examined it thoughtfully, his pale eyes narrowed.

"That's at least five years old, Pons," he said at last. "Hall might easily have forgotten him since then."

"I do not remember saying anything to the contrary," agreed Pons. "But the picture you adduce of a man bent on murder coming calmly to a chess game and himself being murdered leaves some unsatisfactory questions. I submit that murder was not Comrade Propov's primary goal. I suggest that he was in search of something."

Jamison made an all-embracing gesture toward the ransacked appearance of the room.

"Ah, but this melee was not made by someone in search of something," protested Pons. "Surely Hall would not have permitted Propov to ransack his room? And surely, had he done so, Propov would not be sitting at chess. No, the appearance of the room derives from the haste of the murderer to take his leave with such valuables as he could not do without."

"Unless, of course, we postulate a third and thus far unknown murderer."

"Granted. You have looked up Propov?"

"Yes. He was registered at 217 St. George Street as Pyotor Harlov. The area is one frequented by Russian emigres."

"Very probably then Hall knew Propov initially as Harlov."

"We have assumed that Hall recognized Propov only as a fellow-Russian," said Jamison. "This meeting was very likely not their first. Hall, if a Russian, was himself in hiding, and took Propov for another Russian in hiding. What happened, as I see it, was this: in the middle of a game of chess, Hall believes that his life is in danger from the man he knows as Harlov. He rises on some pretext and, passing behind Propov, seizes the candelabrum and strikes Propov down. He then shaves hurriedly, takes only the barest necessities, and escapes."

"Yet he left his wallet, well stuffed with notes, in the pocket of his great coat."

"He may easily have forgotten it," explained Jamison.

"Despite taking the trouble to shave in order to disguise himself? Does it not seem logical that, having gone so far, he should also supply himself with money to take him from London?"

"He may have had other resources."

"Conceivably. You postulate that Propov and Hall were acquainted as countrymen; Propov's London address would be a natural place for Hall to make Propov's acquaintance, assuming both men to be in hiding. Yet, does it not seem somewhat unusual that Hall, a highly cultured man, would frequent a place which is not particularly noted for harboring men of culture, but rather more men of Propov's calibre?"

"Why not?" protested Jamison. "The fellow was in hiding, wasn't he? He was a Russian; it seems natural that he'd seek out other Russians even at the risk of running afoul of the Yard."

Pons raised his eyebrows. "You believe he was in hiding from the police? I submit rather that he was hiding from his fellow countrymen."

"Then how explain his willingness to see Propov?" countered Jamison triumphantly.

"We have no evidence that he was willing to see Propov," retorted Pons. "Rather Harlov."

"Very well," snapped Jamison, disgruntled. "Go on."

"We might as conceivably suspect Hall and Propov of being two Soviet government agents in a quarrel which turned out disastrously for Propov. In such an event, the charge would very likely be murder in the first degree. But if your hypothesis proves correct, would the charge not then be countered by a claim of self-defense?"

Jamison pursed his lips thoughtfully. "I doubt it," he said finally. "He might plead self-defense; wouldn't that be natural? Circumstantial evidence wouldn't prove his claim. Chances are, though, he'd be packed off to Russia, unless he's taken out papers."

"And left to the mercy of the Soviet government, eh?" asked Pons.

"I suppose so."

I had had no difficulty in following this seemingly aimless conversation; clearly Pons meant to establish in his own mind the possible fate of the man Hall, if Scotland Yard found him. Pons, however, having satisfied himself on this score, was now engaged in looking at the chessmen scattered about; he appeared to be counting them, and I, too, began almost unconsciously to add them up – sixteen pawns, four rooks, four knights, four bishops, two queens – but there was only one king. Perhaps the remaining king had been kicked under one of the articles of furniture.

Even as the thought occurred to me, Pons went to the floor on his knees and began to peer rapidly under the table and around the rug at the edge of the chairs. Jamison watched in silence; his association with Pons had been of sufficient duration to teach him a certain tacit respect for my companion's methods. He contented himself only with a routine examination of a chessman, a knight he picked up from the table.

The chessmen were carved in ivory and seemed very solid. The set was doubtless valuable; I should have regretted parting with it, had I owned it, for it appeared to be hand-wrought. But the set was evidently not without blemish, for when Pons came to his feet once more, he held in his hands two queens, one of which he immediately placed upright on the table, the other of which he continued to hold; its perfect whiteness was marred by a faint dull brown line which encircled it in the middle. It had obviously at one time been broken and mended with glue.

"I take it you noticed that one of the chessmen, a king, is missing?"

"I hadn't," confessed Jamison. "I daresay they played with a substitute."

"That is always a possibility, however remote," agreed Pons. He held the queen out to Jamison, who took it. "You have no objection to my keeping this?"

"None at all, provided only you'll have to surrender it if Hall turns up and demands it."

"Quite so," said Pons, dropping the chessman into his pocket.

"I need hardly ask," asked Jamison somewhat stuffily, "whether you and I are working toward the same end. I'm satisfied that anyone with power enough to hold us up for ten hours must be someone of considerable influence; so I'm satisfied on that score."

"Capital!" exclaimed Pons. "Yet there are a few favors I'd like to ask – for your own sake as well as mine. I want you to use the Yard's influence to insert a news paragraph in all the metropolitan dailies. Let the Yard phrase it as they see fit. It should be to the effect that – " He paused abruptly, halted by the dubiety of Jamison's expression. "But, no, let me set it down."

He drew a chair up to the table, moved the chessmen to one side, and found paper in a drawer opposite Propov's body. Since he carried his pen with him, he was soon writing rapidly in a firm, legible hand, with Inspector Jamison and myself reading over his shoulders as he wrote, much to Pons' annoyance.

> The mysterious murder of an unknown person in the lodging house of Mrs. Ottilia Baker, 37 Woburn Place, was taken in hand today by Inspector Seymour R. Jamison, whose capable work in the matter of the Black Narcissus crime only two weeks ago will be recalled. Inspector Jamison quickly discovered that the deceased was Pyotor Harlov, a Russian emigre, registered at 217 St. George Street, Stepney. Spurred by the nature of the facts evident to him, the Inspector has now reached the conclusion that the lodger, Landon Hall, has also met with foul play, since many of his most valuable possessions are still in his lodgings. Mr. Hall may have been abducted, and various addresses in Stepney and Wapping, known to be frequented by Russian emigres, are under surveillance.

> The body of Harlov has been removed, and the guard has been lifted. Mrs. Baker is in a request to relatives of Mr. Hall to step forward and remove his effects, so that she may re-let the room. That the criminal or criminals will not long remain at large is assured by Inspector Jamison's previous performances.

Pons finished; he turned to hand the account to Jamison. "Read it over and send it off at once."

"Very well, Pons," said Jamison, manifestly flattered at the highly complimentary nature of what my companion had written. He did not trouble to re-read the notice, but beckoned to Constable Jones, gave him what Pons had written, and turned back to Pons. "Do you suggest we watch 217 St. George Street for the abductors?"

"By all means, Jamison," replied Pons. "And, of course, you will withdraw your men from here at once."

Jamison demurred. "Do you think that the best course."

"In view of the fact that Parker and I will occupy this room until at least the day after tomorrow, I think it is. If any results are to be expected, that plan is best. And pray observe that such results as I may obtain are yours as well. By all means take all the time you need to remove Propov's body and the evidence collected on that chair, with the addition of the candelabrum, the *instrumentum mortis*."

It was not until after Inspector Jamison and his men had departed that Pons relaxed. He sat down in the chair which had so recently held the evidence Jamison had collected and regarded the empty chair across from him with quizzical interest. From there his gaze went to the mantel behind, and I assumed that he was picturing Hall in the act of striking down Propov.

"Yes, you are right, Parker," Pons said without turning. "I am reconstructing the crime. There are aspects of it which I find nothing short of intriguing."

"Oh, come, Pons!" I protested. "It seems as plain as a pikestaff to me."

"I don't doubt it," he replied dryly. "But think on it for a moment. We are allowed to assume that Propov, the OGPU killer, is on Hall's trail. With what end but that to which so many other White Russians have come – assassination? Yet we have every evidence to believe that the two men, slayer and slain, were engaged in a game of chess before the crime. I submit that if Propov's motive and goal were Hall's death, no good could have come of having a game of chess with his intended victim. The portrait of the gloating killer is, I fear, limited very largely to the penny dreadfuls. No, I fancy, M. Propov's goal was not primarily Hall's death, whatever his secondary goal may have been. This seems to have escaped the good Jamison; I am curious to know whether it escaped M. Parenin as well."

"The circumstances are somewhat peculiar," I admitted.

"It is generous of you to say so," said Pons with a whimsical smile.

"But not half so peculiar as your statement that you knew who Hall really was."

"Ah, it is not particularly difficult to establish Hall's identity. We have been given several leading facts – he is a Russian emigre, he has some royal connections, he lacks one leg or foot, he wore a black van Dyke. Think back to 1917. Picture to yourself a Russian nobleman who fits Hall's description."

The picture was immediately provocative; it called to mind an old portrait-photograph I had seen in a London exhibit. The portrait, I remembered, had been labeled with the name of a gallant Russian count, and newspapers had made especial mention of his having had a leg shot off in a Polish border skirmish in 1914.

"Why," I began, "it would suggest – but no, he is dead."

"You were thinking of?" asked Pons.

"Count Sergei Romanoff, cousin to the Czar."

"Precisely. That is our man."

"Impossible!" I cried.

"Not at all! No one has ever proved his death. Can you recall the circumstances relating to his disappearance?"

"I know of none. I am certain he has never again appeared, though many court nobles of Russia have turned up in Vienna and Paris."

"Allow me to refresh your memory. Rumor prevalent in 1918 announced his 'escape disappearance,' it was then called, a week before the Czar and his family were seized. Through Berlin, Scotland Yard received certain information with which Inspector Jamison might have done well to acquaint himself. The Count did not vanish entirely empty-handed; with him went a rather precious stone, the Orloff diamond, worth about a hundred thousand pounds."

"Ah! Propov's goal!"

"You have hit it, Parker. I congratulate you," said Pons. "I find it difficult to conceive that the Soviet would permit such a jewel to slip through their hands without at least an attempt to recapture it. The assignment is surely a natural one for a man like Propov. Yet the Count must have known the identity of his pursuer, whose search began in 1923, for the clipping he saved so suggests; it is dated 1923, which is additionally informative. The portrait in the clipping might account for the Count's failure to recognize Propov when he first saw him, for the black beard was not characteristic of Propov, who was one of those fellows who fancy themselves to best advantage with a strong lower jaw jutting out like a challenge to their fellowmen.

"Let us, then, reconstruct events as they very probably took place. We can assume that the Count met Propov, perhaps in one of those 'accidental' meetings which Propov could arrange. Propov is in no haste to liquidate the Count; he must first learn where the stone is hidden. So he cultivates the Count, and he is finally invited to the Count's lodgings, where he waits for some betrayal of the jewel's hiding-place. Unfortunately for him, the Count recognizes Propov in the man Harlov, and acts at once, as Jamison concluded, by taking the offensive – rising on some pretext, passing behind his would-be assassin, to seize the heavy bronze candelabrum with which to kill Propov. His next moves are obviously the result of panic. Was Propov alone? Is the house under observation even now? He tries to disguise an identity already marked by his missing leg; he shaves, his panic growing. Finally he takes flight, taking with him only the Orloff diamond."

"I am afraid there is a flaw in the theory, Pons," I could not help pointing out, not without triumph. "There is no logic in Parenin's protection of a former Russian nobleman, the enemy of the Soviet whose government Parenin represents."

"Ah, there is little logic in mankind," answered Pons, smiling. "M. Parenin is, I fear, at heart a Royalist. And with no love for Propov, whose innumerable atrocities serve to give any observer in possession of the facts a sense of the fitness of things at his end."

"Then if Parenin wants the Count to escape, how can you promise Jamison that your results will be his?"

"Surely they have always been, haven't they? Whether I wished it or not?"

"But you don't even know where the Count is!"

"No, nor have I any wish to. If Jamison keeps his word to insert the notice I wrote into the dailies, I expect him call on us without delay."

"Absurd!" I cried. "He will be taken. Why should he come back?"

Pons smiled enigmatically. "Because he took the wrong chessman!"

"What do you mean?"

"Let me suggest that you compare the weight of that queen on the table with this one in my pocket."

He handed both to me.

"The difference in weight is so slight as to be almost imperceptible," continued Pons, "but it exists. The Orloff diamond lies hidden in the broken chessman you hold in your hand."

"But the Count certainly wouldn't make a mistake of that kind," I protested.

"In the circumstances, he did. Look here." He bent and picked up the king. "We assume that the Count took the other king. I submit that this fact is capable of but one interpretation – that the king was also broken. Presumably the Count had originally attempted to conceal the stone in the king, found the king too small, and settled on the queen. In his panic, it was a simple mistake to seize the king instead of the queen: they are not dissimilar in appearance or size. By now he has discovered his mistake; he is therefore certain to return for the broken queen just as soon as he considers that it is safe for him to do so. For that reason alone I persuaded Jamison to send out the notice I wrote out.

"We are therefore unlikely to have a visitor before nightfall, following publication of the notice. We may as well spend the time, if you can be spared from your practice for the day, in sleep."

Shortly after eleven o'clock of the night that followed an uneventful day, I felt Pons reach out and touch me lightly on the arm.

"Don't move, Parker," he whispered, "our man is at the side window."

A slight rustling sound reached my ears. Then, in the whiteness of the fog-square of window, a figure stood for some minutes in absolute silence. Presently the window began to slide up very slowly to a quarter of its length, when there was a pause for listening. Evidently satisfied that he was unobserved, our nocturnal visitor pushed the window up as far as it could go. Again he listened for some moments; then he reached up, grasped the window-jambs, and pulled himself into the room, where he stood for a hesitant moment in the darkness, limned against the white fog outside, before he came slightly forward, walking with a pronounced, though carefully hushed, limping sound.

Without warning, Pons turned on his flash. Its bright light struck our visitor full in the face.

"Count Sergei Romanoff, I believe," said Pons. "Will you be seated?"

The Count made a tentative movement toward the window, but I was there before him, and he turned again to Pons, who had leaped to the button and illuminated the room. The Count stood blinking at Pons in the light; I noticed how well he fitted the description Pons had postulated, and saw too, several places on his chin where he had cut himself while shaving. His hair was somewhat disheveled, and his features were unnaturally pale. His firm lips trembled as he regarded Pons.

"You are not – not police?" he asked hopefully, looking from one to the other of us.

"We are not police," Pons assured him.

The Count sank into a chair. "What do you want of me?"

"You came, I believe, for this," said Pons, extending his hand; the broken chessman lay in his palm.

The Count looked at Pons in sudden terror. "You are not from – the Government?"

"We are not, though we are acting in unofficial capacity for part of it."

"Ahl Who is it then? Is it Parenin? Yes, it is surely Parenin!" he exclaimed.

"Quite so. You know M. Parenin?"

"Yes. As a boy, he was a guard in my father's house. Yes, I know him well. He was the only one in the city who knew of my identity."

"It is unnecessary to tell you that we are in possession of most of the facts of Propov's death. But tell us, how did you encounter him? That is a matter of detail about which we can only speculate."

"In the street, sir. Oh, it was foolish, but I was lonely, very lonely. Parenin could not visit me without arousing suspicion. Propov must have known me at once; he was so unnaturally gracious. I didn't recognize him then, though I knew he had been looking for me since 1923, when I was warned against him in Paris. I clipped a picture of him then; I thought I would always remember him. But he had grown a beard in the interval; so I didn't realize who he was until we sat down to that game of chess. That was his second visit to my lodgings. He was left-handed, and I remembered that Propov was left-handed. I studied him then, and I became convinced of his identity. Once convinced, I did not hesitate to kill him at once. I shaved then, you know, but that was indicative only of my desperation, for I could not change my leg. And then, in my haste, I picked up the wrong chessman. You know about the diamond, too?"

Pons nodded silently.

"I had tried to put it into the king, but it would not fit; so I put it into the queen. You cannot know the bitter disappointment I suffered until I read the account in the papers this morning." He looked up, eyes narrowed. "It was not true, then? I am in the hands of the police."

"On the contrary, the account was put in expressly to enable you to retrieve the jewel."

"And so that you might take me," replied the Count bitterly.

"It becomes my duty to hand you over to the police, I fear." Pons shrugged his shoulders. "But, of course, this is your property," he continued, handing the chessman to the Count. "I will exchange it for the broken king."

The Count silently handed the king to Pons, who gave it the queen's place in his pocket.

"It will take us a few moments to notify the police, Count Romanoff," said Pons. "For your convenience, I have packed your wallet, your most valuable books, and most of your clothes. You will have time, I daresay, to see whether I have forgotten anything."

The Count's eyes met Pons' briefly. He murmured his thanks for Pons' thoughtfulness in packing his things while I had slept. Then Pons beckoned to me, and together we left the room.

In the hall, Pons went directly to the telephone, where he called the number the Russian consul had given him.

"M. Parenin?" I heard him say. "Solar Pons here. I called in regard to our problem of last evening. Our quarry is quite safely in our hands, but it might be well to prevent further official pursuit. Early tomorrow morning, please telephone Inspector Seymour Jamison of Scotland Yard and tell him I have delivered into your hands the man known as Landon Hall; assure the Inspector that Hall is already on his way to Russia in the hands of government agents. Above all, make certain that Inspector Jamison is to receive full credit for solving the crime at 37 Woburn Place."

There was a brief pause. Pons chuckled. "Official notice, eh? Inspector Jamison has a great respect for anything official."

Pons turned from the telephone. "I fancy that will satisfy both our client and the estimable Inspector. Now let us see how our prisoner fares."

He looked cautiously into the Count's quarters. There was no one there.

"Dear me!" he exclaimed, "how careless of us! I am afraid our prisoner has escaped."

On the way back to our own quarters, Pons said, "We must be sure to look at the morning papers, Parker. I daresay we shall find the affair chronicled under some such caption as, shall we say, *Inspector Jamison Scores Again!*"

IV

THE ADVENTURE OF THE DOG IN THE MANGER

"No, Parker," said Solar Pons quietly, without turning around, "I fancy you will not find him in Whitaker's. He might conceivably merit a few lines in some theatre directory. But it is a tribute to the energetic self-adulation and self-seeking publicity habits of the late Ahab Jepson that you should think of looking for him in the *Peerage*."

Despite years of experience with the astonishing deductions of my friend, Solar Pons, the private enquiry agent who has become known as "the Sherlock Holmes of Praed Street," I had not learned to conceal either my surprise or my sometimes nettled admiration. I protested. "I've not spoken a word in the last hour. You can't even see me now. How did you know I was about to look up Ahab Jepson?"

Pons made a clucking sound of disapproval. "Dear me, these elucidations seem so needless. At breakfast you read with manifest interest the *Times*' account of the murder of Ahab Jepson, a minor actor on the London and sometime provincial stage. An hour later, you tossed away the *Daily Telegraph*, folded to the page of new plays in review. You rose and walked to the shelf where I am accustomed to keeping the *Peerage*. No other conceivably useful reference book is kept there. Surely it is most elementary to infer that the reviews in the *Daily Telegraph* reminded you of Ahab Jepson's murder and sent you to attempt the expansion of your knowledge in regard to the victim?"

"The paper's account was extremely sparse."

"I could not help observing it." He turned with a twinkle in his keen, dark eyes. "I doubt that Mr. Jepson would have liked his 'notice'."

"You speak of him as if he were an unsavoury fellow," I protested.

"Not at all. He was hardly more than a troublesome poseur. Our American cousins have a most apt word to describe an actor of Ahab Jepson's histrionic pretensions; in both of its forms, it is a major item in the American diet. The word is 'ham'."

"'Troublesome'?" I repeated.

"He made trouble for almost everyone who had dealings with him. As the son of the distinguished tragic actor, the late Sir Hesketh Jepson, young Ahab conceived that he had a proprietary right not only in such plays as his father wrote, but also in his late father's methods of delivery on stage, his ideas, even his gestures. Ahab, if I recall correctly, once tried to write a play himself – a poor thing, and alas! his very own. Surely you remember the number of actions Jepson instigated against fellow actors whom he accused of invading his proprietary rights by using gestures and methods of delivery similar to those common to his late father? He won none of them, of course, but he was no less a nuisance in chancery with his 'dog in the manger' attitude."

I took the *Times* from the newspaper rack where Pons had deposited it until he had opportunity to clip it for his vast file, and re-examined the notice of Ahab Jepson's death. It was little more than a bulletin and was so presented. It said nothing but that the body of Ahab Jepson had been discovered "hanging above the staircase in the family home near Stoke Poges," and adding that an investigation was in progress. The only detail appended to this brief statement was a sentence or two identifying the victim as the son of a justly famed and popular actor of yesteryear.

Pons watched me, his lean face agleam with interest. "A singularly barren account, is it not?" he asked, when I had finished re-reading it. "What do you make of it?"

"Obviously, there is something here that does not meet the eye," I replied.

"Ah, profound, Parker, profound," he observed with marked irony. "You will have noticed, too, there is nothing more in the *Daily Telegraph*. I submit that is a most uncommon circumstance. Not a word about the identity of the body's discoverer. Not a word, either, about the household. And did he have house-guests? One wonders. It was Sunday. I shall not be surprised if the police see fit to call upon Scotland Yard."

Pons' intuition was not in error.

Within the hour Inspector Jamison of the Criminal Investigation Department had telephoned to say that he was sending to Number 7B, Praed Street, Detective-Sergeant Peter Cobbett of Stoke Poges; he would be obliged to Pons if he would make such suggestions to Cobbett as Pons found possible.

The sergeant himself followed hard upon Jamison's call. He was a gaunt young man with an harassed air. He had a clear-eyed, honest expression, his straw-coloured hair was somewhat disheveled – habitually so, it appeared – and his square-cut face was markedly freckled. Though a stranger to Pons, he knew him by sight, introduced himself without delay, and was in turn introduced to me.

"Pray sit down, and tell me what it is about Ahab Jepson's death that disturbs you so deeply, Sergeant," invited Pons.

"Inspector Jamison has told you, then?"

Pons smiled. "Not a word. I shall hear it from you."

Sergeant Cobbett thereupon began his account without delay. "There are certain circumstances about Jepson's death which are so puzzling as to be most disturbing," he admitted. "We have said very little to the press. That is not only because we know so little, but because what we do know involves some very prominent people."

Pons raised his eyebrows. The ghost of a smile lay on his thin lips, and his almost feral face betrayed the keenest interest.

"To begin with, the murder was reported to us late Sunday night by a house guest – Sir Malcolm McVeigh, whom you will know as the Shakespearean actor, discovered the body when he came downstairs at midnight for a book to read. That is, he allegedly came down for a book – permit me to put it that way. The body was hanging from a beam above the main stairs in a most extraordinary position, and we have not yet been able to ascertain just how anyone could have got him there. However, the police surgeon reports that he had evidently been drinking: this may have been sufficient to have brought him close to unconsciousness; it is impossible to say. Certainly he was somehow placed in position. I should explain that he was hanging six feet from the stairs, directly above the sixth step, in the well of the stairs, which is broad and very gradual to the landing, from which it turns and goes on to the second floor, proceeding thereafter in similar fashion, though somewhat less broadly, to the third floor. The instrument of death, a chain, depended – and still depends – from a beam above the third floor, but appears to be fixed into the wall along the staircase there. There were other guests in the house."

"And you are considerately keeping their names from the papers," interposed Pons. "I assume all have equal standing with Sir Malcolm McVeigh?"

"Yes, Mr. Pons, it is so. The remaining three guests were Randolph Sutpen, Sir John Watkins, and Richard, Lord Barick."

I understand Pons' smile; anyone of these distinguished actors would have been sufficient to make the story of Jepson's death one of extreme prominence – but all four at one time verged on the sensational.

"I'm sorry to have to add that at least one of the guests, Lord Barick, had a physical encounter with Jepson in the course of that evening, and apparently all the guests were on – shall we say uncertain terms? – with their host."

Pons looked over at the mantel clock. "An express leaves Paddington in ten minutes for Slough. I believe we can just make it. No doubt we shall be able to obtain some method of transportation from Slough to Stoke Poges."

"I can wire for the trap to meet us, Mr. Pons," said Corbett eagerly.

"Very well. Let us be off."

He suited his actions to his words as he spoke, rising and divesting himself of his dressing-gown. He put on his deerstalker cap and a checked jacket, over which he wore his Inverness.

When we were seated in a compartment of the train bound for the half-hour run to Slough, Pons invited Cobbett to continue his account. The sergeant obeyed with alacrity, while the countryside flashed past and Pons sat with his sharp chin sunk upon his breast, and his eyes closed, listening.

"In addition to Lord Barick, the fingerprints of Sir John Watkins appear on a box of veronal capsules. There is evidence to indicate, Mr. Pons, that Jepson was given whiskey and veronal to make him sluggish, so that his murderers could the more easily make away with him. He had not been well. He had asked these gentlemen to be his guests for the weekend, begun with last night's dinner, because he wished to let bygones be bygones and to make amends for his conduct. We have the statements of the gentlemen, and two of them have produced letters from Jepson – identically worded – to substantiate that fact. All the gentlemen were in London, though only Sutpen was playing. Even he allowed his understudy to stand in for him and came down. All arrived just before dinner last night.

"Apparently everything went well until dinner was almost finished; then some reference was made to an action at law which had been lost by Jepson. The action had been taken against Lord Barick. There was an acrimonious exchange. As they left the table, Jepson, who had fallen into step beside Lord Barick, is reported to have said, 'You didn't deserve to win that case, Barick. You know you copied those gestures from my father.' Barick struck him. The two were immediately separated. No apology was made. Barick does not deny the incident and is furious enough still to say that Jepson's death is no loss.

"At or about ten o'clock in the evening, Jepson asked Sir John Watkins to look at something in his room. Sir John's brother is a distinguished doctor, and Sir John himself had had some medical training before he went on stage. Sir John says that he was asked to examine some sleeping capsules. He says that he did so and approved their use. There was then some discussion of cures for insomnia, and by devious ways the conversation carried on to some reference to an action brought by Jepson against Sir John, and, of course, lost by Jepson. There were words. A passing servant heard Jepson say, 'Were I more fit, I would challenge you to sabres, sir!' To which Sir John made this answer: 'Say rather broomstraws, Ahab. Those are your forte when it comes to battle.' Sir John does not deny that there were words. He was apparently the last person to see Ahab alive. His fingerprints appear on the box of capsules, which was sheathed in waxed paper; no fingerprints lie over his. Yet it would appear that Jepson was given veronal before he was taken downstairs and hanged. It is doubtful that one man could have done it. It would appear to have taken place shortly before midnight, according to the medical examiner; the method seems to have been that two or possibly three men carried Jepson down the stairs while he was in a stupor, and that they managed to lift him high enough to remove the Caroline Islands mask which was suspended from the chain normally, and hang him there in its place."

"Grotesquely elaborate," I observed.

"But effective," added Pons. "There are certain challenging facets in your account, Constable. Pray inform me – is it customary for the chemists in Slough or the vicinity of Stoke Poges to dispense sedatives in waxed paper?"

"No, Mr. Pons. That was Mr. Jepson's idiosyncrasy."

"Can the gentlemen account for their movements after ten o'clock?"

"All but McVeigh maintain that they were asleep."

"No witnesses."

"None."

Pons opened his eyes. He looked with intense speculation at Cobbett.

"Here we are at Slough, sir," said Cobbett.

The trap was waiting at the station. The three of us got in and set out through some of the most attractive country in the vicinity of London, hallowed by the memory of Thomas Gray, and long distinguished by the residence of Grote, the historian. The day was pleasant for March, and the open trap an ideal conveyance, though Pons was lost in meditation and oblivious to the beauty of the landscape.

In a short time we arrived at the country home in which Sir Hesketh Jepson had spent his last years. It was a large and imposing house, set in the midst of an oak grove, into which had been placed several yews and ornamental shrubs. Entrance to the estate was by means of a gate set into the stone wall which went round it. A constable on guard at the door threw it open at our approach.

We entered a spacious hall and found ourselves at the scene of the murder, for the stairs were before us, the noosed chain was suspended there above the sixth step, darkly suggestive of the burden which had been removed from it before our arrival. The scene, however, was not without an aspect of the bizarre, for both walls of the hall were lined with the trappings of the days of chivalry – suits of armor, hauberks, glaives, jousting lances, helmets, and similar paraphernalia, all of which had been added to the souvenirs and mementoes of the late Sir Hesketh's years on the stage – the signed photographs of his companions of the footlights, of fellow playwrights, and England's great at the turn of the century; an imposing array. Various other ornaments decorated the walls, and the Polynesian mask of which Cobbett had spoken still lay on the stairs where it had evidently been thrown by the murderers who detached it – a great, colorful, almost gaudy representation of some ancient demon feared or worshipped by the natives of the Carolines.

"As a crime," I said, "it has elements which make it seem flamboyant."

"Could one expect other from the stage?" asked Pons, who had mounted the stairs and now stood looking upward at the chain, following its course to the great beam overhead and the extension over the beam toward the wall along the stair. "Or would you say it is unworthy of Lord Barick and his companions?" He flashed a provocative glance at me. "Is this not a most singular method of murder, Parker?"

I agreed soberly that it was.

"I can hardly recall anything similar among the little adventures with which I have been privileged to be associated. I daresay only a very determined man could manage to reach that chain. I measure it at eleven feet above the stair on which I am standing."

"That's right, Mr. Pons," corroborated Cobbett.

"Though from a few stairs up it might be possible to reach it in nine feet. At the same time the mask might bring it still lower. Presumably, then, it would be necessary to raise Jepson sufficiently to slip the chain over his head and tighten it on his neck. I observe there is an adjustable loop or noose there. Has anyone examined the chain?"

"Yes, Mr. Pons. There appears to be some give in it."

"Indeed," said Pons, raising his eyebrows. "Let us just have a closer look at it."

So speaking, he ran up the stairs to the third floor, where the chain was in easy reach from the narrow hallway. He took hold of it eagerly and began to draw it in over the beam, where it was held in place by two iron rods.

"Ah, what have we here?" he cried. "The chain has been oiled." He looked at Cobbett keenly. "Would you say it suggests premeditation, Cobbett?"

"It would seem so, sir."

"Come, come, do not be so cautious."

He released the chain and turned his attention to the bolt to which it was fixed in the wall. The bolt was formidable; it projected just under the ceiling, and the chain was not just hooked to it, but appeared to be an integral part of it, emerging not from the rounded extremity of the bolt, but from the thick stem itself. Pons went catlike down the hall for a chair and brought it back; he mounted it and scrutinized the bolt with attentive fascination, his sensitive fingers exploring the wall around it. Then he grasped the chain at the bolt in both hands and gave it a sharp tug outward.

It gave four inches, bringing with it not only the bolt but a rounded piece of the panelled wall, which fell back into place against the studding there as soon as Pons released it. He leaped off the chair, rubbing his hands together in pleasure.

"It would appear that this is not, after all, the end of the chain. We shall have to look elsewhere for it. Let us just glance into the cellar."

"We have been there, Mr. Pons."

"I daresay a return journey will not be amiss, Sergeant. Lead the way."

The sergeant obediently trudged down the stairs, one flight after another, to the main floor, where he went around to the kitchen, from which a stairway opened into the cellar under the house. With the aid of the sergeant's torch, we made our way down into the damp rooms below.

"Just about here," said Pons, "we are under the bolt. What have we on this wall?"

"A cupboard," offered Cobbett.

"So the eye sees it. But the eye is limited by the surface, not so?"

As he spoke, he opened the cupboard and disclosed shelving bearing narrow rows of preserves. I was so injudicious as to smile. Pons' serenity was undisturbed.

"Some of the country virtues have survived the war, I see," he said. "But I submit that a cupboard tall enough and deep enough to hold two or three men must contain something more than a single row of preserves."

He was already working at the shelving, moving the jars about to peer behind them; but, not satisfied, he seized hold of the shelving and shoved back. It receded from its depth, half a foot or thereabouts, and held there. He gave it an experimental push away from the outer side wall of the cupboard, and it slid noiselessly into place behind the shelving which looked out of the other door of the cupboard. In doing so, it disclosed a space recessed from the cupboard into the wall at that point, and harboring an ordinary winch, fixed to a concrete block. Around the winch was wound a section of chain, one end of which reached tautly upward, the other end being bolted to the concrete. There were several devices attached to the winch suggesting automatic mechanism of some kind.

Pons stepped into the aperture thus revealed and, moving into the wall space, looked upward.

"The chain reaches to the third floor without obstruction," he announced. "Just as I thought. The floor has been cut away widely enough to allow for ease of passage, and the chain is fixed between the joists."

He gave his attention then to the mechanism. After studying it for a few moments in silence, his keen eyes twinkling with fascinated appreciation, he turned the winch by its handle and unwound the chain; it unwound but eight feet, no farther. Then he wound it up once more; it wound up only the eight feet he had unwound it. He examined the automatic device, unwound the chain once more, set the device, and gave a sharp tug at the taut end of the chain. Instantly the device whirred, the winch moved, and the chain wound itself up once more.

"Capital! Capital!" exclaimed Pons delightedly. "Now you will have observed, Sergeant, that one man could very well effectively have hanged Jepson. All he need have done was to unwind the chain, thus letting it down to within easy reach of the steps, slip the noose over Jepson's neck, and pull at the chain sufficiently to start the mechanism. Let us just set it once more and test it for ourselves."

Accordingly, he did so. Then the three of us returned to the main hall. The chain had been lowered, as Pons had foreseen; it hung now only three feet above the sixth stair. Pons looked upward into the gloom of the ceiling at the far end of the stairwell; nothing of the false bolt with its circular piece of the wood panelling was visible in that murk, quite possibly because it was in the shadow of the great beam over which the chain passed. He mounted the stairs, grasped the chain in both hands, and gave it a sharp tug; the chain moved steadily back into its former position eleven feet above the stairs.

Only a waiting ear could have heard the sound of the winch below.

Constable Cobbett stared hard at the chain. "Well, all I can say, sir – only an actor would have figured out something like that!"

"Quite right," agreed Pons.

"It would have been simpler to dispatch him almost any other way."

"But not nearly so effective," replied Pons instantly. "And actors are notoriously fond of their entrances and exits." He favored me with an enigmatic, almost sly glance. "Would you not be inclined to say, Parker, that a good entrance or a good exit more adequately affords us the measure of the actor than any given set of lines?"

I agreed that it was so.

"Now then," Pons continued, "we shall need to examine the problem of how the veronal was administered."

"Evidence indicates that it was given to him in whiskey and soda, sir," said Cobbett. "Perhaps you would like to examine Jepson's room? We've left it precisely as it was found."

In Jepson's room, too, a sergeant was on guard. Cobbett instructed him to stand before the door while we were in the room. The room itself was decorated with all manner of heraldic emblems, oddly mingled with Polynesian masks, considerably smaller than the one which had customarily hung from the chain over the stairs. The bed was a canopied four-poster, an obviously old piece of furniture; it had been turned back, in readiness for ocupancy, but it had not been occupied. There was some evidence to show that someone had sat on one end of it.

Pons glanced only cursorily at the room in general, his eyes lingered a few moments on the bed, darting here and there, from pillows to posts, and then he gave his undivided attention to the dressing-table beside the bed. A decanter of whiskey, a soda-water bottle, and two glasses stood there; two brushes had been pushed back to make room for the tray on which the bottles and glasses stood.

"We have impounded the box of veronal, of course," explained the constable.

"How many capsules did it contain?" inquired Pons.

"Eight. It was made to contain twelve. He had just bought it at Henderson's in Slough the day before yesterday. He was evidently given four of them."

"Sir John Watkins has been questioned in regard to these glasses?"

"Certainly, Mr. Pons. He says that he had one drink with Jepson, while Jepson had three. His prints are on both glasses. He says that he handed Jepson's glass to him; he was closer to the tray and Jepson asked him to fill his glass a third time. It was then that the argument began, says Sir John."

"And where were the servants all this time?"

"There are only two – a cook and a manservant. They are man and wife, and live in a cottage three miles away. They spend their nights there, traveling to and from the house by dog cart when Mr. Jepson is in residence. They were gone last night. Jepson had permitted them to go sometime after ten o'clock, as usual."

Pons nodded absently. Quite clearly he had no further interest in Jepson's house guests. He displayed a marked disinterest in examining them, but instead walked back down the stairs and stood looking once more at the bizarre setting for Jepson's murder.

"Do you remember Randolph Sutpen's melodrama, *The Four Who Returned*, Parker?" he asked suddenly.

"Yes, a little."

"Does not something about this situation remind you of the central situation in that drama? Was it not concerned with four men who 'executed' a fifth?"

"By Jove!" I exclaimed. "So it was. And Sutpen is one of the guests."

"And suspects," added Pons. "I believe, Sergeant, we shall now have to talk to them. I take it they are available."

"Yes, sir. They are in the library, to the right, sir." The suspects came to their feet as we entered the study. All four were between forty and sixty, and they shared one quality in common – all had what is known in the parlance of the theatre as "presence." They were distinguished in appearance, and at the moment of our entrance, as they rose and ranged themselves together, like a phalanx against us, they had a most formidable aspect.

"Pray compose yourselves, gentlemen," said Pons. "I must trouble you with but a few questions."

"We are at your service, Mr. Pons," said Lord Barick, a tall, broad-shouldered man with impressive eyes and mouth. "We trust that this problem can be solved with your usual ingenuity."

"I thank your lordship. Please sit down."

As they did so, Pons took his stand against the mantel at the fireplace, facing them. "First of all," he continued, "there is the question of the letter. Does any of you have his letter with him?"

"I do, sir," said Sutpen, the youngest of the four, and, like all the others, a man of evident physical strength. He handed an envelope to Pons.

While Pons opened it and removed the invitation from it,

I could not but reflect upon the fact that men who looked less like playwrights and more like cricket-players could not readily be conceived. Anyone of them appeared fully capable of carrying the not inconsiderable body of Ahab Jepson up and down his stairs with ease.

Pons read, interjecting comments. "'I take the liberty of imploring you, for the sake of my dead father's memory' – a maudlin touch, – 'to give me the opportunity to make the amends that are due you' – He is not above being ambiguous! – 'and be my house guest for the last weekend in March. There are matters which sorely need adjustment' – How delicate he is! – 'and I welcome the opportunity of adjusting them. I trust you will let bygones be bygones and do me the honour of being my guest.'"

He handed the letter back to Sutpen. "This role did not fit Ahab Jepson well – yet it is singularly in character – florid, pompous, vain, and wholly fraudulent. I take it, gentlemen, that Mr. Jepson's conduct was basically unchanged."

"That is correct, Mr. Pons," replied Lord Barick.

Pons turned to Sir John Watkins, the shortest of the four, though a sturdy, well-muscled man. "You, Sir John, were asked to examine a box of veronal capsules. How many were in the box at the time you looked into it?"

"Eight," replied Sir John without hesitation, his dark eyes flashing.

"When were you last previously a guest here, Sir John?"

"This is the first time I've entered the house since Hesketh Jepson's death."

"That was fifteen years ago on the twentieth of May. Has any of you been here since that time prior to this visit?"

None of them had. Sutpen volunteered the additional information that he alone among the four of them had never previously visited in the house; he had known Sir Hesketh only in the last two years of the actor's life.

"Will you think back to your last visit, Sir John?" suggested Pons.

"Yes?"

"Can you recall any signal differences in the appearance of the house?"

Sir John smiled grimly. "Sir Hesketh would hardly have tolerated the gew-gaws Ahab collected. I mean that though he came from a distinguished family, he had none but family heirlooms about; Ahab went in for all manner of chivalric paraphernalia, and added a line of Polynesian carvings. I am constrained to suggest that the former appealed to him as compensation for his own lack, and the latter to the essentially primitive aspects of his mind."

"Let us not speak ill of the dead," said Sir Malcolm McVeigh quietly. He was the oldest of the group, with greying hair, and wore a monocle in one of his grey eyes. He had an impressively reassuring manner.

Pons turned and looked at him, and without changing the direction of his glance, said, "Now I should like a detailed account of your movements between the time you entered the house yesterday and the discovery of Jepson's body." He spoke with a casual air which suggested that this was only a formality to be got over with.

"I believe I can speak for all of us," offered Sir Malcolm, returning Pons' gaze with an attitude of easy confidence. "We arrived together, you see, and we remained pretty much together throughout the evening. We were shown into this study on our arrival, while our things were packed off upstairs to our rooms. Our host appeared, greeted us pleasantly enough, and himself showed us to our rooms. We were not left any longer than the time it took us to get ready for dinner. Then our host himself led us down to the dining-room. On the way he stopped on the stairs to deliver a lecture about the mask hung there; it purports to be a mask worn by witch-doctors in summoning up the dead – a macabre conceit which seemed to please him. Then we went in to dinner. I believe you have heard already of the disagreeable conversations which were carried on at the table; our host took the occasion to reveal his true colors; with each drink he took, he became more offensive. After dinner we sat for over an hour in the study. Let me see – dinner took until some time after eight; I believe we left the study for our own rooms at nine-forty-five or thereabouts. It was while we were on the way to our rooms that our host asked Sir John to his room.

"As for the rest of us – we went to our own rooms but shortly foregathered in Lord Barick's quarters to discuss our host's aberrant conduct. We were joined there by Sir John, much agitated, in perhaps an hour's time. Lord Barick had turned in by the time we left him. We went on to Mr. Sutpen's room, spoke about his play, and left him disrobing. Sir John sat for a while in my room, still angry at what he termed our host's insolence. I recalled an incident on one of my early visits to Sir Hesketh, when he was obliged to cane Ahab for his insolence, though Ahab was then but a boy. It was eleven o'clock when we parted. Sir John presumably retired. Only I failed to do so; I was myself so upset that I could not sleep. This was in part because at least two members of the party – Sir John and Lord Barick – had not wished to respond to our host's invitation, but I prevailed upon them to come, thinking that perhaps Ahab had had a change of heart or conscience. I walked about or sat in my room until midnight or thereabouts; then I gave up trying and went downstairs. I found Ahab."

Pons had listened carefully during this recital. At its conclusion he glanced from one to another of the other three men, but none volunteered additional information. "Did you hear any suspicious sounds during the hour you were awake before you went downstairs?" he asked then.

"Mr. Pons, I heard nothing."

"Not even, let me suggest, the closing of a door?"

"I do not remember that I did."

"Now, gentlemen, I want you to listen very carefully. Pray excuse me; I will return in a few moments."

Pons left the room.

He was gone only a short time. Just before he stepped back into the room, I heard the distant grinding of the winch; he had evidently set off the mechanism. It was remote even from this floor, which was directly above the cellar; from the second story it would scarcely have been audible.

"Did you hear anything now, Sir Malcolm?" asked Pons.

"Something creaked?"

"What would you say it was?"

"A pump, perhaps?" ventured Sir Malcolm.

"Would anyone care to make a guess?"

No one did.

"Very well. Let us say no more about it at the moment. Now, Sir Malcolm, since you have said you were instrumental in persuading two other members of this party to accept Ahab Jepson's invitation, will you tell us why you did so? We need not pretend that any degree of warmth existed between any of you and your late host. Why, then, accept his invitation?"

"Mr. Pons, I must violate a confidence to tell you, but I will do so," answered Sir Malcolm graciously. "I had learned that our host was a sick man, and that he had prepared an announcement of his retirement from the stage, though only forty-seven. Frankly, I believed this only a bid for some popular sympathy. My own doctor, however, had been consulted by Ahab Jepson; I took the liberty of making an enquiry, and was informed that our host was actually suffering from a heart ailment which compelled his retirement from all activity whatsoever, and which in all likelihood would take him off at any time. I felt sorry for him; so I came and persuaded the others to come, too."

"Thank you, gentlemen. That is all," said Pons.

In the hall, Pons paused to look up once again at the ingenious device which had brought Ahab Jepson to his death. He wore a satisfied smile when he turned to Cobbett at last. "I take it you are quite settled in mind, Sergeant," he said. "Does anything remain to perplex you?"

"Mr. Pons, I confess I cannot imagine which one of them or which two could have committed this crime. It is what has troubled me from the beginning."

"My dear Cobbett, allow me to congratulate you," cried Pons, his eyes dancing. "You are quite right – none of them is guilty. Pray follow your instincts – permit these gentlemen to repair to London without further delay, and say nothing to the press about their presence here."

Cobbett gaped at him, taken aback.

"It was staged with some eye for drama, but the eye was unsure. Ask yourself, as I did, why a box of veronal capsules should be wrapped in wax paper if not to take fingerprints? And why should it be required of Sir John to fill Ahab's glass if not for a similar reason? And surely Lord Barick was provoked into striking his host so that it might be duly recorded! But unfortunately, Ahab forgot something, if you take the trouble, as you must, to look into the matter – you'll find no evidence of fingerprints save only Ahab's and my own on the machinery of the chain – winch-handle and attached mechanism – or on the cupboard concealing it. He overlooked a vital detail, just as he seems to have done in most of his undertakings. He forgot to take his guests into the cellar and reveal the mechanism. But the whiskey and veronal were necessary: the veronal – such capsules as he took were removed from the box before Sir John saw it – to make it look as if he had been drugged into a stupor, the whiskey to screw up his nerve to that point at which he could walk down the stairs and hang himself in order to implicate and throw the dark cloud of scandal shamefully over the good names of four sterling gentlemen he could harm in no other way."

"An elementary matter," observed Pons, once we were seated in our compartment on the return trip to London that evening. "Cobbett himself gave us the initial suggestion of the truth on the way down. He said of Ahab, 'He had not been well.' But Cobbett thought himself confounded with four suspects, each with a motive to want Ahab Jepson out of the way. Nothing could have been farther from the truth – it was not Cobbett's suspects who had motive to want Ahab out of the way – they had won the actions Ahab had brought – but Ahab who had motive to want them injured in such a way as to bring them some mental suffering. I proceeded, therefore, from the opposite basis – that the guests were innocent, and every discovery made at the house only verified it. Ahab's garish and slightly *gauche* touch was everywhere apparent. He was capable of killing them, but he wanted something more of them, and a scandal of such proportions as to involve them in suspicion of murder would have served his purpose very well. It is to Cobbett's credit that he proceeded with such caution. He is a young man who shows promise of some ability in the field."

"But to kill himself!" I protested.

"He lived on borrowed time, Parker; so much is obvious. And whatever his unlovely attributes, he had a sincere love of the stage; to have to leave it was like a sentence of death. Nor could he bear to leave his exit to chance; like every actor, he wanted to plan and execute it himself. He did. He conceived a dastardly plan, set it in motion, and made his flamboyant exit, wholly melodramatic. A poor thing, but certainly his own; it was beyond his guests to have conceived it. It had all the marks of his conception. Alas, poor Ahab! His exit was in keeping with his life – pompous, florid, somewhat ignominious, and in his customary bad taste."

"It is simple enough, now you explain it," I agreed.

A wry smile touched Pons' lips. He turned to look out at the little lights of the English countryside flying past. "Inevitable," he murmured. "As Tacitus puts it, *Omne ignotum pro magnifico*."

For years thereafter Pons was never without complimentary tickets to any London performance in which were displayed the histrionic abilities of the four gentlemen of the theatre who had been so ill-advised by sentiments of common humanity as to permit themselves to be the guests of Ahab Jepson on that fateful weekend at Stoke Poges.

V

THE ADVENTURE OF THE PROPER COMMA

When I look over my notes on the problems which commanded the attention of my astute friend, Solar Pons, during 1922, I find myself faced with some difficulty in the selection of a typical adventure. For that year included, among others, the singular case of Hrenville, the paralytic mendicant, and his remarkable macaw; the perplexing riddle of Lily MacLain and her extraordinary clairaudience; the complex puzzle of the five Royal Coachmen; and the horrible affair of the Tottenham Werewolf. But the story which comes to the fore is none of these; it is rather that lesser adventure which I have filed in my notes as that of the Lady in Grey, though Pons is adamant in maintaining that it is more correctly referred to as *The Adventure of the Proper Comma*.

It came to Pons' attention from an uncommon source; perhaps no other adventure ever reached him by way of the little group of urchins he often asked to assist him, and whom he called his Praed Street Irregulars – bright, alert lads, always willing to lend what unobtrusive assistance they could for an honest sovereign. As boys, they were able to go unnoticed many places where Pons would have drawn attention, and they were thus on occasion of invaluable help to him.

Early one evening in March, David Benjamin, a shock-haired youth, swarthy in the darkness of his skin and the acknowledged leader of the Praed Street Irregulars, came apologetically up the stairs and knocked almost timidly on the door.

"Ah, that is one of the boys," said Pons, raising his head. "Fearful of rousing Mrs. Johnson, I daresay. Open to him, Parker."

I opened the door and revealed David in the act of snatching his cap from his head.

"Come in, David, come in," said Pons with hearty invitation. "What is troubling you, lad?"

"Mr. Pons, sir," said the boy, walking into the room. "We thought as 'ow you ought ter see this."

He handed Pons a stone so small as to be almost a pebble. Pons seized on it with interest and held it under the lamp on the table. I bent forward, ranging myself beside him where he leaned over the stone in his palm. Scatched crudely on the stone, apparently with a pin or similar tool, were two words:

HELP, PLEASE

Pons viewed David with narrowed eyes. "Where did you get this, David?"

"We went down Walworth way today, sir. Bert, 'e's got 'n aunt near the *Elephant and Castle*, an' we went down ter visit 'er."

He began to talk with more animation, now that it was plain that he had not come in vain, for Pons' interest was manifest. Bert's cousin, having shown his visitors all about the premises of his parents, took them on a tour of the neighborhood. They had ended up at a strange, walled place some distance away from the house at which they had been visiting, but in one or two places there were wrought-iron gates breaking the continuity of the stone walls. They had clustered about one of these gates and were peering into the grounds, where men and women in grey uniforms were walking about within the enclosure, all apparently accompanied by guards or companions to watch over them, when suddenly a woman in a grey uniform had run toward the gate, closely pursued by a guard, who reached her just as she got to the gate, which was securely locked and barred. She had caught David's eye – he was the oldest of the four boys – and, as she clung to the bars of the gate, the stone had slipped from her fingers to the ground at David's feet. Her right hand bore a crooked scar across the back near the wrist. The guard had pulled her roughly away, and returned to the gate to chase them away. David had retrieved the stone. As soon as he had seen what was written upon it, he had consulted with his companions, who were unanimously of the opinion that it should be brought to 7B, Praed Street, and delivered to Solar Pons without delay.

"So's soon as I got back home, I came round with it," finished David.

"And quite right, too, David. Here." He fished a sovereign out of his pocket and gave it to David, who smiled gratefully. "Now I'll just keep this stone. I may need you again, and I'll send word to you if I do. We shall just look into this."

David thanked him and took his departure, clattering down the stairs in marked contrast to the stealth of his entry.

"That was surely a wasted sovereign," I said.

"I doubt that any contribution toward the development of the faculty of observation in man is ever truly wasted, Parker,' said Pons thoughtfully, contemplating the stone. "Why do you say so?"

I could not help smiling. "Because I recognized the place from the boy's description. It is the private sanitarium of Dr. Sloane Sollaire. For mental patients, of course. That stone is only a pathetic but typical gesture to be expected from people who are sufficiently deranged to be incarcerated."

"Indeed," murmured Pons, still turning the stone in his fingers. "I wonder that you can be so dogmatic, Parker."

"Medicine is my field, Pons," I replied, not without some satisfaction.

"Ah, I would be the last to dispute it. But I fancy there are nooks and crannies of the torso as well as of the mind about which even our best medical men are not yet comprehensively informed."

"True," I conceded.

"Who knows the vagaries of the human mind? Indeed, I myself am the last to claim such knowledge. I find it constantly refreshing to probe and peer into the depths. At the moment I am intrigued by this message. I could not help reflecting, as I listened to David's account, how slyly it was done, how cleverly."

"Oh, some of those poor people are very cunning."

"Paper is obviously denied them. But pins and a stone! There is tenacity there, Parker."

"They are tenacious, too."

"I daresay they are occasionally everything normal, sane people are, not so?"

"There are times, yes, when..."

"Even grammatical," said Pons, putting the stone before me.

There was an undeniable comma properly placed between the two words scratched so laboriously upon the surface of the stone.

"I submit, Parker, that grammatical accuracy is not a common attribute of deranged individuals, particularly of those who are making so frantic an appeal for help as this."

"My dear fellow," I protested, "there is no hard and fast line between the sane and the insane."

"How true!" He gazed at me quizzically, his dark eyes intent and distant. "We have been in the doldrums recently, and

I fancy this is as good a time as any to improve my knowledge of the insane in our institutions. Tomorrow I will have you incarcerate me in Dr. Sollaire's sanitarium."

"What?" I cried out. "Pons, you aren't serious!"

"I was never more so."

"But it is such a mad scheme!"

"Ah, I shall be mad as a hatter, if necessary. I have always had a fondness for Alice's table companions."

"Pons, I don't like Dr. Sollaire."

"You are trying to prejudice me, Parker," Pons bantered.

"His reputation..."

"Pray permit me to discover it for myself."

"Oh, come," I cried impatiently, "Sollaire is not a man to take lightly. I have reason to believe him dangerous, and his establishment no less so."

"There is always a fascination about danger," countered Pons. "And things have been uncommonly dull of late."

I shrugged and gave up for the evening, determined to talk him out of his mad plan in the morning.

But the following day found Pons up with the sun and about one of his most detestable habits – revolver-practice in the front room which served as our sitting-room and study. The sharp crack of his weapon woke me, and when I came from my bedroom I found not the familiar companion of most of my days but an unrecognizable fellow in the guise of a middle-class merchant of some means and a woeful inability to select his clothing. Indeed, had it not been for Pons' addiction to revolver-practice, I should have had grave doubts that the gentleman into whom he had transformed himself was indeed the companion of my quarters, for he had made up his face so skillfully, and without the addition of any hirsute adornment, that he did certainly resemble far more the slightly deranged individual he had set out to become than Solar Pons. Tossing his revolver to one side, he collapsed his chest, hunched his shoulders, losing height, and clasped his hands nervously before him, thus still further retreating into his role.

"Mr. Samuel Porter, late of Canada, at your service, Parker," he said in a rasping voice, totally unlike his own.

"You are determined to go through with it, then?" I asked, sitting down to breakfast.

"I am."

"On nothing more than a poor lunatic's pebble?"

"On less – so little a thing as a properly placed comma."

He sat down opposite me. "I shall take the role of a retired businessman who has gone over the edge worrying about his Canadian investments, which have recently taken a little drop, as you will see by the financial columns of the *Times*. I have been visiting relatives in London – I leave you to produce them, if necessary – and you are committing me for observation, but not molestation. I must have a relatively free hand within such boundaries as are allowed me."

"Pons, I hope I can dissuade you from this wild scheme," I protested.

"Say no more, Parker. I shall expect to be committed this morning. Pray make the necessary arrangements, and plan to call on me tomorrow afternoon."

Accordingly, since Pons was adamant, and after a lengthy telephone conversation with Dr. Sollaire, I delivered Pons in mid-morning to the private sanitarium in the vicinity of the *Elephant and Castle*, and left him with profound misgivings in the care of a man who, for all his impressive reputation, was little more than a charlatan in medicine.

After a restless night, impatient at the slow passage of time, I presented myself at Sollaire's sanitarium for a consultation with my patient. I was shown into a visiting room, and presently Pons, whom I had described as a patient who was excitable and much given to talking to himself, was ushered into my presence. He stood glowering at me just past the threshold until the attendant left us; then he came forward hestitantly, acting his part perfectly.

"It is Dr. Parker?" he asked.

"Come, sit down, Mr. Porter," I replied. "Are you enjoying your rest here?"

Pons came forward, saying in a loud voice, "They treat me very well. But it is expensive, is it not? And who is to pay for it?" To this he added in a whisper, "What a model of fusty stuffiness you are, Parker!"

"Please speak freely," I said.

He gave a barely perceptible shake of his head, by which I understand that we might be under optical or auditory observation, but he seated himself near me and began to talk a farrago of nonsense, dropping his voice from time to time ostensibly to mutter to himself but in reality to convey to me some vital information. The lady with the scarred hand, he had discovered, was the second wife of Dr. Gerald Buxton, a well known Park Row practitioner. She did not believe herself insane, but did not actually know her condition, which was not typical of a deranged condition. Pons had caught her attention and would manage to talk to her again. He intended that he should remain here for another day, until the hour at which the patients were permitted to walk about the grounds, which was between three and four o'clock in the afternoon.

Having imparted this information, he proceeded to give me a set of instructions, which, stripped of the nonsense he talked in character, came to this:

"Present yourself here at three-fifteen tomorrow afternoon to remove me either temporarily or permanently. You will employ a cab, preferably with Alfie More driving it. Alfie is to be told to follow my orders no matter what occurs. You may be knocked down and left behind, as much a victim as Mrs. Buxton's attendant. Reach David Benjamin and persuade him to have the Irregulars at the carriage entrance to create a diversion as soon as the gate is opened for us, and generally to impede pursuit."

Since all this was put to me sotto voce, I could not protest. "But, my dear Mr. Porter," I said in some alarm, "if the conditions for you here are not satisfactory, what do you intend I should do for you?"

"I'm going back to Canada," he announced in a loud voice, and added, "I intend to abduct Mrs. Buxton."

I gasped. "Think it over for another day, at least," I implored.

"I have have made up my mind," replied Pons, and rose.

I presented my compliments to Dr. Sollaire, a tall, ascetic man clad in a black frock coat, wearing a Van Dyke beard on his weak chin and pince-nez over his grey eyes, and made a report to him.

"Your patient – " he glanced at a file on his desk – "ah, Mr. Porter – makes no complaint, Dr. Parker?"

"None, sir," I answered. "But he is restless. I have persuaded him to take an additional day. He now believes that he wishes to go back to Canada, and I may sanction the journey."

"There is no history of violence?"

"None, Doctor. The man is utterly wrapped up in himself and his troubles. He may be given every liberty, except, of course, his freedom. I will expect to call for him, unless he changes his mind, tomorrow afternoon."

I rose. Dr. Sollaire came to his feet also, leaning forward with his grey eyes fixed on me.

"Tell me, Dr. Parker – we have your office address, but not your home address – are you not the same medical man who makes his home with Mr. Solar Pons?"

I saw no reason to deny a fact which could have been discovered so readily.

"An extraordinary man," murmured Dr. Sollaire.

"There are those who think so," I agreed.

He raised his eyebrows. "Do I detect a note of hesitation?"

"I could not say. But Pons' methods are certainly not those of a physician, sir," I said with heat I did not find it necessary to manufacture.

He smiled. "Very well, Dr. Parker. We shall wait upon your wishes in the best interests of the patient."

I went about following Pons' instructions with profound doubt of his wisdom. While it was manifest that he intended to exclude me as a suspect in his plot – so much was in his plot – so much was in his promise that I might be knocked down and left behind – I was nevertheless gravely uneasy over the part he required me to play in a scheme which was fundamentally illegal.

Promptly at the designated hour, I presented myself at Dr. Sollaire's sanitarium, paid my respects to its director with a request that a statement be sent to me, and then sat to await Pons' coming. He came presently, arguing volubly with his attendant, and I immediately asked him whether he had determined to leave and attempt a trip to Canada. That he had was evident, for the attendant carried the small bag he had taken with him to his voluntary incarceration. Remaining in character, he answered that he had, and went on to talk such nonsense that the attendant shrugged and grinned.

The three of us made our way from the grim building into the walled yard, where other patients now walked about together with attendants. Alfie More and his cab waited at the carriage entrance, toward which the attendant spurted ahead in order to open the gate and stand on guard against any attempt at escape of any other patient.

Just as we were about to pass from the grounds, Pons stopped doggedly before the opened gate.

"I won't go," he cried. "They've kept my razor."

"Come, come," I said soothingly. "I'll get you another."

"I want my own. It was my father's. I hid it in the table drawer in that room."

The attendant came forward. "He's mistaken, Doctor. He didn't bring any razor. He hasn't touched his face, and we didn't shave him. Your orders."

"Yes, yes, I know," I answered nervously.

During this altercation, a young and not unattractive woman had moved in our direction, accompanied by her attendant, a burly fellow who promised to offer Pons more difficulty than he had bargained for. Just a few steps away stood Alfie More's cab, the door swung wide, waiting on our entrance; no one was in sight save an elderly woman walking down the far side of the street, which was a narrow side street debouching upon the thoroughfare beyond.

"Come now, Mr. Porter," I said persuasively. "We're off to Canada."

At this moment, the lady in grey came up rapidly, crying,

"Oh, what are they doing to that poor man?" with her attendant at her heels, calling, " 'Ere, now, Missus. 'Ere, come away from that gate."

Suddenly Pons leaped from his role. With one sweep of his arm, he knocked me against his own attendant with such force that both of us went sprawling. With a sharp jab of his fist, he floored the lady's attendant. Almost in the same movement, he took her by the hand and hustled her into the cab even as both attendants were coming to their feet. As if by magic, the Praed Street Irregulars materialised from nowhere, crowding, with shouts and cries, between the cab and the attendants, tripping, pummelling, and generally harrying them, as well as myself, for I had come to my feet and run, shouting, after the fast-vanishing cab. Behind us an alarm bell had begun to ring, but the cab was already out of sight, and with its passage from the narrow side street, the Irregulars, too, melted away like mist.

I turned to face Dr. Sollaire, who stood controlling himself as best he could.

"The address of his relatives, quickly, Doctor," he said. "We must lose no time. That woman is dangerous – dangerous."

I gave him the address of the mythical Samuel Porter's "nephew," amid my protestations and apologies, to which Sollaire paid not the slightest attention. He hastened off with the address, leaving me to stand in the street as if I had ceased to exist.

It was two hours before I returned to my Praed Street lodgings. I had not thought it prudent to go anywhere but to my office, having paused *en route* only long enough to telephone a warning to "Porter's nephew." I found Pons alone in the living-room, his lean figure bent over a reference volume I could not at once identify. He did not look up at my entrance, but manifestly recognized my step.

"Ah, Parker, I fear I was too rough with you this afternoon. My apologies."

"It's nothing," I answered. "But what the devil are you up to? The police have been at my office, putting me through it. Porter, of course, has disappeared."

"Vanished without trace," he agreed. "That is what the papers will say."

"What have you done with Mrs. Buxton?"

"I have given her a sedative and allowed her to sleep. She is in your room."

"My room!"

"Pray do not alarm yourself, Parker. You will double with me tonight."

"Have you notified her husband?"

"I fancy he will pay us a call before too long a time has elapsed." He gave me a long, searching glance. "What do you know of Dr. Gerald Buxton, Parker?"

"Oh, Park Row connections. Dowagers' doctor. Exorbitant charges. A high liver who throws away his money at the races and elsewhere."

"He himself had his wife confined."

"Of course. Pons, I warned you that you were making a mistake."

"Ah, but the lady made none. Mrs. Buxton is his second wife. She was the former Angeline Magoun. Does that convey anything to you?"

"Oh, yes, of course. Daughter of the late soap magnate, Andrew Magoun. An only child, too."

"An only heir," added Pons dryly. "Dr. Buxton's first wife died in a sanitarium in Bristol. I submit that it is more than a coincidence that two of his wives should go mad. I submit, moreover, that it is even more of a coincidence that both the ladies should be heiresses – in a minor way, of course, but yet, heiresses – and well insured, leaving Dr. Gerald Buxton beneficiary."

I stared at him open-mouthed for a minute before I found my voice. "Pons, Buxton may be what medical men tend to call a 'hand-holder', but he has no need to be what you are suggesting he is."

"And, finally, I respectfully draw your attention to recently published gossip that Dr. Buxton has been seen escorting yet a third young lady, likewise an heiress, to Covent Garden and certain imported American plays. Dear me, but he is an enterprising man!"

"He has a devoted following."

"Indeed! As Despreaux says, *Un sot trouve toujours un plus sot qui l'admire*. Above all else, pray remember that Dr. Buxton must not know of his wife's presence in our quarters. I daresay the man is no fool; he will not spend much time looking for Mr. Samuel Porter when once he learns of your connection with me."

"And his wife – what had she to say?"

"Buxton had her committed three months ago. She has lost weight; her dresses no longer fit her. She believes she is being slowly and systematically poisoned. Buxton sends in her own medicines; Dr. Sollaire and his staff discreetly look the other way. He is not a pleasant man, your Dr. Sollaire, but alas! one who has managed to keep himself out of the hands of the law for the time being. If she is to be believed, her husband has no such elite practise as to justify his lavish expenditures; he has had himself declared her guardian, and forced her to sign a power of attorney to him. She and her fortune are thus at his mercy."

At this moment a cab which had been coming down the street at a swift pace drew up at our door, and within moments the outer door of our lodgings was wrenched open with some violence, followed by the pounding ascent of the stairs.

"A big man, in a hurry," said Pons tranquilly. "Pray contain yourself, Parker. He would appear given to violence of word and deed."

The door of our quarters was opened without ceremony, and our visitor thrust himself into the room where we stood. He was certainly a big man, large of frame, porcine, with a florid, full face, sensuous lips surmounted by a bushy moustache, and protruding eyes, which glared at us in fury.

"Dr. Buxton, I presume," said Pons, smiling.

"Ah, you know me. That is not a coincidence," said Buxton from between tight lips. His lower jaw thrust out, and his fingers trembled on the heavy ebony cane he carried.

"I make it my business to know a good many people, Dr. Buxton." Pons nodded in my direction. "My companion, Dr. Lyndon Parker."

Buxton gave me a contemptuous glance. "Your lackey, sir. I am not deceived. Where is my wife?"

"Do you have reference to the wife already disposed of or the one whose case is under disposition?"

Buxton grew almost purple with rage. He raised his cane and shook it at Pons, but in a moment leaned forward, one hand flat on the table between him and Pons, and said in a choked voice, "I know you, Mr. Solar Pons. You meddling busybody! I warn you – don't get in my way, or I'll break you – like this."

He dropped his cane to the table as he spoke, snatched up a broom which our long-suffering landlady had left behind, and broke it with one angry motion. In answer, Pons reached down, took up our visitor's heavy cane, snapped it in mid-air, and handed the pieces to Buxton.

"Pray do not forget your stick, Doctor."

For a moment the two men faced each other in silence. Then Buxton turned with an inarticulate growl of rage and made his way out of our lodgings as stormily as he had come in, flinging the pieces of his ebony cane to the floor.

"A dangerous man," I said, after the outer door had slammed. "And an angry man."

"Say rather a badly frightened man," retorted Pons.

He went around, picked up the pieces of Buxton's cane, and threw them into the fireplace. Then he returned to the table, taking something from his pocket.

"Mrs. Buxton had presence of mind enough to bring along two of the capsules she has been taking at her husband's direction. An analysis of their contents might prove interesting and informative."

"Pons, he would hardly dare poison her."

"Would he not, indeed? Dr. Sollaire sees only what is convenient for him to see. She has not been mistreated; every attendant can and would testify to that. Dr. Sollaire can produce a case history to show her steady decline and physical deterioration. If Buxton raised no question, no one else would be likely to; no near family relatives would survive her. You are too willing to suspend the faculty of belief, Parker. This man is wilful, devious, dark; he brooks no interference. He may well return here with a warrant within twelve hours; by that time Mrs. Buxton will be in the care of Sir Francis Jeffers, to whom I explained the circumstances over the telephone. I daresay Buxton will think twice before challenging the opinion of so distinguished an alienist."

"Pons, he will find a way to get her back."

"I think not. She will see her solicitor after Sir Francis has seen her. Once she has gone that far, Buxton is finished. It remains to be seen to what lengths he may go before then. I have a surprise or two in store for him yet." He rubbed his hands together with evident relish. "Now then, Parker, let us get on with an analysis of Dr. Buxton's medication."

When I returned from Thorndyke & Polton with an analysis of the capsules Mrs. Buxton had carried with her, I found Sir Francis Jeffers listening to Pons' story. Sir Francis, an austere, bemonocled man past middle age, nodded gravely to me, his narrowed eyes flashing only briefly in my direction.

"Dr. Parker has had Mrs. Buxton's medication analysed," explained Pons. "Come, Parker, tell us what you found. I observe my guess was not wide of the mark."

"Sulphonal. Each capsule contained 0.64 gram."

Sir Francis gazed at me speculatively. "Ah, the design is to prolong life for some months. What was the prescription?"

"I think we can ascertain that by asking the lady," said Pons. "If I am not mistaken, I hear her stirring."

He rose as he spoke, excused himself, and vanished in the direction of my chamber, from which he returned in a few moments escorting a raven-haired woman of thirty or thereabouts, who clung to his arm almost tenaciously.

"Mrs. Buxton, may I present Sir Francis Jeffers and Dr. Lyndon Parker?"

She nodded without speaking, her eyes looking warily from one to the other of us. Her hands were trembling, her thin-lipped mouth was stubborn, her wan face clearly betrayed ill health.

"Mrs. Buxton, how long were you with Dr. Sollaire?" asked Sir Francis gently.

"Six weeks, I think."

"And the capsules your husband prescribed for you? How often have you taken them?"

"Daily – until I began to think there was something wrong."

"Will you tell us how you came to be where Mr. Pons found you?"

"My husband put me there."

"Against your will?"

She smiled tiredly. "No. But he kept me there against my will. He had always been very kind to me, very considerate. I had no reason to distrust him. He told me I was not well, and I did feel unwell after a while. He said there was nothing physically wrong, but that my mental health might be affected. He suggested a short stay at the sanitarium. I did what he asked. But I did not feel that I was so unstable as to justify his keeping me there; yet every time I asked him to move me, he put me off, and at last I understood that he did not mean to take me away from there at all. I was closely guarded most of the time. My letters were not delivered; I could not telephone or wire, nothing. I tried everything. Once I threw a letter over the wall, but they recovered it, and after that I was denied paper and pen. Then, that little stone – oh! I am so grateful to that boy, whoever he is, and to you, Mr. Pons."

"Give me your hands, Mrs. Buxton," commanded Sir Francis.

Unhesitatingly she surrendered her hands. He held them for a few moments in his, gently touching her palms, then clasped them together and patted them reassuringly.

"You are nervous, tired, ill, Mrs. Buxton. I am sure it is not serious – now that we can dispense with your husband's capsules. Will you put yourself in my care?"

"Certainly," she answered at once. "But I must see my solicitor to cancel the power of attorney I gave my husband."

"And who is he?"

"Leonard Runciman. He will be at his home at this hour, I am confident."

"Very good. My car is downstairs. May I send you to Mr. Runciman with my driver? I will join you there in a little while."

"If you will, please."

"I have telephoned him," said Pons.

"Thank you."

Sir Francis saw her solicitously from our quarters. Pons shielded her from weather by shrouding her in his Inverness, and stood at the window looking down to see that she was safely dispatched.

"One never knows the extent of a brute like Buxton's persistence," he murmured. "Ah, there she goes. Sir Francis is coming back."

He turned from the window to face the door in the familiar pose with his hands clasped behind him, and his feral features almost hauty in their strong aquilinity. He spoke as soon as Sir Francis crossed the threshold.

"What do you make of her, Sir Francis?"

"I cannot be certain, but I think she is as sane as you or I. She has been through an ordeal, she is extremely nervous, she is unsure of herself. But she has a hard inner core of resistance; she will come out of it all right. You did her a singular service, Mr. Pons."

"Her condition is consistent with the symptoms of sulphonal poisoning?"

"Certainly. Sulphonal probably accounts for it. She will need care. What a fiendish plan! I can hardly conceive of her husband's doing it."

"Not only once – but twice. His previous wife, too, died in an institution."

"Good God! What manner of man can he be?"

Pons' alert ears caught the sound of wheels outside. He smiled grimly.

"If I am not in error, you may find out," he answered.

Once more the outer door was flung open with a crash; once again came that insistently demanding pounding up the stairs; once again the door of our quarters was opened without the formality of a knock, and Dr. Gerald Buxton stood there – somewhat disheveled, carrying a new stick, his porcine features flushed with anger still.

"Mr. Pons, I've come for my wife. I should warn you – your quarters are surrounded."

Pons stepped tranquilly to the windows facing Praed Street and gazed down. "Ah, you have brought your bully boys," he murmured. "I had thought you might be so unwise as to go to the police."

"Sir, my wife!" repeated Buxton.

"You are too late, Dr. Buxton," answered Pons. "She is in the care of Sir Francis Jeffers, who is, I fancy, a better authority on sanity than you, sir."

"You prying scoundrel!" shouted Buxton in a rage, half raising his cane in a threatening gesture.

"Ah, yes, I think to pry farther still, my dear fellow. An application to the Home Office for an exhumation of the body of your first wife might be in order."

Buxton smiled sardonically. "You must think me a fool, you meddling detective." His voice dripped contempt.

"On the contrary, I have a high regard for your abilities, if not your methods, Dr. Buxton," replied Pons. "You were doubtless clever enough to avoid the use of any poison which might be detected so late. But there is little need to prolong this painful scene. The capsules you were giving your wife were analysed this evening, and the sulphonal in them, at least is still evident. Your wife has cancelled your power of attorney, and will begin an action against you tomorrow. Your little plans, Dr. Buxton, will not materialize this time in quite the patterns you designed. The capsules, together with your wife's story and my deposition, will be in the hands of Scotland Yard before midnight. Pray allow me to bid you good evening"

Buxton stood briefly as one transfixed. Not a flicker of emotion crossed his face, and one arm was still upraised in a gesture of threatening defiance. He might have been statuary for the moment after Pons had finished speaking. If he saw his house of cards collapse, if he visualized what the newspapers would do to him, if he saw his private world destroyed, he gave no sign. Then his face whitened, a kind of explosive sound burst from his thick lips, he turned and ran down the stairs without troubling to shut the door after him.

Sir Francis broke the silence with a discreet cough. "Paranoid," he said with conviction. "Certifiable."

"A man given to violence. But his wife is now beyond his reach. Upon whom will he turn next?" said Pons. "We shall hear of him again."

Nor was Pons in error. The morning papers carried word of Dr. Gerald Buxton. He had shot himself in his Park Row quarters.

VI

THE ADVENTURE OF RICOLETTI OF THE CLUB FOOT

It was on a wild and windy night in autumn of a year shortly after my fortunate chance encounter with Solar Pons led to our sharing quarters at 7B, Praed Street, that Pons was introduced to the curious affair of Orso Ricoletti, the reclusive crytographer. I had fought my way home from a professional call through a driving rain which came down in sheets of such intensity that the street-lamps shone through only as indistinct blurs of light. Few vehicles were abroad, and even fewer pedestrians. Yet, when I reached our quarters at last, grateful to be shut away from the equinoctial gale outside, I found Solar Pons standing on the hearth in an attitude of the keenest expectation. He was clad in his blue dressing-gown and worn slippers, and stood with his hands clasped behind him; that he had been smoking shag was evident in the pungence which lingered in the room. His almost feral face with its sharp features – the aquiline nose, the piercing grey eyes, the thin-lipped mouth, and the heavy brows – was bent upon the door as if he expected it to open at any moment and present to him the agent of another perplexing adventure.

"Aha, Pons!" I cried, "you were anticipating someone else!"

"Say rather I am," he replied, a smile touching his lips. "I could hardly mistake that familiar tread of yours for anyone else's."

"It is not fit for beasts outside, to say nothing of men," I said, shrugging out of my rainproof. "Who but a doctor would be out on a night like this?"

"Or a policeman," added Pons, with a dry chuckle. "I daresay you have heard me speak of my brother, Bancroft?"

"It is he who is in the Foreign Office?"

"Yes, he holds a position which is apparently as important as its nature is ambiguous. He is about to honor my humble dwelling with his presence. Since he is devoted above all else to his physical comfort, it requires no great intelligence to divine that only a matter of marked significance would bring him out on such a night. From there it is but a step to the conclusion that the matter is at least quasi-official, for no personal concern would move Bancroft sufficiently to venture against such weather. I confess I anticipate his arrival; I have spent a dull day adding to the scrapbooks, and puzzles on paper have no such attraction as the problem in life."

Even as he spoke, the door to the sitting-room opened noiselessly and disclosed a tall, heavy, almost massive man, who might in physical appearance have been an inflated replica of my companion, save that his eyes were rather sleepy in their expression than keen, like Solar Pons', and his mouth was proud and sensuous; withal, he was an impressive figure of a man as he stood for a moment on the threshold before coming forward without sound, lightly, into the sitting-room.

"At your favorite pastime, eh, Solar?" he murmured with amused tolerance.

He crossed the room and appropriated Pons' own chair, letting himself down into it and promptly sprawling at his ease, stretching his legs toward the hearth. He moved with remarkable grace for so large a man.

"I fancy I am not wide of the mark," said Pons. "I believe you have not met my companion, Dr. Lyndon Parker. My brother, Bancroft."

Bancroft gazed languidly in my direction, but his air of the casual did not conceal the alertness behind. "A medical man. Back from an obstetrical case within the hour, I see. Your cuffs are still wet. And babies carry with them a singularly lingering smell, I have often observed, Solar."

"I have never been aware of it," I said.

"Of course not. You exist in these auras, Doctor; one would not expect you to be aware of them. My brother, however, delights in these little conclusions which are so effective because they are devoid of the simple intermediate steps. The average listener never fails to be impressed at his deductions because he is himself too slackwitted to follow the peregrinations of my brother's nimble thoughts. If I were to tell you, furthermore, that you had just delivered a nine-pound boy to a dark-haired woman in her late thirties in a comparatively easy delivery, which you had expected to be difficult, you would no doubt be amazed."

"I would indeed," I said in astonishment.

"Yet it is perfectly simple," continued Bancroft, with a twinkle in his blue eyes. "For the delivery was made to the wife of one of our officials in the consular service and a report of it duly reached our office just before I set out for these quarters. That, I submit, is evidence of the triumph of instruction over deduction, but my brother would go through a comprehensive recital of each little clue the long dark hair adhering to your trousers, the contented satisfaction so evident on your features, and so on – until he had reduced the whole to such patent absurdity that you could not help being disappointed in yourself for having failed to draw similar conclusions and thus, of necessity, angry at Solar for having so underscored your manifest shortcomings."

"I can hardly believe you came through wind and rain to instruct Parker," said Pons.

"No, I did not," agreed Bancroft amiably. "I came on a very different mission indeed." As he spoke, he took out a gold watch and consulted it gravely. "I am sorry to disturb your comfort, but I must take you out in this weather; I fear there is no alternative. I want you to see Ricoletti."

"Is he unable to come here?" inquired Pons.

"Ah, forgive me. I should have said 'view'. He will not know you are seeing him. He is in our cryptography department at the Foreign Office, and I have arranged matters so that he will be leaving his office within a quarter of an hour. I have a cab downstairs; if you hurry, we can just make it."

"Pray do not expect me to recount his life history from the brief glance we will have of him running through wind and rain to his car," said Pons, stepping from his bedroom slippers.

"You will have ample time to view him, weather or no," retorted Bancroft imperturbably.

In a few minutes we were on our way to Whitehall. We rode in silence, Bancroft with his chin resting on his hands, folded over his cane, his eyes dwelling on the street before our cab, Solar Pons in the familiar attitude of contemplation, his chin sunk upon his chest, his deerstalker drawn down over his eyes.

Bancroft Pons had given the driver detailed instructions and in a short while the cab drew up opposite the Foreign Office building in Parliament Street. Lights still burned in the building, despite the lateness of the hour, for it was now nine o'clock by the booming of Big Ben, the notes loud in the wet, windy night. The rain was abating, though the wind blew as violently as ever. Three or four cars were parked in the vicinity, one of them directly before the Foreign Office building, with a driver sitting at the wheel.

"That is his car," whispered Bancroft. Peering up at the building, he added, "There. His light has gone out. He will be along in a few moments, and you will have an excellent opportunity to see him when he crosses to his car; there is adequate light there."

"We sat waiting silently for a few moments more. Then Bancroft touched his brother's arm and murmured, "Ricoletti."

"Ah," said Pons, "a deformity of the right pedal extremity. A club foot!"

A short, thin, sallow-faced man came from the building and made his way under the brilliant street-lamps toward the kerb.

He moved with almost agonizing slowness, aided by a cane, buffeted by the wind, and impeded by a heavy briefcase he carried, dragging himself across the pavement with patent effort.

"A native Briton," said Pons.

"Born in London in 1868 of Italian parents," said Bancroft. "He has been in foreign service."

"Consular. In the West Indies."

"How long ago?"

"Eleven years. He is now fifty-three."

"There is obviously no question of his loyalty."

"None," assented Bancroft.

"Very well, then," said Pons. "He is a conscientious, able servant of His Majesty's Government. He is sufficiently moneyed to enable him to own a Daimler and support a chauffeur, as well as, presumably, a house in the suburbs."

"Hampstead. He lives on the edge of the heath in relative seclusion."

"Nevertheless, the Foreign Office has uncovered some reason for concern and, since you have stirred yourself to inquire into it, Bancroft, I have no doubt there is a valid basis for such inquiry."

"My dear Solar, you are unusually verbose. Come."

The Daimler had driven off with the deformed Ricoletti; it was out of sight beyond the corner of the street when we left the car and crossed to enter the Foreign Office building, where Bancroft was instantly recognized by the guards there, and we were passed through. He led the way to the lift and we were taken up several flights before we debouched upon one of the floors above. Bancroft went directly to a front office, which he opened by the use of three different passkeys, to reveal an austere little room, brilliantly lit at the touch of a button.

The room was devoid of everything but the steel desk, a filing cabinet, three chairs, and a wall shelf of apparatus clearly designed to be of use in the research which Ricoletti did for his government. A wastebasket stood beneath the opening of the desk.

"Spare to austerity," murmured Pons. "Mr. Ricoletti is not given to ostentation nor is he a slave to the comforts of the flesh."

"He lives like a Spartan," agreed Bancroft. "But we will return to him later. Pray consider the room. How readily do you believe it might be entered?"

"It would not be easy," said Pons. He strode to the single window it contained and looked down. "The window is all but impossible. The door has a triple lock. The desk has a similar sequence of locks."

"Yet it was entered last night. And Ricoletti's desk was opened. Only a purely fortuitous circumstance revealed that fact to us, for nothing whatever was taken and there was subsequently no evidence of the slightest disturbance."

"Except in the Foreign Office," said Pons dryly.

"The affair reflects no credit upon our operatives," admitted Bancroft with a grimace. "Yet there is no occasion for any alarm. It is true, up to three days ago Ricoletti was at work on the deciphering of a new code recently put in use by the Japanese War Office, as well as at the construction of a new code for the Admiralty. Both might have been of interest to someone outside, particularly the Admiralty code. But all work on the Admiralty code was stopped three days ago, and all papers removed from Ricoletti's office, and he had decoded the Japanese cipher two days past. So there were no papers of serious moment to be had in his desk last night."

"What was the incident which caused the Admiralty code to be withdrawn from Ricoletti?" asked Pons shrewdly.

Bancroft smiled. "Elementary, my dear Solar. I shall come to that in good time. Let us first consider the incident of last night. Entrance was effected between two and three o'clock in the morning. The single guard was summoned to the street by a diversion – a woman's cry for help. He was certainly not away from his post for more than two minutes. Yet in that time someone entered the building and Ricoletti's office. The guard presently suspected that something might have been designed to take him from his post, and he began a systematic search of the building.

"When he came to Ricoletti's room, he flashed his light cursorily across the desk. He swears that he saw sitting there a horrible beast with long black hair and a bulbous, warty face, so terrible of aspect that he stumbled backward, his flash fell or was knocked from his hand, and in his shocked confusion, he was struck a blow on the temple which temporarily knocked him out. He says that his light disclosed papers on the desk, but when he came to and put on the overhead light, all was in order in the room. There was nothing whatever to indicate that anyone had been here since Ricoletti left. Of course, he reported the matter at once. We were over here within the hour; we went through the room and Ricoletti's papers with the greatest diligence. We made one disturbing discovery, and that, too, was in the realm of the conjectural, as was the guard's experience."

"What was it?"

"A faint odor. Faint enough to be imaginary. Of civet." Bancroft shrugged. "The guard spoke of a beast, an animal.

The odor gave tenuous confirmation. Now, the whole tale is incredible, and has the sound of a perfervid imagination. But I call to mind one of your own maxims, Solar – that the most prosaic matters may be most untrue, and the most incredible be true. Moreover, there was an incident which took place three days ago, as you deduced. As it happened, I was in an adjoining office at the time.

"Ricoletti had just come to his office that morning and had begun to go through his mail. His door was standing open. He had been carrying on a conversation with McAlester, who is in the office across the corridor, and McAlester had just come to the door in time to see Ricoletti standing at his desk, as pale as death, holding in his hand a personal letter. McAlester was just about to ask Ricoletti what the matter was, when Ricoletti collapsed in a swoon, from which we could not rouse him for ten minutes. I heard him fall, I heard McAlester's cry, I was there in a moment.

"The letter was instantly photographed and replaced, since it appeared to concern a personal matter. I examined the envelope; it had been posted in Limehouse, but there was no address, neither on the envelope nor on the letter. The letter, however, appears to be perfectly innocuous; our experts have been over it with no result; it is certainly not in code, and a cryptogram has eluded them. I have a photostat of it here, together with a dossier on Ricoletti. Ricoletti, of course, accounted for his swoon by saying that he had suffered a great disappointment. Will you look at this letter?"

He took it from a manila envelope in his pocket and flattened the photostat on the desk. Pons and I bent above it. The letter was written in a loose, irregular script.

London, 17th Sept.

Dear Rico,

£1,000 does not seem to me quite enough for so substantial a property. I spoke to C. and he did not think so either. After all, the house is in excellent shape, and it has all the seclusion you desire – far more than you may now be occupying.

In a week or so C. and I will have an architect appraise the property with more detailed care, for there may quite possibly have been errors made which ought to be rectified. There are so many factors which enter into a picture like this and no one ought to suffer at another's expense.

Ten days from now should see the matter settled in one way or another. Or would you prefer to select an architect yourself? It would be perfectly agreeable to us, you know, though I don't know that the picture would be much changed.

I am sure that whatever your decision will be, C. and I will go along with it. We just feel at the present that the price you have offered is not enough. Perhaps we could compromise at £1,200? Or does that seem too much?

Reverse of the wainscoting in the living-room, about which we talked, shows that the wood is ash. The paint can be removed, but of course there is no telling what the removal of the paint will show. The reverse is in good condition, however.

Address C. in care of Guy's if you want to write to him directly.

He has as much interest in this as I have, perhaps more, though his principal concerns are elsewhere nowadays.

Soon I hope to see you and settle the matter. I know you want the house preserved until you can make a decision.

Sincerely, A.

"It seems anything but a profoundly disturbing letter," observed Bancroft. "Yet its effect on Ricoletti was indescribable. He destroyed it immediately on returning to consciousness, unaware that we had had it photographed. He was offered the rest of the day as a holiday, but he refused. From that moment he was under observation, but this revealed nothing, for Ricoletti is a man of methodical habits from which he does not deviate. Nevertheless, the Foreign Office cannot afford to take any chance whatsoever, and until we can be certain that this affair does not concern his work, we must be vigilant. If, indeed, it is personal, we need not look into it; that it may not be is indicated by the nocturnal visitor of the early hours of this morning. Let me tell you something about Ricoletti."

"Later," said Pons. "Give me a few moments to examine the room."

"Very well."

Pons began an intensive scrutiny of desk, window and door, crawling about on the floor beneath the desk. Bancroft picked up the photostat, folded it once more, and restored it to the envelope; he viewed Pons' activities with something akin to patient tolerance, glancing at his watch from time to time.

"Come, come, Solar, we are wasting time," he protested at last. "We have been over the room with every instrument

Scotland Yard has at its disposal. There was nothing to be discovered. We have dust from Hampstead, which is hardly unexpected. We have lint from McAlester's trousers; that is not an earth-shaking discovery."

Pons, I saw, was inclined to agree. He came to his feet.

"But you will want to know who had keys to this room and Ricoletti's desk," continued Bancroft. "The guard, to the room only. Ricoletti, of course, and the Chief to both room and desk. There are thus but two sets of keys for the desk, three for the door. The Chief's keys had not been disturbed – unless they were taken and returned. The remaining possibilities are evident."

"The guard's story is untrue; someone took an impression of a set of keys; or someone used Ricoletti's keys," replied Pons. "Let us begin with the guard. I will talk to him."

"I thought you would like to. He is in the Chief's room waiting for us. I should tell you that Ricoletti was under observation last night; he cannot drive a car, and did not leave the house until his chauffer came for him this morning. In fact, the only movement from the house at all was an old woman who had evidently been visiting Mrs. Ricoletti; she left before midnight."

"Where is Ricoletti's car kept?" Pons put in.

"It is not at the house, but in a rented garage down the street a few hundred yards away and around the corner. Are you finished here?"

Pons nodded.

"Then come."

The guard was a young man, fresh-faced and manifestly eager to be helpful, though at the moment ill-at-ease and unhappy. Yet his intelligent brown eyes were alert, and his soft full lips were pursed expectantly.

"My brother wishes to ask you some questions, Mr. Steward," said Bancroft without the formality of an introduction.

"Yes, sir."

"Your name?" asked Pons.

"Frederic Stoward."

"You've seen service, I notice. Decorated for bravery."

"Under fire, sir."

"Mons."

"Yes, sir. And Ypres."

"And wounded."

"Twice."

"You were in action for some time."

"Almost the entire course of the war."

"You must then have seen some soul-shaking sights, Mr. Stoward. Did any of them send you reeling?"

"No, Mr. Pons. They made me ill at times, but, of course, you expect things like that at the front. Not here."

Pons smiled grimly. "Will you just tell us what took place last night?"

"Yes, sir. I was on duty. Came on at midnight. At about a quarter past two o'clock this morning, I was standing in the doorway – the night was very warm, with a light fog – when I thought I heard a woman calling for help. I ran outside at once as far as the kerb, but there was no recurrence of the call and no disturbance. I returned to my post immediately. It occurred to me somewhat later that the call might have been a ruse."

"How much later?" interjected Pons.

"Ten or fifteen minutes. I immediately began to make a routine examination of the building. When I came to Mr. Ricoletti's room, I saw nothing to indicate that his room had been entered. I unlocked the door and flashed my light from one side to the other. I saw something sitting at the desk; It appeared to be examining papers. I did not then believe it could have been a human being. Mr. Pons, it had long, black hair, and a horrible, warty skin, out of which shone small, gleaming eyes. I was so astonished that I staggered backward, tripping as I reached for the light-button. At the same time, a little pencil of light struck upward from the desk and I saw the horrible swollen travesty of a face for the second time. It seemed to rise up from a blackness which might have been its body. While I was groping for the light-switch, something struck me, and I was knocked out.

"When I came to, I switched on the light. The room was undisturbed; there were no papers on the desk; there was nothing to show that anyone had been there, except a bruise on my temple."

Pons fingered the lobe of his left ear thoughtfully. "You have mentioned the animal-like appearance of the room's invader. Did it suggest any specific animal to you?"

"Mr. Pons, it was like nothing I have ever seen before," said Stoward earnestly. "Except that it recalled certain hospital cases I encountered during the war."

"Something has been said of a peculiar odor in the room. Did you notice any unusual smell?"

"Yes."

"A perfume?"

"Rather a musk. It was very strong just when I was struck."

"The smell of an animal," said Bancroft curtly. "It lingered."

"Have you any idea what struck you?" asked Pons. "You mentioned 'a pencil of light'. Could it have been a flashlight?"

"Yes. Or a paperweight."

"Very well. That is all, Mr. Stoward."

Bancroft Pons was gazing impatiently at his watch again. "Let us be on our way, Solar. I can add what remains to be said on the way back to Praed Street."

Outside, the rain had now entirely abated, and the wind was beginning to diminish. Our cab still waited where we had left it and, once we were inside, moved off toward Praed Street somewhat more slowly than we had come from our quarters, at Bancroft's explicit directive.

"I have no desire to repeat data which can be found in our dossier on Ricoletti," said Bancroft. "That carries you up to the time of his employment in our crytography division. Since coming to London, Ricoletti has lived a most circumspect and secluded life. He bought his home in Hampstead, had certain alterations made there, and then sent for his wife to join him; she was then waiting in Barbados. Since her coming, neither of them has moved about socially at all. Ricoletti leaves the office, is invariably driven straight home, and does not stir from the house until his chauffeur comes in the morning to take him back to work. His routine never varies.

"At work he remains at his desk save for two interludes: he takes his lunch away from his work, and in mid-afternoon he goes out and indulges in one solitary drink, usually a scotch and soda. He takes tea in his office at four. He leaves customarily in time for dinner at home, but on occasion, when special tasks are assigned to him, he is kept later. Whenever he is so detained, he faithfully telephones his wife that he will be late."

"A man of singular habits," mused Pons. "And since he received this disturbing letter, what variations have been observed in his behavior?"

"In the major pattern, none. But there are upsetting and, I hold, indicative minor variations. He has abandoned his mid-afternoon drink. He has seemed frightened, furtive, shrunk together, as if he expected some blow to fall. On two of the three days since then, he has not taken his lunch, and he has shown a marked apprehension of the post, though he has been unable to ignore it."

"He did not seem furtive this evening," said Pons thoughtfully.

"You anticipate me," replied Bancroft testily. "I will tell the story in my own way, if you please. We notified Ricoletti this morning of the invasion of his office last night. He was profoundly upset. He immediately examined all his effects and declared that none of them was missing. Yet his agitation was in no way diminished. I was present at the time, and I watched him closely. Now, Solar, Ricoletti first examined the top drawer of his desk, in which presumably he keeps papers pertinent to work in progress. He then went through every other drawer methodically, after which he examined his filing cabinet with great care. He stood for a moment in honest perplexity, as far as I could ascertain his attitude. Then, quite suddenly, he picked up his wastebasket, emptied it on his desk, and pawed through the crumpled papers and envelopes with shaking hands. Only after he had finished, did he assure us that none of our papers was missing."

"Let me interrupt," put in Pons. "Surely, after Ricoletti's receipt of that disturbing letter, you had his mail watched?"

"Dear me, yes. We were, of course, watching for the recurrence of the photographed script. Ricoletti received another letter in that same hand yesterday morning."

"You did not examine the letter?"

"No. There was no reason to believe that letter was not a personal matter. There are certain limitations we must observe."

"And his reaction at its receipt?"

"There was no reaction."

"Ah," said Pons cryptically, and smiled.

"But I should add," continued Bancroft, "that Ricoletti was entirely his old self after lunch today."

"He took lunch today, then?"

"Yes. He went to Piero's. He ate alone. He spoke to no one, except the cashier on his way out. Oh, the waiter, of course." He peered from the window of the cab. "Here we are at 7B. Are there any further questions, Solar?"

"Only one suggests itself," replied Pons. "Is there any manifest reason why the Ricolettis do not take part in social activities?"

"There is evidently some sensitivity about Ricoletti's deformity," replied Bancroft. He hesitated reflectively. Then, shrugging, he added, "His wife seems to share his desire for seclusion. I need hardly tell you that the Foreign Office considers a reclusive cryptographer rather an asset than otherwise. There is some unsavory gossip about Mrs. Ricoletti; I once heard someone speak of her as 'that abominable woman.' But then, as you will learn from the dossier, she was a West Indian, and one might expect her presence in Hampstead to arouse prejudice in some quarters."

As the cab came to a stop before our lodgings, Bancroft handed Pons the manila envelope containing Ricoletti's dossier. "If you need me again, you have my number and have only to call," said Bancroft.

"I hardly think it will be necessary, apart from presenting you with the solution of this intriguing little riddle."

"Which is no doubt already completely obvious to you, my dear Solar?" said Bancroft, smiling.

"That is not beyond the realm of the possible," agreed Pons amiably, and bade his brother goodnight.

Once again comfortably ensconced in our quarters, Pons turned to the dossier on Ricoletti. There were not many papers in the manila envelope, and most of them were photostats. The recent letter, Pons laid to one side. He took up the first two pages of biographical data.

"Hum! An education at Oxford. Balliol," he murmured presently. "He would appear to have been the only son of a fairly prosperous green-grocer in the West End. Some Continental post-graduate work at Bonn and Prague. He entered the foreign service at thirty, and spent two years at a consulate in Brazil. Another year at Pekin. He is evidently a master of languages. Two more years in Dutch Guiana, and finally to the Dutch West Indies. Consul at Willemstad, Curacao, for seven years. Then to his present position, in which he seems to be contented."

He turned to several of the other enclosures, scrutinized them briefly, and cast them aside. "Ricoletti seems to be an admirable servant of the government. Here are copies of commendations from several official sources and a record of a decoration by His Majesty. He would appear to be singularly devoted to his work, and has achieved an enviable position as perhaps the outstanding crypto-analyst in the realm. Does he have the sound of an intriguer to you, Parker?"

"Emphatically not."

"I agree. Nevertheless, there are several points of interest which can hardly be overlooked. The description of the 'beast' in Ricoletti's office, for one. Did that convey nothing to you?"

"I thought it had the sound of an hallucination."

"Well, the guard's story is either true or not true. If not true, he could certainly have imagined a more credible tale. His complicity would then also be involved. But nothing was taken – at least, nothing official was taken. You will bear in mind that Ricoletti told Bancroft that none of 'our papers' was missing; he did not say 'nothing' had been taken. I submit that while the negative does not necessarily postulate the positive, there is a very strong probability that something of Ricoletti's was taken. Yet it does not seem to have been anything of intrinsic value, for Ricoletti's actions, as observed by Bancroft, suggest that it was removed from the wastebasket. I think we can proceed, therefore, from the assumption that the guard's story was true as he told it. He saw something which made him think of an animal. That suggests nothing to you, Parker?"

"Someone in disguise, I daresay."

"Come, come, Parker, try again. The sight was enough to shock an experienced ex-soldier like Stoward. But Stoward himself suggested a comparison."

"I am not unaware that he did," I retorted. "But if you expect me to believe that any person so badly diseased as to shock into semi-paralysis a man like Stoward could pass about London streets without exciting comment, you will have to try again. I am afraid, Pons, that whatever theory you have, it is untenable. Consider the risks of breaking into a room in the Foreign Office building for nothing more than a scrap of paper in a wastebasket!"

"Or the information on it. That might be a different matter, Parker. I submit that Ricoletti might well have worked out a complete code on a scrap of paper and thrown it away after transcribing it, though his previous diligence suggests that as unlikely. And the risks. What are they?"

"The keys, for one thing," I replied with spirit.

"Yes, the problem of the keys has certain points of interest. Of the three sets, none appears to have been used. Yet one set was undoubtedly in use last night. We can eliminate the guard's, since we have begun by accepting his story as objective truth. This leaves Ricoletti's set and those in the office of the Chief; of these, the likelier set to have been used is Ricoletti's, though a wax impression might have been made of the Chief's set just as well. The guard's set, however, might be eliminated on more than his story's count – he had no set of desk keys, and the intruder evidently did, though we have no direct evidence that this is so, for the guard's story corroborated only part of Bancroft's. Moreover, the conclusion is inescapable that if anything was taken, it was something of personal concern to Ricoletti; if someone had made a wax impression of the Chief's keys, then it is reasonable to suppose that the interloper had an interest in official papers.

"The guard recounted, you will remember, that when he flashed the light toward the desk, it was covered with papers. Only a short while later, the desk was in order. Now, then, if the contents of the drawers had been placed on the desk, I submit that it could not have been got back into order in the little time that the guard was unconscious. Therefore, it is not amiss to conclude that the papers the guard saw on the desk were the contents of the wastebasket; these could have been swept back into place in the space of moments. But actually, there is little mystery about the invasion of Ricoletti's office."

"Indeed!" I cried. "Next thing you will be telling me you know who entered it."

"Let us say, rather, I am reasonably certain of his identity," replied Pons. "No, the mystery lies primarily in the letter. And daresay I detect its point of reference in this paragraph of Ricoletti's dossier."

I looked to where Pons indicated and read:

> "Ricoletti requested transfer from Willemstad in 1910 after the unfortunate death of Cyrus Cryder, a colonial who was shot in self-defense by Ricoletti, following an attack made on Ricoletti by Cryder. Though the testimony of a clerk in Ricoletti's office exonerated Ricoletti of all blame, Ricoletti persisted in his request for transfer. His ability in analysis and composition of cryptograms having come to the attention of the Foreign Office, Ricoletti was ordered to London to be prepared against crises on the Continent."

I gazed at Pons in undisguised astonishment. "And how does the letter refer to this? Perhaps it is a cryptogram, but I confess it seems only a casual letter about the purchase of a house."

"Come, come, Parker, Ricoletti, to the best of our knowledge, is not buying a house; he owns one. No, the letter is a little masterpiece of subtle menace. Pray examine it again."

I took the photostat and read the letter carefully a second time.

"I can hardly imagine a more innocuous communication," I said at last. "If there is a cipher here, it is hidden too deeply for me. But I am no cryptographer; I do not pretend to be."

"The message is so simply presented that the experts at the Foreign Office failed to understand it for its very simplicity. It looks out at you, Parker, though doubtless the experts were looking for something quite different. Pray read it carefully once more. Meanwhile, I will just have a look at the newspapers."

With some exasperation, I turned once more to the letter, while Pons began to look rapidly through the morning and evening papers, all of which were faithfully brought to our lodgings, for Pons carefully clipped them for his voluminous files on crimes of London and the Isles, together with summaries of Continental and American crimes.

In but a few moments Pons gave a sharp cry of delight, and placed before me a morning paper folded to a brief bulletin.

MURDER IN LIMEHOUSE

> A body identified as that of Andrew Walton, a seaman, late of Barbados, was found early this morning in a room at the Wander Inn, Limehouse Causeway. Walton, who had taken lodging at the Inn a week ago, was off the freighter, *Captain Christensen*. Evidence indicated that he had been strangled in the early hours of the morning, for his body was still warm when it was discovered shortly after six o'clock. Metropolitan Police have received reports that an animal-like person was seen in the halls of the Wander Inn between three and four o'clock this morning. Police are investigating.

"I submit it is no coincidence that a human being described as 'animal-like' should be reported twice in one evening," said Pons. "They are surely not two, but one. And this crime, which followed chronologically upon the entry of Ricoletti's room at the Foreign Office, was surely the occasion of Ricoletti's attitude after lunch today. He spoke to no one but the waiter and the cashier; but almost certainly he saw a paper, for the story was there, and he is too conscientious to read his paper during working hours."

I handed the letter back to him. "The problem only becomes more mystifying," I said.

"On the contrary, it is now entirely explicable," reported Pons.

"Oh, come, Pons, you cannot be serious!"

"I have never been more so. Let us examine the problem from its beginning. The letter. If we take the initial word of each paragraph, we have the following sequence of words:

"'£1,000 In Ten Or I Reverse Address Soon'

"Now this enigmatic letter becomes clear as daylight, and Ricoletti read its full meaning at once. Small wonder that he fell into a swoon, for the letter told him that the clerk who had testified in his favor at the inquiry into Cyrus Cryder's death was now prepared to reverse his testimony unless Ricoletti paid him a thousand pounds. For what else could be 'reverse' but testimony, that would do Ricoletti harm? So what his brief message amounted to was an ultimatum to Ricoletti to deliver a thousand pounds in ten days, or he would reverse his testimony. He would send his address soon, so that Ricoletti could deliver the money to him. It did not matter that eleven years had gone by, and that such a reversal might be seriously questioned; Ricoletti's career would be ruined, and Ricoletti had more than usually strong reasons for preventing such a contingency, as the writer of this blackmailing letter well knew. But let us give the writer his name; he signs his letter simply A., for Andrew Walton, late of Barbados.

"With this knowledge, turn to the letter again and you will understand that all this casual writing of a house has a double meaning. The house is nothing more than Ricoletti's life;

the C. to whom reference is made, is the late Cyrus Cryder, who can be addressed, note the irony of it, in care of 'Guy's'. Ricoletti understood it full well; he realized its implications, too – that once he began to pay Walton, he would be subject forever after to his demands. But what else could he do?"

"What he did," I put in. "Kill him."

"Dear me, Parker," murmured Pons in protest, "you have a disturbing faculty of leaping to conclusions. Ricoletti could do only one thing, as he saw it; he must prepare to make the payment demanded of him. So he began to do so, waiting upon another communication which would convey the address to which the money must be sent. But in doing so, he aroused suspicion in other quarters than those of his employment. Whether he was aware of having done so, none can say. But you can well imagine his delight at discovering this noon that the predatory Walton would plague him no more. Small wonder that he was once again his old self, as Bancroft observed."

My patience with Pons was wearing dangerously thin. I protested. "If Ricoletti did not kill him, who did?"

"Someone who looked like a beast," replied Pons simply. "The same individual who invaded Ricoletti's office. Let me hazard a guess, though I may well be in error. The murderer is a sufferer from a disease uncommon in these latitudes; you will recall Stoward's description – a 'horrible, swollen travesty of a face'. It suggested something to me at once, rare even in the latitudes where it occurs. Sometimes a commoner form of the disease is called 'Barbados leg'."

"Elephantiasis!" I exclaimed.

"Capital, Parker, capital!" cried Pons. "I submit that *elephantiasis arabum*, or *filarial elephantiasis*, of the face, with its characteristic coarse, wart-like skin, with possible varicose ulcers, would excite the descriptions we have encountered."

"But surely such an individual could be discovered with ease," I protested.

"Perhaps," said Pons enigmatically. "I fancy the man to identify Walton's murderer is Ricoletti himself. I propose to ask him without further delay."

He came to his feet as he spoke, a gleam in his eyes that would not be gainsaid.

"But the hour," I cried. "It is almost midnight. You could call on him at his office tomorrow."

"No, no, Parker," Pons answered impatiently. "It is the house I am most desirous of seeing. Must it not indeed be a veritable paradise that man would seclude himself within its walls with no desire to leave it save for the monotony of his work? If you will be so good as to telephone for a cab, we will be on our way without waiting upon the Underground."

The house which belonged to Orso Ricoletti brooded darkly on the edge of Hampstead Heath, from which came the aroma of wet foliage, for, though rainfall had ceased, a thick fog was beginning to rise, and carried with it the multiple odors of the city and, in this place, of the surrounding countryside. I had remonstrated with Pons all the way in vain; he had set his heart on knocking up Ricoletti, and no other time would do.

We made our way to the front door, upon which Pons beat a rattling tattoo. Beyond the house, the undulations of Hampstead Heath, with its birches and poplars, shone spectrally in the semi-darkness, for there was a moon behind the now thinning clouds, and a kind of iridescence illuminated the scene. The house, at the end of the street leading to the Heath, was attractive yet simple, without ornateness in its exterior. Pons knocked again; there was no bell-button to be seen, for Pons had struck a match to search for it.

We waited yet longer, but presently a light went up inside.

"Ah, it is Ricoletti himself," whispered Pons. "He has stopped to put on his shoes. What a pity he should be so inflicted."

The door opened suddenly and the cryptographer stood there, clad in a dressing-gown, his feet shod, and carrying in one hand a stout cane, leaded at one end, and in the other an electric lantern.

"Mr. Ricoletti," said Pons softly.

"I am Ricoletti."

"My name is Solar Pons. My companion is Dr. Lyndon Parker."

There was a sharp intake of breath from the sallow-faced man on the threshold. "Ah, Bancroft's brother. I have heard of you, Mr. Pons. Please come in."

He stepped aside as he spoke, waited until we had passed him, then closed the door behind us and walked around us to lead the way in his slow fashion to a sitting room, which he lit by pressing a button with his cane. Soft, diffused lights, set low around the walls, came into being. The room was comfortable and well-appointed, but its furnishings were distinctly foreign, save for such added pieces which contributed to physical comfort and did not conflict with the West Indian theme of the decoration. There was present in the house a marked, animal-like musk, not unpleasant, but provocative.

I forebore to ask about it, but Ricoletti himself mentioned it at once. "I trust the pungence does not offend you. I am used to it. It is a West Indian perfume my wife likes to use." He turned, having reached the farther wall of the room. "Please sit down. I know you would not have come to see me except on a matter of the utmost urgence to you."

"And to you," said Pons.

Ricoletti sighed. His dark eyes seemed infinitely weary and sad, his sensitive mouth was twisted as if with pain. "Of course, it is about the office," he said. "I told them none of the papers had been taken; I assured them solemnly there was no occasion for concern. But I know the Chief; he will not rest until he knows."

"He waits only on my assurance, Mr. Ricoletti," said Pons. "That is why I am here."

"I give you that," said Ricoletti passionately. "Pray believe me, Mr. Pons. The entire matter has been explained, and nothing further will come of it."

"But there are a few minor points," Pons went on relentlessly. "There is a reasonable probability that your keys were used to effect entrance to your office last night."

"Impossible. My keys were in my pocket when I went to bed; they were there when I woke up."

"Could someone not have abstracted them in the night?"

"Sir, my wife and I live here alone."

"Did you by chance have visitors last evening?"

"We never entertain visitors, Mr. Pons. Except for an urgent messenger from the office one night in 1914, no one but you two gentlemen has ever been inside this house," said Ricoletti gravely. "How can I assure you, so that you, in turn, can convince the Chief there is no reason for their concern?"

"Ah, there is no need to assure me, Mr. Ricoletti," said Pons. "I know very well that the matter was an entirely personal one. The only question which remains is this: was Cyrus Cryder's death self-defense, or was it not?"

"Sir, the evidence at the trial was satisfactory."

"Ah, but you see, I have read Andrew Walton's letter," said Pons softly.

Ricolleti's head jerked up, his lips parted in dismay. Then he covered his face with his hands and rocked his slender body to and fro in despair.

"I might have known," he said at last. "They photographed the letter."

"And now that Andrew Walton has been slain," began Pons.

"Mr. Pons, I beg you to believe me. Cryder had made overtures of the vilest kind to my wife. He came to my office one day, drunk, and attacked me; I shot him. I was unable to prevent his death. Walton's testimony was true, but he had fallen on evil days. He had written me from Barbados, asking for money; I had sent him some, but not at the urgence of a threat; he had previously not uttered any threats. I had not heard from him for years, believe me; his letter came like a bolt from the blue against which I had no defense. Everything would have been lost, my position – though that did not matter – my home and my wife, and that did. I had to pay, or be involved in scandal which would have ruined my life, no matter how certainly I might have been cleared, and I would have been. I am glad Walton is dead, but I did not kill him."

"My visit here is entirely unofficial, Mr. Ricoletti," said Pons. "I know nothing of any murder you may have committed."

There was a sudden rustle from the adjoining corridor, and in a moment a woman stepped into the room.

"I think you gentlemen are looking for me," she said in a harsh but steady voice.

Then I saw her face. It was a horrible, blasphemous mockery of a human face, swollen and coarse, warty and ulcerous; its features were askew, as were it a grotesque and repulsive mask; it was more than twice as large as it ought to have been, making a further mockery of the well-proportioned body beneath it; if ever it had had any natural beauty, that beauty had vanished without trace. The woman was dark-skinned, younger than Ricoletti, and despite the grotesquerie of her head, she walked with lithe grace to where Ricoletti sat and reached down for his hand.

I controlled my features only with the utmost effort.

Pons came to his feet. "No, Mrs. Ricoletti, we are looking for no one. We came only to assure your husband we could convince his superiors that there was no further cause for alarm at the invasion of his office which someone made last night. Neither of us is an official, and if I were to guess that someone had drugged your husband, taken his keys, taken his car, driven to his office to find the address of the man who was blackmailing him because he would not himself reveal it, and then gone there to that inn in Limehouse and strangled him to protect your husband, I would be too far from being able to submit proof to dare offer the hypothesis."

For a long minute the two of them faced us – he sitting there with his malformed foot before him, she standing at his side, their hands clasped, her horrible face turned in our direction but seeming to look beyond us.

"Fifteen years," whispered Ricoletti then, and only clasped her hand more tightly.

"Please tell them," said Mrs. Ricoletti, "that my husband has done nothing, that no one is interested in his work."

"I shall have nothing other to report," said Pons.

"Thank you," said Ricoletti.

In the cab Pons leaned back, his chin sunk upon his chest, his eyes closed.

"Was there from the beginning the possibility of any other solution, Parker?" he asked. "I daresay not. The keys were Ricoletti's, certainly; he might have suspected that they had been used. He might have known. We shall not know. But I am certain that what happened can readily be imagined. It would have been impossible for Ricoletti to conceal his agitation from his wife, after he had read Walton's threat, however much he might strive to keep from her anything to worry her. But she must have divined when Walton's address reached her husband, perhaps by his actions – the preparations to send Walton money without further delay, a kind of lessening of his tension undoubtedly. He had not brought it home; he meant to deal with Walton on Walton's terms. She, too, foresaw Walton's ultimate plan and forestalled it. She may have drugged him; I think it likely that she did, taken his keys, gone for the car – you will remember that she was seen to leave the house, but the guard thought it was some late visitor – and found Walton's address in her husband's wastebasket at his office. She lost no time going to Limehouse and strangled Walton.

"Who can say where the largest measure of guilt lies? I loathe a blackmailer above all other criminals; he preys upon the weaknesses of his fellow-humans. And can you put yourself into her place? Conceive what torture she must have endured through these years, looking like an abomination on the face of the earth, a solitary by necessity, but still sharing a love that did not falter throughout her adversity. That house was their haven; their security lay in each other. Walton threatened it. She knew that if Walton had his way, their security would soon be gone; she knew that if she were caught, then, too, that precious security was lost, they would be parted, perhaps forever, since neither is any longer young. It did not matter. Perhaps she tried to reason with Walton; but I doubt even that. She went there to kill him and did so."

"But if she did kill him, Pons," I remonstrated, "it was murder. You have an obligation to lay your evidence before the authorities."

"Ah, but I have no evidence," said Pons, smiling. "My only obligation is to Bancroft and the Foreign Office in this matter; I can give them the assurance they want and need. I can do no more. My conjectures are of no interest to the police or Scotland Yard, and I have no desire to pursue them to actionable proof. No, Parker, I detect in this little matter the hand of Providence; and I have no desire to interfere with her inscrutable workings."

VII

THE ADVENTURE OF THE SIX SILVER SPIDERS

Perhaps one of the attitudes in which I have seen my friend Solar Pons most often is that of poring over a book or studying the agony columns of the daily papers, a broadside or something from his extensive files, the keen, dark eyes intent under their full brows, the thin lips pressed together, the almost feral face grim, presenting nothing so much as the aspect of a bloodhound on the scent. It was thus I found him late one afternoon in October early in the fourth decade of this century, when I came in out of a dense white fog that lay especially heavy along Praed Street.

Pons' dark eyes flashed up from and back to the object of his scrutiny. "You came by Underground, I see," he observed.

"I suppose my cuffs are showing Underground dust," I replied with some asperity.

"Nothing so crude, my dear Parker, but quite as elementary. You are too wet to have taken a cab, and not wet enough to have walked very far. Paddington station is near enough to account for the degree of moisture."

By this time I had removed my topcoat and hat; I had unbuttoned my waistcoat and taken my place at the table.

"Mrs. Johnson will have supper soon," Pons continued, in leaning back now. "Tell me, what do you make of this, Parker?"

The object he handed me was clearly a leaflet or small brochure issued by a bookseller.

"A request for bids on the private library of Paul Guillaume, Comte d'Erlette," I read, opening it to glance at the statements which preceded the listing of books. Pons said nothing, but his sharp eyes were fixed on me not without a glint of humor. I read the dignified announcement. "Mr. John Amworthy, having acquired the private library of occult literature formerly the possession of the Comte d'Erlette of Erlette, near Voyonnes, France, will dispose of it to the highest bidder on the 13th September. Bids are to be sealed and sent to Mr. Amworthy in care of the Boar's Head Book Shop, 17 Princes Street, Edinburgh, Scotland. All bids will be opened in the presence of bidders or their duly accredited representatives at three o'clock in the afternoon of 13th September, on the premises of the Boar's Head Book Shop." There followed an account of the death of the collector and former owner, together with a statement explaining Mr. Amworthy's fortunate possession of the rare volumes "herein described."

"There is surely nothing extraordinary about this," I said.

"Pray examine it."

Somewhat nettled at his determination, I turned to the titles listed, and dutifully read through the first entry. "Al Hazred, Abdul: *Necronomicon*. Tr. from the Arabic into Latin by Olaus Wormius. With several woodcut tables of signs and mystic symbols. Madrid, 1647. Small folio, full calf with ornamental overall stamping in blind, including date, 1715. Binding somewhat stained and rubbed. There is a slight foxing, but only in first ten pages. In fine condition, and one of only six known copies of the first Latin edition. Only copies known to be in existence are in the Bibliotheque Nationale of Paris, the Widener Library at Harvard, and Miskatonic University

Library at Arkham, Massachusetts, U. S. A. Only privately owned copy known to have been in existence disappeared from the library of the Massachusetts artist, R. U. Pickman. Only two copies in Arabic known to have existed. According to Von Junzt in *Unaussprechlichen Kulten* (see number 17, page four this catalog), '*es steht ausser Zweifel, dass dieses Buch ist die Grundlage der Okkulteliteratur*'."

I glanced at several of the other titles listed – d'Erlette, Paul Henri, Comte de: *Cultes des Goules*, Rouen, 1737; Prinn, Ludvig: *De Vermis Mysteriis*, Prague, 1807; *Liber Ivonis* (Author Unknown), Rome, 1662; – all manifestly occult literature. The four-page brochure was printed in singularly good taste, with the appearance of being set by hand. Some of the books were described in the most minute detail, and many were "with a lock" of silver gilt or gold. In all there were but twenty-seven items, and only two of them were represented at all in private libraries; while many of the rare books listed were believed to be only copies. For the library intact, explained a concluding notice, no bid under two thousand pounds would be accepted.

"It seems to be an extremely rare, possibly unique collection," I said at last, with that caution which comes of experience.

"It does indeed. It suggests nothing to you?" asked Pons with that sometimes irritating insistence which indicated that he was aware of information I did not have.

"Nothing, except that only a wealthy collector could afford to bid on the collection intact."

"So much is evident," agreed Pons. "Have you ever heard of the library of the Count de Fortsas?"

I confessed my ignorance of it.

"Some ninety years ago a sixteen-page pamphlet-catalogue of the exceedingly rare books in the library of Jean Nepomucene-August Pichauld, Comte de Fortsas, were offered for sale at Binche. The catalogue was printed at Mons, and was sent out to collectors in several countries. It excited bibliophiles in

England as well as on the Continent; bids came in to the printer at Mons, who had issued the catalogue. So did collectors; on the day of the sale in August, 1840, there were so many strangers in Binche that the gravest suspicions were aroused among the police, who thought these curious-looking characters might be dangerous fellows planning an émeute. But, my dear Parker, there was no such library, there were no such books, there was, in fact, not even a Comte de Fortsas; all existed only in the brilliant imagination of a certain antiquarian, M. Render Chalon, who wrote books on numismatics and had a fancy to amuse himself at the expense of his fellow bibliophiles."

I took up the pamphlet again. "Pons, you cannot mean...?" I cried.

"Indeed," said Pons, smiling, "but I fear such is the case. All these books have a precarious existence only in the writings of certain minor authors of American origin, all apparently followers, in a remote sense, of the work of Edgar Allan Poe. The catalogue is, in short, a hoax."

"But the Count d'Erlette?" I protested.

"Erlette is a provincial name in France. The family existed in some numbers before the Revolution, but the last member to carry a title died in 1919. The Boar's Head Book Shop is real enough, but clearly only an accommodation address. I fancy we are dealing with a gentleman of extraordinary cunning, who is not unwilling to take the greatest pains to achieve his end."

"And what is that?"

"That is the problem, Parker. We shall hope to elucidate it." He tapped the catalogue. "This was sent over by messenger in mid-afternoon by Baron Elouard de Baseuil. I expect him immediately after supper. And here, if I am not mistaken, is Mrs. Johnson with our supper. Come in, come in, Mrs. Johnson; Parker and I are famished."

Our long-suffering landlady bustled in as he spoke, murmuring plaintively that someone had better induce Pons to eat or he would waste away to a shadow. "Always studying, always figuring things out, and always forgetting to eat. This lamb is stewed in white wine," she ended with emphasis.

"Ah, my dear Mrs. Johnson," said Pons, drawing the lamb toward him, "in these rooms it is more than customarily true that, as the French have it, '*De la main a la bouche, se peril souvent la soupe*.'"

"That lamb won't be lost, Mr. Pons," said Mrs. Johnson, and, sighing, left us to our supper.

The dishes had just been removed when our visitor arrived. "A man of decision, impatient, and at the moment in haste," said Pons, listening to the steps on the stairs.

Mrs. Johnson ushered in a gentleman in evening dress. He was a tall, imposing man, with a square face on which he wore a Van Dyke and a monocle over one of his clear blue eyes. His beard was streaked with grey, as was the hair of his head, for he carried his opera hat in his one hand, and his stick in the other.

"I have the honor to address Mr. Solar Pons?" he said, looking unerringly at my companion.

"Pray sit down, Baron de Baseuil. Dr. Parker is eminently trustworthy."

The Baron acknowledged the introduction with a formal bow. He sat down. His eye had caught sight of the catalog, which had reappeared on the table after Mrs. Johnson had removed the supper dishes, and he now indicated it with his stick.

"You have had opportunity to examine this, Mr. Pons?"

"I have. I perceive it is an elaborately conceived and skillfully executed hoax. But do let us hear your story, for it is evident that you are on the way to an engagement for the evening."

"Mr. Pons, it is simply told," began the Baron with animation. "Six of us responded to the lure. I myself journeyed to Edinburgh. So did Colonel David Wade, Sir Austin Mannell,

Kester Roxbrugh, and representatives of Lady Monica Jevrons and Alan Thomason. We arrived at the Boar's Head Book Shop only to find a message awaiting us, telling us that the entire collection had been bought by a barrister representing an heir to the estate of the late Count. You will have observed the resemblance to the Fortsas hoax. I regret to say that we did not do so until then. The books listed, you see, have a certain kind of spurious existence in the writings of little known American and British writers, and the fact is that the books have been held by some readers to be real volumes. In the case of the title which heads the list, every reputed fact supposedly 'known' about this rare volume has been skillfully added to the customary data one always finds in descriptions of books up for sale to make the paragraph, thus lending it still more superficial reality. Mr. Pons, I am not a man to be hoaxed. I want to know the identity of the man behind this hoax."

Pons sat now with his eyes closed and his chin resting on one hand. Without opening his eyes, he asked, "And the owner of the Boar's Head? Presumably you questioned him?"

"Of course," replied the baron. "All arrangements had been made with him by mail. He was promised that the books would be brought in just before the hour of the sale on the thirteenth. A handsome retainer was sent to him with the initial letter from Mr. Amworthy, who is doubtless as fictitious as his catalog."

"In name only," said Pons. "Was there no occasion to make enquiry by post?"

"None. The catalogue, as you see, is explicit."

"I have read it, yes. And your fellow bibliophiles – you did not think it strange that only six were represented?"

"Mr. Pons, we are the best-known collectors of occult lore in the British Isles, and our collections are the most extensive."

"You went up by train and returned when?"

"The following day. We had anticipated that some time would be lost in the opening of the bids and the disposal of the books. All but Colonel Wade had engaged rooms, and he followed suit after he reached Edinburgh."

"So you were out of London, then, for most of two days and a night?"

"That is correct."

Pons meditated for a moment. Then he said, "I fancy this little matter holds promise of an entertaining chase, Baron. Will you be so kind as to set down immediately an order permitting me to examine your collection?"

"I will be at home in the morning, Mr. Pons."

"We have already lost three weeks, sir. I propose to begin tonight."

Baron de Baseuil came to his feet. "Very well, Mr. Pons. Permit me to excuse myself so that I can take leave of my host for the evening. I will be at your service in an hour at my home in Portman Square."

He took his departure, and at once Pons flung aside his casual air.

He went swiftly to his shelf of references and came back to the table with a slender book entitled *The British Bibliophile*. "We should be able to find our client in this little work," he murmured, as he leafed through the pages. "Ah, here we are!" He flattened the book out under the lamp and stood above it, hands flat on the table, looking like a great bird of prey as he read.

"'de Baseuil... born August 21, 1871: Paris, France. Son of former consular official in London. British citizen since 1912.' Hm! this is primarily biographical. Let us see. Ah, here is a paragraph pertinent to his collecting activities. 'Possesses one of the largest private libraries in England. Specializes in occult literature, esoterica, books relating to ancient civilizations. Fine collection of miniature books, including one of the six spiders of the forger, Yeovil. Some fine bindings, calf, vellum, and so forth. Also interested in all incunabula (before 1650) – subject immaterial. Value of library estimated at £40,000."

"Not particularly informative except to a collector," I said.

"You caught nothing of interest?" asked Pons as he jotted down a few notes from the book.

"Not particularly."

"Nothing which ought to have occurred to you as uncommon?"

"No," I retorted.

"I submit to you it is not just a coincidence that the number 'six' should occur twice within so short a time. Our client informed us that only six collectors were represented at the sale; I submit that each of the others he mentioned is likewise the owner of one of the six spiders of the forger, Yeovil."

Pons replaced the book.

"What the devil are 'spiders' doing in a book collection?"

"Ah, my dear Parker, they have an honored niche. Yeovil was a forger of no mean ability. He forged not only sovereigns and guineas, but also books and works of art. The six silver spiders – they are actually scarabs – are hollow and each contains part of a chapter from the *Book of the Dead*, in miniature book form, supposedly written by an Egyptian priest of the time of Amenhotep. One of Yeovil's most skillful forgeries."

"They have a certain value then?"

Pons shook his head. "Only as curiosa. They are hardly worth stealing, if you are contemplating their theft as a possible motive."

"What about this fellow, Yeovil?" I asked then.

Pons was already divesting himself of his dressing-gown and eyeing his Inverness. "It would not be an exaggeration to look upon him as one of the most fascinating figures in the entire annals of British crime. I fancy he is somewhat before your time, Parker – he has been in Dartmoor for the past two decades, and must be an old man now. Had it not been for his impetuous slaying of a bobby in the attempt to take him, he might well be a free man today. He was without doubt one of the most skilled forgers in history, with a talent that permitted him to enter many fields. He might have been a great artist, had he not chosen a career of crime instead. Many of his effects were never recovered, but his forgeries have never been duplicated since his time, which is fortunate since his guineas and sovereigns particularly were almost flawless and very difficult to detect. Inspector Jamison had occasion to mention him only a few months ago; copies of Yeovil's correspondence are carefully examined by experts at the Yard, where they have not given up hope of recovering the rest of his effects. But come, let us be on our way."

Since the distance from our lodgings to Portman Square was not great, Pons elected to walk by way of Edgware Road and Upper Berkeley Street. "There is a sense of adventurous expectancy about a London fog," he often said. "One can expect anything to come out of it." But tonight he walked in silence, deep in thought. His long, imposing stride, his slightly open Inverness, his height all lent him an impressiveness which was manifestly felt by passersby, who instinctively swerved aside on meeting us. He walked, indeed, like a solitary pedestrian whose kinship with the fog swirling around us was several degrees more substantial than any relationship he might have had with his companion.

Our client awaited us at his sumptuous dwelling. He was still in evening clothes and had obviously not long preceded us. He had given instructions that we be shown to the library where he kept his collection of books, and we found him there, standing with hands folded behind him, dignified despite an air of impatience.

"I am at your service, Mr. Pons. What can I show you first?" he asked.

"I fear I may disappoint you, Baron," replied Pons. "But I have a fancy to see the silver spider miniature of the forger, Yeovil."

"By all means, sir." He favored Pons with a curious and surprised glance, but asked no question.

Baron de Baseuil walked to a nearby case, opened it, and took out a little box of the kind in which jewelry is kept. He opened it and turned it toward us. Cushioned inside lay an exquisitely wrought silver scarab which, save for its unusual bulk, looked almost genuinely alive.

"The miniature, of course, is inside," said the Baron. "Pray examine it at your leisure."

Pons took the scarab and turned it over, disclosing a tiny door. Under our client's eyes, Pons opened the little door.

The scarab was empty.

A cry of mingled anger and shock escaped Baron de Baseuil. He took the silver container from Pons' fingers, his hand trembling; he turned it over, examining it from all sides. Then he cast an apprehensive glance toward the remainder of his treasures.

"Do not alarm yourself, Baron," said Pons softly. "I daresay this is the only object which has been stolen."

"Sir, I have been informed of your powers," said the Baron. "How did you guess?"

Pons smiled enigmatically. "Surely it was obvious that the elaborate hoax of the Boar's Head catalogue was perpetrated for the purpose of taking you sufficiently far from London so that someone might have access to your collection, Baron. Six of you were present or represented at the sale; there are in existence six of Yeovil's miniature forgeries. I dislike to believe in coincidence, Baron. The deduction is almost inevitable that your companion dupes were very probably the only other persons to receive the spurious catalogue and that they, like yourself, possess one of Yeovil's silver pieces."

"It is true, we own the six spiders among us," said Baron de Baseuil thoughtfully. "But, of course, it is really absurdly simple, now you explain it. Yet there is little reason for having taken this; it has no great value."

"As to that, we shall see. Let us discover what manner of man we have to deal with."

The Baron rang for his manservant, who came with commendable promptness. He was a gaunt individual, slightly stooped, and already well along in years. His dignified correctness suggested long service.

"Bateman, on one of the days I was in Scotland, someone called," said the Baron. "Who was it?"

"No one called but Mr. Wootyn, the appraiser from Sotheby's."

"What did he want?"

"He said he had come in response to your request to appraise several small pieces in the collection, sir. He was here perhaps ten minutes, and said that he would write to you in a few days. I assumed he had done so. I did not leave him out of my sight, sir."

The Baron held up the silver scarab. "Did he examine this, Batemen?

"Yes sir, I believe he did."

"The miniature could be abstracted easily," observed Pons. "It would require but a slight manual dexterity."

"Is anything wrong, sir?" asked Bateman anxiously.

"Telephone Wootyn at his home. I'll speak to him from here."

"Very good sir." He left the room.

"This is amazing, Mr. Pons," said Baron de Baseuil. "I have known Wootyn for twenty years."

"I take it you did not instruct him to make an appraisal for you. I'm afraid you will discover that Mr. Wootyn made no call here last month."

The telephone rang; Baron de Baseuil reached for it at once. Our client spoke but a few minutes to ascertain that Pons was indeed correct – Mr. Wootyn had not called at the house in Portman Square since April.

"I cannot understand it," muttered the Baron, as he turned from the instrument. "The miniature has no great value."

"We are dealing with an exceedingly clever man, Baron. He has apparently familiarized himself sufficiently with your habits to have succeeded in impersonating Wootyn so cleverly as to deceive Bateman. I rather think there is no time to be lost, if we are not already too late. I must have sight of the remaining miniatures without delay – if any do remain. I recall their owners and took the trouble to jot down their addresses before I left Praed Street. Lady Monica Jevrons was one of the two who did not go to Edinburgh."

"She was ill, Mr. Pons."

"I fancy her home will be the most likely place for our next visit. Will you be so good as to telephone her and ask her to receive us immediately? Please also ask your other fellow-bibliophiles to see us briefly in the course of the evening."

"Certainly, Mr. Pons. Permit me to put a car at your disposal."

"Thank you. It will facilitate our movements. Perhaps with good fortune I shall be able to recover your miniature." So saying, Pons led the way from the house. We stood briefly on the kerb until the Baron's chauffeur brought his car around. Pons gave the address of Lady Monica Jevrons to the chauffeur and we rode away, Pons urging the driver to hasten.

"What manner of chase is this, Pons?" I asked dubiously.

"I have taken a shot in the dark, Parker," he replied. "But I daresay, unlike some of us who venture, I have come close to the mark."

It was midnight when we returned to 7B, Praed Street.

"A most entertaining evening," said Pons jubilantly. "A delightful character, this fellow who is able to transform himself in the space of a single day from Mr. Wootyn of Sotheby's to Colonel Wade's cousin from Bristol, from Sir Austin Mannell's solicitor to Kester Roxbrugh's business manager. I am impatient to meet him. He has made no less than four separate attempts to reach Lady Jevrons' collection, and six to get at Alan Thomason's. Apparently he disdains simple breaking and entering. But I am confident that he will not despair; he will continue to try. Let us have a look at our catch."

He had removed his Inverness and deerstalker cap. Now he placed on the table the tiny books, so beautifully made, which, with the permission of their owners, he had taken from the "spiders" of Lady Jevrons and Alan Thomason. I confess that, being tired and irritable after our wild chase over London, I eyed them with profound disfavor.

"I cannot pretend to understand collectors," I remarked. "They pay fabulous sums for comparative trifles."

"There is much in what you say," replied Pons, shrugging into his dressing-gown. "Yet you have a kinship with them, Parker – you are no less assiduous in assembling notes for these trifling adventures of mine."

He drew forward his magnifying glass and bent to the first of the books.

I stood behind him, looking down. The tiny books, which were approximately an inch by three-fourths of an inch were singularly beautiful in craftsmanship. They appeared to have been written in a script with the aspect of print, and the pages were decorated with hieroglyphics which had an indisputable look of authenticity. They were bound in limp leather, with decorative end-sheets, intricately scrolled. To Pons' face now had come that intentness of expression so characteristic of him; he was plainly "on the scent" – the keenness of his eyes, the pursed lips, the angular line of his jaw all gave evidence that the miniature books challenged his imagination. In a few moments he was lost in contemplation; he might have been unaware of my existence; so I left him shortly after and retired.

How long he sat up studying the tiny books I had no way of knowing in the morning, for when I came to breakfast, he sat at table, obviously waiting for me. His eyes had a glint of satisfaction in them, and the moment I appeared he proffered one of the miniatures.

"Take a look at the end-papers, Parker. What do you make of them?"

I took the book, waiting upon Mrs. Johnson to bring breakfast, and scrutinized the end-paper decoration with care. The elaborate design which Yeovil had worked into the pages was planned for a single page, and repeated thus four times on the two end-papers.

"The motif looks Egyptian," I said at last.

"It is meant to," replied Pons.

"There appears to be a numeral worked into the design," I ventured.

"Capital, Parker! What is it?"

"6." I hesitated. "But, of course, there are six books. This is manifestly the sixth of the group."

"Then there would be a numeral, too, in this one, would there not? What do you see?"

He gave me the second of the miniatures. Look as I might, I could not discover any numeral on the end-papers of the second miniature. But that there was something to be seen I could not doubt; Pons had discovered something, and he meant that I, too, should do so. I studied the design with the greatest attention and ultimately found what appeared to be the letter "B". I said as much.

"Excellent, my good Parker! So, indeed it is."

"But what significance does it have?" I asked.

"I have worked upon the problem half the night. If you will study the text, you will observe that the book with the letter in it would seem to be the concluding volume of the set of miniatures. An examination of the text in the volume featured by the numeral suggests that it is the second of the series. We have thus to suppose that the numeral or numerals in addition to the letter or letters compose a message of some kind. I submit that not very much of a message could be contained in six letters or numerals. But they could very readily convey such a message as an address. Proceeding, therefore, on that deduction, we begin with this arrangement – " Here he thrust before me a piece of paper upon which he had written:

"– 6 – – – B"

"Now, either the message to be conveyed is an address or it is not. If it is not, then we are left with the suggestion of a code which must be extremely limited, and must therefore also be known to very few persons. Yeovil has been in Dartmoor for so long a time that the possibility of anyone's reading such a code with ease is appreciably diminished. That it is an address is much the more likely probability. Accepting that assumption, we do not find any very great difficulty confronting us. It is not likely that more than the first three spaces are occupied by numerals, and the probability is that the '6' is the last numeral of two; the first is then, necessarily one of but nine numerals. It is manifest, furthermore, that there is no designation for street, road, lane, square, court, or place of any kind; I submit that this very absence suggests an address which ought to be relatively easy to discover. 'B' is then the last letter of an abbreviation; presumably, it is either the third or fourth letter of the abbreviation. I began with the assumption that it is the fourth, and proceeded to consider the streets and byways of London, with particular attention to the vicinity of Yeovil's sphere of greatest activity, which was not far away. I began with Barbers Hall in Monkwell Street, and went steadily down the list of all the streets which might satisfy the requirements. There is scarcely any need to burden you with all the details of my search, but I concluded finally with Holborn. I had then the following – "

He handed me yet another slip of paper upon which he had writing: "– 6 H O L B".

"However, when I had applied each digit from one to nine in turn to this address, none seemed to me likely as the repository for the kind of – shall we say 'treasure'? – I expected to find. Yet I was loath to discard Holborn Street. It was squarely in the center of Yeovil's sphere; it was certainly the likeliest of streets from any points-of-view; yet the numerals did not satisfy. It occurred to me finally that by only a slight alteration, to High Holborn, I arrived at this – "

A third slip of paper was forthcoming: "– 6 H H L B".

"And at once it was evident that the address must be 16, High Holborn. That is the address of the Soames Museum, an institution supported by funds out of a private trust, and open to donations of pieces fitting the various exhibits. What could be more ideal as a repository than a semi-private museum? If your practise permits, we shall just take a run over there this morning."

"And where does Yeovil, the forger, fit into all this?"

"I talked to Dartmoor in the telephone this morning. Poor Yeovil, alas! is not long for this world. He was stricken with a fatal malady in August, and his death is but a matter of a fortnight away. I submit that the long arm of coincidence dangles too insistently upon the scene. Surely it is too much to consider it only coincidence that the onset of Yeovil's malady in August should be followed within a month by the appearance of the Boar's Head hoax and the purloining of four of the miniature book forgeries created by Yeovil before his capture?

No, Parker, the matter strikes me as essentially simple – Yeovil had kept his secret against the hope of escape. He revealed it only when he realized that the secret would no longer serve him. How he did it, I do not yet know. The cipher experts at the Yard are not amateurs, and Yeovil was certainly aware that his effects were sorely wanted. I have reason to hope that we have anticipated Yeovil's wishes in the course he desired his correspondent to follow."

"But what 'treasure' could Yeovil have hidden?"

Pons shrugged. "We shall discover that, I hope, in good time. We shall also find out to whom Yeovil revealed his secret. I asked Dartmoor for the names of those people with whom Yeovil corresponded, and I have their promise to send along the names and addresses just as soon as they can be ascertained. I fancy that a life-long prisoner at Dartmoor is not likely to have many friends who correspond with him with any regularity after so long a time in quod."

At this moment Mrs. Johnson entered with our breakfast, her plain, honest features beaming with pleasure at the contemplation of our enjoyment of the food she prepared with such maternal concern for our welfare.

Immediately after our meal, we made our way to the Soames Museum, in advance of opening hours, for Pons had made arrangements with the curator for our admission. The building housed the one-time collection of the late Sir Rowley Soames, and such pieces as had been added by various doners since his time. It was open to the public five afternoons each week. It was not a large museum, but three guards and the curator were regularly employed there, though at this hour of the morning only one guard and the curator were present.

The curator was a corpulent man of middle age, with thinning hair and a pinkness of complexion common to people who are seldom in the sun. He wore *pince-nez*, which lent him dignity, but failed to conceal the anxiety with which he greeted us.

"I know you by reputation, of course, Mr. Pons," he said. "I do hope that your visit here will not result in the appearance of any unfavorable publicity."

"I am confident that we can keep the matter from the papers, Mr. Fredenthal. It is highly confidential, and this visit, if I am correct in my assumption, may actually forestall precisely the kind of public notice you seem to fear."

"What can I do for you, Mr. Pons?" asked the curator apprehensively.

"I should like to know what pieces were added to the museum in the years 1911 and perhaps 1910, either by a gentleman named Yeovil or anonymously. There is a more remote possibility that the pieces I am seeking were sent to the Museum under some other name, but the probability is that they were sent anonymously."

"Stolen?" asked Fredenthal immediately.

Pons smiled. "Dear me, how we do fear the worst! I think not."

"Well, that should be easy, Mr. Pons," replied the curator then, and bustled about to take from his desk a volume labeled *Acquisitions*. "That was before my coming to Soames, but the record should be here." He was turning the pages as he spoke. "Now, let us see – 1911 was the year, I think you said. We don't ordinarily receive many accessions, as perhaps you know. Ah, here is 1910. Six accessions in that year – only one anonymous, however, which is dated December, a set of four books bound in vellum, purporting to be thirteenth century volumes, illuminated."

"You say 'purported'?" asked Pons.

"There is some question about their authenticity, Mr. Pons," He turned another page. "Here we are in 1911, and again we have but one anonymous donation, early in the year – a Norse seaman's chest."

"I would like to examine both books and chest, Mr. Fredenthal," said Pons without hesitation. "I fancy they are the items in which we are interested."

"I will have them here in no time at all, sir."

The curator was as good as his word. In but a few minutes the set of books, bound in hand-tooled white vellum, and the chest, a small, squat object, painted a dull green with a flower decoration, and secured by bands of wrought iron, were put down before Pons.

"These are Yeovil's," said Pons without a moment's hesitation. "Here is the same precision of craftsmanship." He took up one of the books, put it down, and picked up another. In this fashion, he handled all four of the volumes. He opened each one in turn. "These are surely uncommonly heavy," he reflected. "Yet none has many pages, though the parchment appears to be genuine. But it was always so of Yeovil's work." He gave his attention to the binding of the book. The front and back covers were unusually thick; each cover represented a thickness of almost an inch and, while the outside appeared to be soft and padded, the inside cover was firm, with a sheet of parchment pasted over an end-paper. "A pity that so good an artist should have turned to crime," murmured Pons.

He turned to the sea-chest. It was not locked. He opened it and looked inside. It was quite empty.

"I observe this chest has a great deal of weight, also," said Pons. "I know comparatively little of Norse customs. Are such chests commonly weighted?"

The curator nodded. "They are usually taken on sea voyages, and they are made weighted, usually with a thick, heavy bottom. This chest is no exception, you see, Mr. Pons. We have considered it authentic."

"I fear I shall be obliged to commit an act of vandalism, Mr. Fredenthal. I believe the bottom of this chest is not solid."

"But certainly it isn't hollow, Mr. Pons."

"No, sir, it is not. But I submit that it is not entirely wood. The chest has too much weight to be accounted for in the heavy bottom or the iron bands. The books, too, have more weight than they should have. I regret this necessity, but the only alternative would result in a distressing kind of attendant publicity."

The curator acquiesced, and Pons set to work.

In a short time he had taken the chest apart, and there lay revealed a heavy block of wood which had served as its bottom. But it was evident now that it was not a solid block, for it was made up of two layers, the bottom layer very thick, the top thin and mortised in. Pons lost no time in removing the top layer and exposing the bottom – and its contents, a set of tools and dies, laid into the solid block.

"Great heavens, Mr. Pons!" exclaimed the curator. "What are those objects?"

"They represent something sought by Scotland Yard for twenty years, Mr. Fredenthal – the tools and dies used by the forger, Yeovil, to perfect the almost undetectable forgeries of sovereigns and guineas which made their appearance in 1909 and are still turning up here and there today. We will find the rest of the paraphernalia in the covers of these books. I shall take these things along with me, Mr. Fredenthal, and dispatch them with my compliments to Chief Inspector Titus at Scotland Yard; he was the sergeant in charge at the time of Yeovil's arrest. I fancy it will not take too much trouble to repair these spurious antiques. I should add that they deserve some sort of niche of their own; I doubt that all England is likely to produce a craftsman of Yeovil's ability more than once in a century."

Back at number 7, we found a message from Dartmoor. Mrs. Johnson had scrupulously copied it in her laborious script.

Pons took it up and read it aloud. "'Yeovil has had only two regular correspondents since the death of his brother in 1927. They are a sister, Mrs. Clement Jones, 13A Lord Street, Bristol, and a nephew, Alastair White, 33 Gerrard Street, London.' – I daresay it is White we want; the impersonations would have been beyond Yeovil's sister, surely. We should manage to reach his place during the lunch hour. His quarters are not far from the theatrical district, and it is entirely likely that he is an actor. If we take the Underground at Baker Street we can go up to Leicester Square from Piccadilly."

I protested. "But to what end, Pons? We have the dies."

"And I will send them off to Titus within the hour by messenger at the same time that I return the miniatures to Lady Jevrons and Alan Thomason," answered Pons. "Some kind of report ought to be made to our client, as well. But I submit that the primary problem is not the recovery of the dies and tools, nor yet the solution to the intriguing mystery of the Boar's Head catalog hoax and the six silver spiders, but the ultimate future of a young man who has already shown a brilliant if erratic talent. Stay at home if you like Parker, but I want a look at Alastair White."

It was clearly Pons' plan to gain access to Alastair White's rooms before that young man himself returned. In this he had no difficult task; he represented himself as a friend of White's, and, with knowledge of the easy familiarity that maintained among members of the theatrical profession, White's landlady readily admitted us to his rooms, a second-storey suite, furnished in excellent taste.

Once inside, however, Pons' casual air dropped from him. He stood in the middle of the sitting-room looking all about him, his keen eyes missing nothing.

"A man of method and determination," he murmured. "He would seem to be scrupulously neat, for everything is in its place, including – " he moved swiftly forward as he spoke – "his letters." He lifted them from the rack on the desk as he spoke, and carried them with him to a chair next the window, from which he could watch the street below.

"What now?" I asked, though it seemed evident what he meant to do.

"I am going to read his mail," said Pons without compunction.

"Like any common bobby," I said.

"You impugn our police, Parker. Say rather, 'like any common detective.' But add in what cause."

He was already scanning the letters. For some moments he read silently, rapidly finishing one letter and turning to the next. "Ah, these are subtle," he said at last. "Yeovil has been doing his best to persuade his nephew that security on the stage is difficult to achieve, that it is difficult in all walks of life save crime."

"Surely he does not say so!"

"Not in so many words. But the effect is manifest, particularly when these letters are read cumulatively. They are insidious – they appeal to vanity, attack integrity, undermine courage. Ah, Yeovil is clever, far too clever! And how many letters there were before this group, which dates from May of this year, it is impossible to say. But here we are in August." He read for a moment. "Yeovil has had his attack of illness; he suspects it is to be mortal. Yes, yes – he writes: 'They have not given me any reason to hope here in the prison hospital that I will leave here alive. In the last few days I have been thinking more and more often of the life I have led, and I could wish I could resume it where I left off – not the criminal life, my boy, but the creative life. Or that someone else could pick it up where I ceased to live. But the race, I say again, as I have said before, is to the ingenious, not to the brute. It is as true in one walk of life as in the other, in art as in crime, and indeed, perfect crimes are always works of art. The challenge is before you, as it is before all of us at a given but seldom foreknown time in life. When I consider the beautiful things I have made – in imitation, it is true – but in some cases the imitations were even better than the originals – I believe that the treasure I would like to see most of all is my little set of six silver spiders and their miniature books. If ever you get the chance, by all means look them over. You will understand what your old uncle meant when I write that I regret having relinquished that work.' He could hardly have been any plainer, and yet he makes no gift of his treasure to his nephew; he must exercise his utmost ingenuity to achieve it," finished Pons.

He restored the letters to their previous position, and then began a systematic search of Alastair White's quarters. He opened drawers, looked through the closet, examined all the books on the shelves, and finally returned to look at the little group of books set up between bookends on our quarry's desk. He took them up, one after another, reading their titles, until at last he gave a little crow of triumph, and turned with an ancient-looking little book in his hands.

"This one seems out of place, eh, Parker?"

I read its titles *Sermons du Pere Bretonneau de la Compagnie de Jesus.*

Then, with an easy gesture, Pons opened it past its seventieth page and disclosed a box; the book was a cleverly made dummy, and the box thus revealed contained four more of the tiny miniature books which had been taken from Yeovil's six silver spiders. Pons took them carefully from their repository and put them into his pocket.

In half an hour, the owner of the rooms came. Pons saw him from the window, and was on his feet in the middle of the floor to greet him when he entered.

He was a man approaching thirty, not ill-favored in looks, with singular presence, and a personality which was at once apparent. His brief uncertainty at sight of us was controlled and dissipated in a moment. His dark eyes took in first one, then the other of us, measuring us as he put his walking-stick away.

"Mr. Alastair White, I believe," said Pons. "We are recent admirers of your work, particularly your splendid impersonation of Mr. Anthony Wootyn of Sotheby's."

The smile of pleasure which had begun to grow on his face was arrested; it faded. He looked at Pons in sharp alarm. "Permit me," said Pons, bowing. "Mr. Solar Pons, at your service. Allow me to present Dr. Lyndon Parker."

"Ah, the detective," said White with an almost dramatic air. "Mr. Pons, I have committed no crime."

"Surely not yet – if we discount the abstraction of the four miniature books from your uncle's silver scarabs and the impertinent hoax perpetrated upon six of the city's most illustrious bibliophiles. It would seem to be a pity, however, that so imaginative a gentleman, so accomplished an impersonator, should consider even for a moment yielding to the subtle blandishments of his dying uncle, no matter how much he may have admired him in his childhood and youth. Tell me, Mr. White, were you aware of the nature of the 'treasure' you were seeking?"

White looked warily from Pons to me and back again, saying nothing.

"Pray do not be wary. I am not here to place you under arrest. Not yet. That alternative lies with you. I have recovered the miniatures and will return them to their owners. I have read your uncle's letters, and I should like to ask you again whether you know what 'treasure' he had hidden for you to find?"

"No, Mr. Pons, I did not. I thought perhaps it was money."

"I have recovered the 'treasure' but two hours ago; it is now at Scotland Yard. Mr. White, it consisted of the tools and dies your uncle used to make those excellent counterfeit sovereigns and guineas for which he is justly famed in the annals of crime. He has led you to the brink of a career of crime. The tools and dies are now out of your reach – but you might well have been faced with the decision of whether to use them or not. The high place is still before you, however. I suggest that your uncle's insidious letters do not tell all the story or even offer you the alternatives. I should consider that the mind which conceived and executed the Boar's Head catalog hoax would be lost on crime – even as your uncle's was. May I extend my invitation to join us at dinner and let me present the alternatives to your uncle's suggestion?"

"Mr. Pons, whatever I say can be turned against me."

Pons chuckled. "Mr. White, pray excuse me. I will wait on the walk below for five minutes. If you should elect to accept my invitation, I hope to see you soon. If not, you may be sure that we will ultimately meet again, in less pleasant circumstances. Good day, sir."

Three minutes after we reached Gerrard Street, Alastair White came from the house. He came striding up to Pons with outstretched hand and a pleasant, sunny smile on his handsome face.

"Mr. Solar Pons," he said. "I believe we have an engagement for dinner."

VIII

THE ADVENTURE OF THE LOST LOCOMOTIVE

Early one morning during the first year of my residence in the quarters of my friend, Solar Pons, the private enquiry agent, I was startled from sleep by a commanding assault on the outer door of No. 7, Praed Street. I jumped out of bed, groped into my dressing-gown and slippers, and came out of my room hoping to anticipate my companion, for he had sat up late assembling certain facts relative to my notes concerning the dramatic adventure of the Haunted Library.

But Pons had preceded me. Indeed, he was even now turning from the window, his keen grey eyes alight with expectation. Clad in his purple dressing gown and velvet slippers, he stood rubbing his hands together in that habit he had, and favored me with a light smile.

"Ah, he has wakened you, too, Parker," he said. "I had hoped to prevent his disturbing Mrs. Johnson, but she sleeps like a cat and wakens at the slightest sound. If the matter is commensurate with the to do which announces it, I fear we shall be asked to look into a formidable problem."

"It is surely no night to be out," I said. "It is still raining."

"But the fog, I think, is thinner," answered Pons.

"Was there a car below?" I asked. "I saw you looking out."

"A limousine. But there are two people on the stairs, and one, unless I am grievously in error, is our old friend Jamison."

The door was tapped upon, and, at Pons' reply, thrown open.

Inspector Jamison loomed behind a portly figure of considerable presence. Our client was a man of perhaps sixty summers, with closely-cropped greying hair, keen dark eyes, and a square, impressive jaw dominated by a wide, thick-lipped mouth. His appearance, however, was that of a man who had undergone but recently events of a most upsetting nature. Without waiting for Inspector Jamison's introduction, he strode toward Pons.

"Mr. Solar Pons," he said, extending his hand gravely.

"Sir Ernest McVeagh, I believe," replied Pons. "Director of the Great Northern Railway, as well as of several other corporations of considerable importance to the Empire."

"I trust you can forgive this unseemly and untimely interruption of your rest..."

"Think nothing of it, sir. I observe you, too, were aroused from your own bed by the events which have brought you here. Pray allow me, sir – your vest is buttoned askew."

"It is of no consequence, Mr. Pons. Let us waste no time in coming to the point," said our visitor in some agitation. "One of our locomotives has vanished."

The light quickened in my companion's eyes. "From the round-house or the line?"

"From the line!"

Pons' eyes fairly danced: "The details?"

"At ten-thirty last evening, a gentleman who gave his name as James H. Mason appeared at our district manager's office; he represented himself as having but recently arrived at Croydon from New York. He stated that it was urgently necessary for him to be in Sheffield at the earliest possible moment, preferably before dawn, certainly not later than ten o'clock. All air travel had been canceled because of heavy weather; he had been unable to hire a car to take him so far from London; he had missed the fast train to Sheffield; so he had come as a last resort to implore our arrangement of a special train or locomotive to transport him to Sheffield. Money was apparently no object. Since he carried but a dispatch case, we were naturally curious to know something more about him. He was unusually reticent, but he disclosed that he had registered at Bohn's; inquiry soon corroborated his statement. He had remained in his room only long enough to deposit a bag, which Scotland Yard has impounded."

Inspector Jamison's rubicund face managed a smile and he nodded gravely. "Nothing in it," he said. "That is, nothing that would tell us much about him, except that he appeared to be in the law."

Our client continued. "His request was a most unusual one. It was not impossible for us to transport him to Sheffield, however costly the operation might be. As he made clear, he did not quibble at the cost of a special, nor did he object when he was informed that it might be impossible to make up a special at such short notice, but that a locomotive was available for his use as soon as we could find an engineer and fireman to man it. It would take at least an hour to clear the line and make the necessary arrangements; he chafed at this delay, but did not stir from the office while arrangements were being made.

"As a matter of record, our registry number 177 left Euston Station at eleven-thirty-seven; it had to run on a very close schedule, of course; for at least part of the way a slow passenger train followed, and the line had been cleared only for the time necessary to make the special run. Each station, therefore, had been informed of the approximate hour of number 177's passing, with instructions to wire the central office as soon as it had gone by, so that we might be fully informed in regard to its keeping on schedule. Wires accordingly came in at the expected intervals, with Number 177 running on time, until the locomotive had passed Girton, which is approximately seventy miles from London. The next station on the line is Kendon-on-Lea; it is just fourteen miles beyond Girton. Since the special was traveling at about seventy miles an hour, it should have passed through Kendon-on-Lea in ten minutes or so after it had gone through Girton.

"But there was no wire from the agent at Kendon-on-Lea. There was no further announcement of the special's passing whatsoever. The central office immediately dispatched an inquiry to Kendon-on-Lea; Jeffries, the agent there, replied by wire that the special had not yet passed. Within half an hour came another wire from Jeffries reporting the passing, on schedule, of the slow train which had been following the special. Naturally, since there had been no report of an accident, the district agent thought that there had been remissness or an error somewhere along the line; at least the special might have left the rails sufficiently far to have escaped the notice of the engineer of the following train.

"At our district agent's instructions, therefore, a party of inquiry was sent back along the line to Girton. Mr. Pons, despite the most diligent search, no trace of the locomotive could be found. The only certain facts were that the special had gone through Girton but had not reached Kendon-on-Lea. Subsequently, however, the fireman, Stanley Meybreck, was found wandering in a dazed condition in the vicinity of Chadwick, the station before Girton on the up-run; and only twenty minutes before we set out for your address, the engineer telephoned from Chisborough; he had found a telegram announcing the collapse and imminent death of his father waiting for him at Chadwick, together with a substitute driver, and had gone rushing off only to discover that nothing had happened to his parent. It would seem that some premeditation is thus indicated, though it is puzzling to believe, and even more perplexing to explain.

"That, Mr. Pons, is the sum and substance of this extraordinary affair. We communicated at once with Scotland Yard, and Inspector Jamison has been working diligently since that time. Though he has not been on the scene, the tracks between Girton and Kendon-on-Lea have been examined with the most minute care, and so have the spurs, though only two of them are any longer in use."

"How many are there?" asked Pons.

"Three. One leads to a colliery, another to a mine, the third to a yards owned by the line but abandoned some time ago to a salvage company."

Pons gazed toward Jamison. "You have had reports on the spurs?"

"Of course," said Jamison with self-assurance. "The colliery line is clear; there is nothing on it, and the guards at the colliery report no disturbance on the line. The line to the mine ends in a block; that has not been disturbed; it too is clear. The other spur is no longer even connected to the main line; the tracks for a short distance from the spur were taken up two years ago."

Pons sat for some moments in deep silence, his head sunk upon his chest, the fingers of his left hand toying with his ear. "A locomotive can hardly vanish into thin air," he observed presently.

"Elementary, my dear Pons," said Jamison heavily.

Pons smiled.

"The fact is," continued Jamison, "that is exactly what it did do. It passed Girton; it did not reach Kendon-on-Lea. It did not return through Girton; it did not go forward through Kendon-on-Lea. The through train which followed met no resistance on the line between Girton and Kendon-on-Lea. I believe it was you who once said that if the possible explanations are shown to be inadequate, then the only remaining explanation, however, untenable, must be true. The locomotive has disappeared as completely as if the earth had opened and swallowed it up."

"Let me see. There are no tarns, canals, lakes along the line," mused Pons.

Jamison smiled with an annoyingly superior air. "My dear fellow, that was the first thing we thought of. We are not amateurs."

"'Pity 'tis, 'tis true,'" murmured Pons. "But the locomotive is not in London; so a visit to the scene of the crime is indicated."

"We can arrange for a special for you, Mr. Pons," said our client.

"I hardly think it will be necessary. There is surely some train on its regular run that will convey us to Girton. From there, we shall enlist such services as you may direct your agent at that station to lend us. We shall need a car – preferably not a hand-car – to go out over the line."

"The next train leaves Euston in scarcely half an hour, Mr. Pons," said Sir Ernest with some anxiety.

"We shall be on it," promised Pons.

Our client was somewhat uncertain, but in his anxiety he could not afford to disregard any proposal Pons might put forth. An examination of the ground was inevitable in the circumstances; that Pons intended no delay could not but please Sir Ernest McVeagh. If Inspector Jamison was dubious, he masked his dubeity well; still, there lingered in his eyes an almost triumphant smile, as if to say that this time, certainly, my companion's much vaunted powers would not help him.

"We shall give you every assistance in our power, Mr. Pons," said Sir Ernest.

After our client and the portly Inspector Jamison had taken their leave, Pons threw himself into the feverish activity attendant upon our departure for the north. Throughout our rapid preparations, Pons said not a word. Yet he made ready with the keenest anticipation; the problem Sir Ernest McVeagh had brought him was one which intrigued him, and even the prospect of going out into so unpleasant a night did not dismay him. Not until we were safely ensconced in the compartment of the train which was to take us north of London did Pons speak.

He looked quizzically over at me, his left eyebrow raised. "What do you make of it, Parker?"

"Well, it is obviously moonshine," I said. "A locomotive simply can't disappear without trace."

"Yet it seems to have done so," retorted Pons. "I am afraid our good Inspector Jamison has proceeded on the theory that you have just advanced, that the locomotive did not actually vanish. Let us, on the contrary, assume that it did; it is no more difficult to adduce an explanation for the one as for the other, whatever Jamison may believe."

"Very well, then," I said, nettled. "Perhaps it was lifted off the line from the air."

Pons, however, did not smile. "Until we have evidence to the contrary, no theory, no matter how absurd it may seem, can be discarded. I fear, in view of the attendant weather, that an airlift is out of the question. Let us ask ourselves what possible motive could there for causing the locomotive to vanish."

"Mason needed it."

"Ah, now we are being facetious," said Pons, wagging finger at me in admonition.

"Well, Pons, I am no good at this sort of thing," I replied. "I should like to hear your explanation."

"Ah, it is beyond my poor powers at this point. But I submit one or two little aspects of the problem for your consideration. The object of the disappearance, I think we are safe in taking it, was not the locomotive, but its passenger."

"Mason?"

"James H. Mason, an American. Now, I submit that is a significant detail. He is not a tourist, for his course is fixed and purposeful. He is evidently a man of means, but he prefers to travel alone; he registers at a hotel like Bohn's, instead of one of the larger and costlier hostelries, where he might be more easily seen. We are not far wrong, I fancy, in assuming that he would like to keep himself as unobtrusive as possible. He is a man with a mission; he must get to Sheffield as early as possible, at least by ten o'clock. Why ten o'clock?"

"He has an appointment," I ventured.

"But would not an appointee wait upon an envoy come from so great a distance? I am afraid, Parker, that if our Mr. Mason flew to England to be in Sheffield at ten o'clock, this was a mission which could not be delayed. Very well, then, what sort of mission might it be? That, too, is not difficult to guess."

"You know?" I demanded incredulously.

"In matters of this kind, one can make certain deductions. I rather think they are not wide of the mark. Sheffield is an industrial city, and I daresay there are important meetings held in that city every day. Does not the hour, ten o'clock, suggest some kind of business meeting?"

"It does."

"Just hand me the *Financial Times*, will you?"

He took the paper and studied its columns. But he was not long in finding what he sought.

"Ah, I fancy this is what we want. 'Northern Steel Stockholders Meeting.' The hour is ten o'clock, in the office of the President of the corporation. I submit, Parker, that a stockholders' meeting is not to be delayed by the non-arrival of such stockholders as are interested enough to want to attend. Such a meeting could hardly be postponed by any other means than a majority vote of the stockholders themselves."

I pondered for some moments what my companion intended to suggest. "But who would have any reason to want to prevent the American's attendance?" I protested. "After all, if it is a matter of votes, he is but one man against a certain majority."

"Ah, you are back on the airlift," said Pons dryly.

"And, if it were meant to abduct him, what possible excuse could there be for waiting until he got so far out of London?"

"Oh, that is elementary indeed, Parker. It must surely be obvious even to you with a little thought."

"It is very easy to brush my objections aside, Pons," I said. "That is not answering them."

"They answer themselves if only you will give yourself time enough to think about them."

With this, Pons turned to the front page of the *Times*. "There is nothing in the paper," I said. "I looked."

"So I see. I observe, however, a paragraph on corporate difficulties in Northern Steel. 'Lord Delapoer, Chairman of the Board, has indicated that he anticipates no change in the policies which the Board has followed in the administration of the Northern Steel, despite the agitation of Balfour Danals, who is, according to Lord Delapoer, only a minority stockholder.'" Pons lowered the paper and gazed thoughtfully over at me. "That suggests nothing to you, Parker?"

"Nothing."

He smiled fleetingly, folded the paper, and threw it down. "My concern at the moment is primarily about the locomotive," he went on. "I am satisfied about Mason, but the locomotive perplexes me."

"I am surprised to hear it."

"I don't wonder. Of course, it is evident that it was taken over one of of the three spur-lines of the road between Girton and Kendon-on-Lea. I daresay we shall discover which one in due time."

He lapsed into silence and sat with his head sunk upon his chest, his eyes closed, his restless fingers beating a tattoo on the arm of the seat. In this fashion he rode into the dawn to our arrival in mid-morning at Girton where a special investigator for the Great Northern awaited us in the company of the stationmaster.

The investigator, a rotund, red-cheeked man in his late middle years, introduced himself as Robinson Melward. The station-master was a transplanted Cockney, James Byron, who looked very harassed and tired at the moment of our arrival, though the presence of Solar Pons seemed to stimulate him to renewed wakefulness, and he was eager to explain his role, however negative, in the puzzling problem of the missing locomotive.

"I seen her go by, like I reported; I sent in my report by wire, and first thing I knew there was the home office calling for more information. Had I seen her go back? No, sir, I had not. Then the wires begun to come hot and heavy, and first thing you know the regular went through. So I reported that and everything broke loose. Next thing I know Mr. Melward showed up, and a detective-inspector assigned by the Yard, and the lot of us couldn't find a trace of old 177 anywhere."

Pons did nothing to stem his loquacity, which did not last long, for he was obliged to telephone up and down the line in order to ascertain that traffic would be slowed and warned of our presence on the line. Then we set out, leaving the assistant stationmaster in charge at Girton. Our conveyance was a motor-driven car, similar in construction to a hand-car, but shielded on three sides from wind and weather, with an open back, allowing for freedom of movement to and from the car.

The rain had ceased, but a fine mist stung our faces despite the slowness of our progress along the line. Pons was so constantly off the car, examining the roadbed, that he might as well have walked the distance. The first spur to which we came found us switched off the main line.

"The regular from the north is due down," explained Byron. "We'll just wait here."

Pons looked along the length of the spur, which vanished into a denser mist.

"Which of the three spurs is this, Mr. Byron?" he asked.

"It goes into the Green Star Colliery, Mr. Pons, Not much used. Just for the cars now and then. The vein's about petered out."

A locomotive's whistle sounded from the north, and in a moment the rumble of an approaching train rose out of the mist.

"Here she comes," said Byron with a proprietary air. He looked at his watch. "Right on time, too."

The train which swept by was evidently the night train out of Scotland, for it included several sleepers. While we were watching it pass, my companion vanished along the dense, foggy spur-line.

"No need to walk, Mr. Pons," said Byron. "We can take the car in."

Forthwith he started up the car. We caught up to Pons, who was running along the line, bent and hunched in an almost ape-like manner, peering intently from one side of the line to the other, as if he hoped to discover some evidence that previous investigation had failed to disclose. In this fashion we reached the mine itself, and the car stopped at a block across the line. This Pons examined with singular intentness, observing the mouth of the mine yawning blackly ahead.

"We thought it might be large enough for a locomotive to get into," said Felward, observing Pons' interest. "But the plain fact is the block hasn't been moved. Guards were here all the time; there's one over there right now if you want to talk to him."

Melward beckoned the guard toward the car. He was a heavyset man, with a porcine face which was set and determined; his aspect was unfriendly. Pons gazed at him intently; a little smile touched his lean lips.

"Porker Kelvay, isn't it," he said. "On your good behavior now, eh?"

The guard backed away.

"Nothing happen here last night, Porker?" asked Pons.

"Nothing, Mr. Pons. I swear to God, Mr. Pons, that's the straight of it. That's the way it was. I was here..."

Pons swung up to the car once more and directed Byron to go ahead, leaving the guard to stand open-mouthed behind him.

Melward was immediately curious. "You know that man?"

"He served a brief term for assault and robbery ten years ago," said Pons. "I appeared against him."

We returned to the main line and went along as before. There was no sign that the mist was altering in density; it grew neither thicker nor any less dense. The humid air was strongly aromatic; briefly, after the passing of the train from the north, of the acrid smoke from the locomotive; thereafter of the dampened landscape, of water and earth.

Pons continued to move off and back on to the car. At the second spur he repeated his examination, going into the mine it served, and marking the semi-abandonment of the line, which came to a dead end, and had evidently not been used for some time. Then once again we waited on the spur for a slow train to pass from the south.

At last we reached the place on the line to which the Company's spur had been attached. Byron would have gone on to Kendon-on-Lea, had not Pons interposed objection.

"Was not that 'points' we passed, Mr. Byron?"

"Yes, sir. Tracks taken up a year or two ago, sir."

"All the way?"

"No, sir – just part."

"Let us just have a look at it."

Byron obediently reversed the car and we returned to the "points."

Pons sprang off. He examined the earth about the switch with great care and then the "points" itself.

"It has been oiled recently," he said.

Byron agreed that it was possible the "points" had been oiled. "The men come along and oil it the same as always. You gets into a kind of habit, you might say."

"The abandoned yards lie over in this direction, I take it?" asked Pons.

"Yes, sir."

"How far?"

"Oh, just around that bend. A mile, hardly more."

"Let us take the car off the line and leave it while we walk over to the yards."

"We have been there, Mr. Pons," said Melward, faintly reproving.

"Doubtless. If it is all the same to you, however, I will have a look for myself."

We bent to it and swung the car off the tracks to a standard which had been constructed along the tracks not far from that point. Then, with Byron leading the way, vociferous in his perplexity at Pons' wish to examine the abandoned yards, we made our way to the yards, which were far more extensive than we had imagined.

Here we found a virtual graveyard for outmoded and worn equipment which waited being broken up for scrap. Quite clearly, in one part of the yards, a salvage company had been breaking up equipment, for a truckload of scrap iron waited being moved. Meanwhile, however, the tracks in the yard were occupied by freight cars, tank cars, flat cars, and even three locomotives.

"These locomotives do not look worn out to me," said Pons.

"One can see you're not a railroad man, Mr. Pons," said Melward good-naturedly. "These locomotives have been here for some time, and they are ready to be broken up. Look at this one – this is old number 169. Over here is 305, and there is 729. All ready for the scrap-pile.

"And who undertakes their disposal?"

"That is out of my department, Mr. Pons. A scrap-iron company has taken over everything in these yards. Whenever they break up an engine, we are notified so that our registry shows its ultimate disposal. I think even you will admit that it would be impossible to break up a locomotive like this in the interval since its disappearance; it could not be done."

"Perhaps not impossible, Mr. Melward," replied Pons imperturbably. "But I concede it is highly improbable. One ought not to confuse the impossible with the improbable."

So saying, Pons went from one to another of the locomotives, popping in and out of the cabs. Melward looked wordlessly from Byron to me, restraining his astonishment with difficulty. In the grey morning the flickering of Pons' flashlight could be seen from time to time. When he came back to where we waited presently, he offered no explanation of his curiosity.

"I don't know what you may be thinking, Mr. Pons," said Melward. "But these three locomotives have been here for quite a time. Their numbers check with those in our reports; no locomotive has been dismantled here for two months."

"Has anything at all been dismantled here recently?" pressed Pons.

"Nothing but three tank cars. Would you like to examine the rest of the cars?"

"I think not," replied Pons, with a smile. He took out his watch and consulted it. "We have made good time. But we shall have to make better. When is the next train due for the north?"

"To what point, Mr. Pons?"

"Sheffield."

"Within half an hour. If we hurry, we can just make Kendon-on-Lea, Mr. Pons," said Byron.

"Then by all means let us hurry."

For the remainder of the distance to Kendon-on-Lea, Pons gave but scant attention to the line. He seemed to be preoccupied, and stood with his hands clasped behind his back, his head lowered into the now thinning mist, his eyes extremely thoughtful.

We reached Kendon-on-Lea just in time to catch the north-bound train. We had but a few moments to side-track the car, obtain tickets, and bid farewell to Melward and Byron, who were to return to Girton as soon as the north-bound train had passed. The through train came in, flagged to a stop through the good offices of Oscar Jeffries, the agent at Kendon-on-Lea; we boarded it, and were off.

"According to the schedule," said Pons, "we should reach Sheffield at about eleven o'clock."

"I confess I am at a loss to know why we are going to Sheffield," I began cautiously. "If the locomotive could not have reached London, it could hardly have reached Sheffield."

"That is an excellent deduction, Parker," answered Pons, his keen eyes twinkling. "No, it is not the locomotive we are now seeking; it is its missing passenger."

"I am afraid you have the advantage of me."

"Surely not by much, Parker. Certain facts are salient. Let us consider that it was clearly intended that Mason should not reach the stockholders' meeting of Northern Steel. It is not too far-fetched to assume that no matter what means Mason used to reach Sheffield, his enemies would have made certain that he did not reach his goal. That presupposes the most elaborate planning, to take care of any contingency, for we cannot doubt but that Mason was shadowed from the moment he landed at Croyden. Such preparations, in turn, suggest that if money was no object to Mason, it was even less so to his enemies. Powerful men involved in a jousting for power, Parker.

"No matter, then, what avenue to Sheffield Mason took, his enemies were prepared. If he came by car, I have no doubt he would have been abducted even sooner. If he came by the regular train, can you question but that the determined men who oppose him would have managed somehow to take him. As soon as it was evident that he was traveling by special train, the information was passed on to the particular crew detailed to take care of this contingency. That crew would have to take care of such little niceties as luring the engineer from the locomotive and substituting one of their own men with forged credentials, as well as of knocking out the fireman and throwing him from the locomotive, to say nothing of the actual removal of the locomotive itself, by way of tracks laid down and then taken up again."

"You suggest that a large number of people have been employed in this venture."

"I submit that it could not have been done otherwise. Consider, no one could know in advance just how Mason would attempt to reach Sheffield. Every possible contingency would of necessity have to be covered. Since that is true, a large number of people must necessarily be employed. Such employment, in turn, suggests that a very large sum of money is at the disposal of the engineers of this daring plan. I think we shall find that Mason was serving in the capacity of a far more important emissary than our friend, Jamison, for instance, conceives."

Pons said no more. He rode the rest of the way to Sheffield in complete relaxation, his eyes closed. At the station in Sheffield he dismounted with alacrity, hailed a cab, and gave the address of the building in which the stockholders' meeting of Northern Steel was presumably now in progress.

"Surely Mason is not there!" I cried.

"Just as surely someone there is in a position to lead us to him, unless murder too has been done."

"By what means do you hope to find him, Pons? This is rash!"

"Frontal assault, my dear Parker. There are circumstances in which no other course is possible – or desirable."

At the Northern Steel building, Pons asked for Lord Delapoer, representing the nature of his business as urgent.

In the face of an adamant clerk, Pons wrote a brief note, and sent it by the clerk's hand into the meeting.

Within a very few moments, an angry middle-aged man came bursting from the stockholders' meeting to confront Pons.

"Mr. Solar Pons!" he exclaimed. "What is the meaning of this outrageous message?"

"Lord Delapoer," replied Pons. "Pray do not underrate my intelligence; I have not underrated yours. If my message had no bearing, it would not have seemed outrageous to you. Since it does seem so, it is manifestly pertinent."

"'*In the matter of James H. Mason. All is known*,'" read Lord Delapoer, his white moustache bristling still. "You have signed it."

"Let us not fence, your lordship. Either you will direct us to Mason by letter, which is in your power to do, or I will lay the facts before Scotland Yard and the newspapers. I am beyond the power of all the wealth in England."

Lord Delapoer gazed with stony fury into Pons' eyes; then he crumpled Pons' note and threw it to the floor. "Wait here," he said, and turned on his heel.

In a very short time another clerk appeared from the room into which Lord Delapoer had vanished and brought Pons a letter enclosed in an envelope, addressed to Leopold Manadal at an address in Sheffield.

Once outside the building, Pons unceremoniously opened the envelope, and took out the note inside.

"Delapoer is likely to think that violence may dispose of us," he explained. "It is a possibility we cannot obviate." He read the note. "Ah, he has considered his position; he does not know, after all, how much we may already have disclosed. 'Admit the bearer to see Mason,' he writes, and signs it simply, 'Delapoer'. I daresay this will do."

In less than fifteen minutes we were being shown into a darkened room where a tall, broad-shouldered man lay bound and gagged on a bed. Despite the objection of his burly captor, a dark-skinned foreigner to whom Pons' note from Lord Delapoer had been given, Pons unceremoniously ripped the gag from Mason's mouth and cut his bonds.

"Permit me, Mr. Mason – Solar Pons, at your service. I fancy we are regrettably too late to save your proxies, but by an immediate appearance at the stockholders' meeting of Northern Steel you may yet avert Delapoer's coup. There is a cab below."

"What else could Mason have carried to make his absence from the meeting important save proxies from American stockholders who, like Balfour Danals over here, are dissatisfied with the present directorship?" explained Pons on the train back to London.

"Of course, now you have pointed it out, it is obvious."

"It was from the beginning," rejoined Pons. "No other explanation was tenable in the circumstances."

"But if I might be so bold," I went on, "it seems to me that the crux of the problem remains unsolved. Sir Ernest McVeagh will still want his locomotive."

"Ah, as for that, you laid eyes on it yourself earlier today, Parker. It stands in the company's abandoned yards as number 729 – which is only number 177 renumbered, for these numerals lend themselves very easily to such an alteration in haste. The real number 729 was converted to scrap at the time that the company received a report of tank cars having been cut up; I think you will find that Lord Delapoer's company also controls various plants for the accumulation and disposal of scrap iron, and unquestionably the yards between Girton and Kendon-on-Lea are under the control of Northern Steel.

In foreseeing every contingency, the real 729 was cut down earlier.

"The locomotive could not, after all, have vanished into thin air. It was not sunk into a mine shaft, no tarn or lake offered itself for the convenience of Mason's enemies, and the locomotive was clearly not run back past Girton or on past Kendon-on-Lea. We have as yet no lorry large enough to load up and cart away an entire locomotive, and anything other than a lorry would have been obvious even in the darkest night. So there remained only the spurs along the road. And what more simple and efficacious than a locomotive yard, where the stolen locomotive might be left to stand in plain sight without being suspect?"

Three days after our search for the missing locomotive, Pons greeted me at breakfast with a marked copy of the *Financial Times*.

"Our little adventure has had an epilogue," he observed dryly.

I read the account he had marked for clipping. "Balfour Danals New Chairman of Northern Steel," read the small caption. The story itself was succinct and clear, though it failed to tell all.

"Following the dramatic appearance of James H. Mason, an attorney from New York City, representing American stockholders of Northern Steel, charging irregularities at the meeting three days ago, stockholders voted to hold a new meeting yesterday. As a result of the new meeting, Lord Delapoer lost the chairmanship of the Board of Directors to Balfour Danals, to whose supporters rallied Mr. Mason with proxies obtained by cable from American stockholders..."

"And, if I am not mistaken, I daresay the new directors will soon expose gross mismanagement, if nothing more serious, under Delapoer. The loss of the chairmanship of itself could mean nothing if it were not for the possibility of damaging disclosures to follow."

Nor, as time and events made show, was Pons in error, any more than he had been in any other aspect of the remarkable abduction of the Great Northern Railway's special locomotive.

IX

THE ADVENTURE OF THE TOTTENHAM WEREWOLF

Very few of the problems which occupied the attention of my friend, Solar Pons, came to him through sources close to him, but at least one of them, the singular adventure of Septimus Grayle, the Tottenham Werewolf, I myself brought to his notice, however unwittingly. During Pons' absence on the Continent one summer, I had got into the habit of taking dinner at the Diogenes Club, and had observed there from time to time a porcine, well-muscled individual of middle-age, who made me uncomfortable by the forthright manner in which he examined me. In turn, I found myself wondering about him, and I determined to ask Pons to join me at dinner as soon as he returned from Prague.

Accordingly, one evening I ushered Pons to my table at the Club.

"Ah, we are in luck, Pons," I said. "He is here."

I placed Pons so that he might obtain an excellent view of our fellow-diner in one of the mirrors which reflected the room beyond our table, and the keen grey eyes of my companion fixed upon the reflection in the glass, though his lean face was ostensibly turned toward me. The object of Pons' scrutiny was leisurely engaged in eating his meal, but he had observed our entrance and his expression had unquestionably quickened; yet he had returned to his meal with the assurance of a man who knows he will complete his dinner before you and be well on his way before you can take leave of your table. He was somewhat warmly clad this evening, but as always, he bore no evident clues about himself, and I was thus all the more interested in Pons' reaction.

"What do you make of him?" I asked presently.

"There is not much to be said," replied Pons, much to my satisfaction. "Though it is evident by his colour that he is an ex-colonial – Egypt, I should say, if the scarab ring he wears is any indication – that he has not long been back in England, that he is very probably not a member of the Diogenes Club but has a guest-card, that he is at present living outside London, since his visits here are periodic compared to yours, which are hardly regular, that he is a man of approximately fifty-five years of age, very clearly accustomed to administrative work – work, I submit, dealing in a large measure with native labor, that his interest in the Diogenes Club lies in something other than its cuisine, which is not exceptional."

"My dear fellow!" I protested. "I can follow most of your deductions with ease..."

"Dear me! How familiarity does breed contempt," murmured Pons.

"But how in the world do you arrive at the conclusion that his visits here have an ulterior motive?"

"You have not mentioned his interest in anything apart from yourself, Parker. I submit, therefore, that you are the object of his attentions."

"My dear Pons!"

"Because the gentleman has been observing you with a most definite purpose. Consider – he comes in from the country at regular intervals; you do not recall his interest in anyone else."

"You flatter me."

"Ah, do not say so, Parker. I fancy his interest in you is dictated by my absence from London."

"You, Pons!"

"I submit that our fellow-diner sought me some time ago, failed to find me – you will recall that Mrs. Johnson, too, spent these past weeks with her sister in Edinburgh, and then discovered your whereabouts either through the medical directory or by accident. He concluded that my return to London would be marked either by your absence from the Diogenes Club or by my appearance in your company. And now, if I am not mistaken, we shall have corroboration."

Our fellow-diner had finished his dinner, and was now coming to his feet. But instead of leaving the dining-room, he turned purposefully and came over to our table, beside which he stood in a few moments, a short, compact figure, bowing slightly.

"I beg your pardon," he said in a low, husky voice, "I believe I have the privilege of addressing Mr. Solar Pons, the private enquiry agent. I am Octavius Grayle, of Tottenham village, near Northallerton in Yorkshire."

"Pray be seated, Mr. Grayle," said Pons. "I believe you know Dr. Parker."

"By sight, yes. I fear I have been making a nuisance of myself by watching for your company. I could rouse no one at 7B Praed Street; so I concluded that sooner or later Dr. Parker's movements would give me some indication of your whereabouts."

"I have been out of London," said Pons. "But you are not interested in my itinerary."

"I have no doubt that you have already exercised those powers of yours which are so remarkable and correctly concluded that I am an ex-Colonial from Egypt, not too long – a year – back in England, and that I am not a member of the Club, but a guest on my brother's card. It is about my brother that I would like to consult you."

"By all means," answered Pons with a mirthful gleam in his eyes. "Your brother is Septimus Grayle..."

"The Tottenham Werewolf," finished our client, for manifestly such he had become. "I am afraid, Mr. Pons," he continued dryly, "that we must concede so much – my brother at least is convinced that he is a werewolf, very probably because he has certain extremely distressing compulsions, the most startling of which is a habit of loping about on all fours on moonlit nights and baying at the moon."

"Incredible!" I cried.

"But you apparently have some familiarity with the case, Mr. Pons," continued Grayle, as if oblivious to my exclamation. "You will then know that in the course of the past year a young man, William Gilton; a girl, Miss Miranda Choate; and our own uncle, Alexander Grayle, have been mysteriously slain, all discovered with their throats literally torn out. The last death, our uncle's, occurred only a month ago, and now my brother has been placed under what is called 'protective custody.' In short, he has been arrested, he has been all but charged and removed from the house. Mr. Pons, my brother may have the compulsion to believe that he is, and even in part to act like, a werewolf, but he is no murderer."

"What are your brother's circumstances, Mr. Grayle?"

"The three of us – my brother, my sister Regina, and I – live together. Each of us is independently wealthy, in a modest way, of course, and each of us lives rather independently of the other, though my sister and brother have naturally grown closer together during my long absence in Egypt. My brother, I should hasten to add, is aware of his affliction, but he is not more than ordinarily depressed by it from time to time, and he does not permit his knowledge of it to cloud his small pleasures. He is somewhat younger than I am, and our sister is younger than he. It is she who manages the servants and runs our household. My brother's situation is such that the mere fact of his arrest would precipitate a local scandal of great proportions, since our family is perhaps the oldest in Tottenham – and perhaps also the wealthiest. My late uncle was the largest landowner in the country, and his death has been widely chronicled, as you know. It is therefore implicit in the situation that the real murderer must be found. Detective-Sergeant Brinton is dogged and persistent, but he lacks any genuine acumen, and the county police are far more accustomed to dealing with traffic regulations infringements than with matters of this kind. Can I prevail upon you to join us at Grayle Old Place in Tottenham as soon as it is convenient for you to do so?"

"You may expect us in the morning, Mr. Grayle," said Pons. Thereupon our client came at once to his feet, bowed with almost military precision, thanked Pons, and took formal leave of us.

Pons, his eyes twinkling, turned to me. "There is as engaging a fellow as I have laid eyes upon for some time."

"A man like that would be capable of anything," I said.

"Precisely. You have done me a good turn, Parker; I have been interested in the case ever since first I saw it in the papers. Indeed, I am carrying it with me."

So saying, he reached into his pocket and came forth with a neatly folded batch of clippings, through which he riffled without delay, selecting one finally, and drawing it forth.

"Ah, here we are. 'Murder of Prominent Landlord,'" he read. "'Alexander Grayle, sixty-seven, of Tottenham, near Northallerton, Yorkshire, was found dead on a country lane not far from his home...' And so on. 'His death is the third in a series. Two previous victims were discovered in similar circumstances...' A curious, if somewhat gruesome, business, this. And clearly, I should venture to guess, intended to point to Septimus Grayle."

"The torn throat, yes," I agreed. "It would suggest the werewolf concept. Doubtless all the villagers are fully aware of Grayle's aberration."

"Unquestionably. All the deaths have been nocturnal; all have taken place on moonlit nights, when Grayle is known to yield to his strange compulsion. I submit, Parker, that this is no mere coincidence, but rather evidence of a design, which, if the facts are as Octavius Grayle has presented them, has already had the desired effect upon the local police who have proceeded, however deferentially, against Septimus. I fear there is devil's work afoot, Parker. Something dark and devious that troubles our client more than he has confided."

He looked up speculatively. "Can you go, Parker?" Or is your practise too demanding?"

"I have a *locum tenens*," I answered. "You know I would be delighted."

"And your wife?"

"Constance is visiting her mother in Kent. She would urge me to go."

"Capital!" exclaimed Pons. "Wifely concurrence in these little adventures is always advisable. I have not looked up the railway timetable, but I believe we can entrain in the morning and arrive in good time. Let us have breakfast together and set out after."

Accordingly, early the following morning we met at 7B Praed Street in the familiar quarters which we had shared for so many years prior to my marriage, and partook of a hearty breakfast prepared by Mrs. Johnson, who served us with many assurances of her delight at seeing us together once again. Pons had already gone through the morning papers, and at the time of my arrival he sat in the midst of a host of newspapers scattered around his chair.

"There is nothing further on the Tottenham puzzle," he said when at last Mrs. Johnson had left us. "The local police sergeant has given out the customary statements – fortunately in nothing like the volubility of his American counterparts. This time, however, I have no doubt that an arrest is imminent. There are delicate hints that the culprit is to be found in a high place, which presumably has reference to people of the Grayles' position in a village like Tottenham. Yet there has been no further outbreak."

"Do you expect one, then?"

"There will certainly be a fourth victim – possibly even a fifth," he said enigmatically.

"You sound very positive."

"Ah, Parker – how it used to annoy you! But it is not so. The speculation takes its rise in a logical deduction. Septimus Grayle either is guilty or he is not. Octavius does not believe him to be guilty. Supposing that he is correct, then I venture to guess that a fourth victim is inevitably meant to follow – obviously, that is Septimus himself. If he is not correct, there may well be another crime. And, remotely, yet one more beyond that. Contrary to the official position, there is very definitely a pattern in the crimes at Tottenham."

We set out directly after breakfast and were soon on the train en route Yorkshire. It was a fine summer morning, with an early fog lifting rapidly before the sun, and the landscape, green and rolling, beyond the cars. But Pons was unaware of it: he sat throughout the journey with his hawk-like face turned away from the window, his chin sunk upon his chest, his eyes half-closed in an attitude of cogitation into which I did not break.

On our arrival at Tottenham, we sought rooms at the Boar's Head, the only local inn of any size. There we paused only long enough to enable Pons to set down and dispatch to the local sergeant of police a note informing him that Pons would appreciate the opportunity to discuss the Tottenham murders with him. Then we ventured forth in search of Grayle Old Place. We found our objective within a short time and without difficulty, for it was one of the two most imposing houses in the village, the other being the abode, until recently, of the third victim of the Tottenham murderer, Alexander Grayle. It was a house set well back into its grounds, with a gate at the driveway, and a sweep of lawns reaching to the Victorian building in which our client lived. Beyond the house lay gently rolling fields and woods. Its setting at the edge of the village was so idyllic that the very thought of the crime which Pons had come to look into seemed alien.

The massive door was opened to us by a dignified butler, hard upon whose heels came our client himself. He walked down a wide hall, the walls of which bore portraits of Grayle ancestors, his hands extended in welcome.

"You are just in time for tea, gentlemen." To the butler he added, "Crandon, rooms for our guests."

"No," said Pons at once. "We have put up at the Boar's Head. It will give us greater freedom of movement."

An expression of disappointment crossed our client's face, but he said nothing. He turned on his heel and led the way into the drawing-room, where we were introduced to the other members of the family – Miss Regina Grayle, a woman whose dark, melancholy eyes belied her youth, a woman who clearly existed on a precarious line between youth and middle-age, and whose austerity of dress, black with a high collar relieved only by a cameo, and coiffure, her hair drawn tightly about her head, accentuated rather middle-age than youth; Randall Grayle, a brash young man, not long back from Canada, the son of yet another brother to our client's father; and Septimus Grayle, a tall, hawk-nosed man, lean almost to gauntness, who viewed us with frankly hostile eyes, in which brooded an unconcealed torment. Septimus wore his hair long; it was greying now, but his face was still young, save for the scars of what appeared to be a fencing accident along his right cheek near his ear.

It was not readily evident whether our client had informed the household that he had retained Pons. Miss Regina made an inquiry as to whether Pons was assisting Sergeant Brinton to which Pons made an oblique reply; he was accustomed, he said, to lend the police all assistance within his modest power. This reply seemed to satisfy her. Not so Septimus, however; he continued to glower at Pons above the specious conversation which took place before the subject of the crimes in Tottenham was introduced.

"This terrible, terrible sequence of events," said Miss Regina passionately, clenching her hand about a handsome, old-fashioned back-scratcher she carried, "is all the more shocking when one considers that the police are actually concerned about our own Septimus, who would not harm a soul."

Septimus favored his sister with a wan smile.

"Our dear uncle was an almost saintly man," continued the lady, "and I could not imagine who would have wished him harm. And little Miranda Choate, while she has been known for sauciness, could hardly have inspired so heinous a crime. And Mr. Gilton, a young man of estimable character – indeed, it is not so many years since I went about in his company quite often – who could have desired his death? Of, it is madness, Mr. Pons, madness."

At the mention of madness, Septimus Grayle underwent a ghastly alteration. His face greyed, became chalk-like, his lantern-jaw fell, and he drew his breath with a rushing sound through his quivering lips. But this transformation was soon again masked, though the unpleasant impression it had given us could not be concealed so easily. I observed Pons watching him surreptitiously, and, beyond him, young Randall Grayle, whose singular brawniness found no complements even in his cousin Octavius's manifest strength. The expression on Randall Grayle's features was puzzling; I could not determine whether he hid disgust or triumph, cunning or naivete.

"Forgive me, Septimus," said his sister quietly.

Our client looked over at Pons judiciously, as if to make certain that he had caught the interchange.

"Surely the police have not exhausted the avenues of inquiry," said Pons thoughtfully. "The press has set forth the lack of connection among the victims of the Tottenham murderer."

"There is none, Mr. Pons," said Octavius Grayle decisively.

"I submit that the choice of the victims may have a pattern."

"Homicidal mania reveals no pattern, Mr. Pons," said Miss Regina primly, reaching behind her to claw her back with the back-scratcher she was holding.

Pons inclined his head. Then he turned to Septimus Grayle. "Tell me, Mr. Grayle, did your late uncle leave a family?"

Septimus, who had hitherto not been directly addressed by Pons, was disagreeably startled. He gazed reproachfully at his brother, imploringly at his sister, and finally looked reluctantly at his inquisitor, who had not removed his eyes from him.

"No, no," he said hastily, with a marked uneasiness in his manner, "Uncle Alexander was not married. He was the one who wasn't, of the three brothers. Like us – none of us is married – except Randall; he's going to be. I think?" He looked to Randall for confirmation; the young man nodded and smiled. "We are all who are left. All the Grayles. We were never a large family. We have none of us married." A fine dew of perspiration made its appearance on his high forehead. Quite suddenly his voice changed. "And you know why, don't you, Mr. Pons? You know it. Everybody knows it!" he almost shouted. Then, biting his lip until it bled, he added almost in a whisper, "Madness! Madness! Madness!"

Abruptly he sprang to his feet and ran from the room.

Miss Regina rose, shot a punishing glance at her remaining brother, excused herself, and followed Septimus Grayle from the room.

"It was not what I would call a successful interview," said Randall Grayle dryly. "In Canada we do things differently – and perhaps more effectively."

Octavius looked angrily at his cousin. "May I remind you, Randall, that a gentleman always maintains the proper attitude toward guests?" He turned to Pons. "Pray excuse my impetuous cousin, Mr. Pons."

Pons lifted himself from the depths of his chair. "I fear we have exhausted our welcome, Mr. Grayle."

"Not at all, let me assure you," protested our client.

Randall Grayle said nothing at all. He had lit a cigarette and was watching curiously to see what Pons would do.

Pons began to walk from the room. "I am at your service at the Boar's Head, Mr. Grayle. Pray call on me there."

With this, we took our departure.

"What do you make of it, Pons?" I asked once we had got clear of the gate.

"A most interesting family, did you not think, Parker?"

"Oh, yes. But the murders?"

"Everything in good time, Parker. Do not be impatient. Let us just hurry along; unless I am greatly in error, Sergeant Brinton will be waiting for us."

Sergeant Brinton was indeed waiting for us at the Boar's Head. He was a young man, still, tall, big-boned, and sturdy in appearance. His manner was frank and co-operative, yet neither deferential nor condescending, though it was impossible for him to conceal entirely the impressiveness of this association with Solar Pons, whose reputation had long since spread the length and breadth of the British Isles.

"I was happy to have your note, Mr. Pons," he said without preamble. "I had learned from Mr. Octavius Grayle that he contemplated asking you to step into the case, rather than intercede with Scotland Yard. I am afraid, though, that there is little to be discovered."

"You are convinced it is Septimus Grayle?"

"I can conceive of no other solution. The crimes are very obviously the work of a homicidal maniac. All have taken place on moonlight nights, just such nights as those on which Septimus has his seizures. He imagines himself a dog, he bays at the moon..."

"Pray enlighten me," interrupted Pons. "For how long a time has Septimus Grayle been the victim of this strange compulsion?"

"For most of his life, I believe."

"It does not occur to you that this additional, shall we say, pastime, of his nocturnal repertoire – the tearing out of throats – is comparatively recent?"

"Obviously."

"You do not think it strange that this proclivity did not manifest itself before this?"

"Insanity, Mr. Pons, is unpredictable."

"Is it not, indeed? I should not have thought so, would you, Parker?"

"Certain forms, of course," I agreed. "But the majority of cases follow a fairly well-defined pattern. It is perfectly possible to predict a course of action."

The sergeant gazed at me thoughtfully and, I thought, a trifle impatiently, as if he thought I did not know what I was talking about. He forebore to say so, however.

"I submit that it is suggestive that this series of crimes took place within a relatively short time after the return of two of the Grayles from foreign parts," continued Pons.

Brinton gazed at him in candid astonishment. "You refer to Mr. Octavius and Mr. Randall." He did not wait for Pons' confirming nod. "But, of course, you do not mean to be serious. The suggestion is patently absurd – neither of them is a homicidal maniac."

"Ah, it is one of the characteristics of homicidal mania that it reveals no distinctive traits, such as those clearly associated with Septimus," said Pons. "But let us put aside this question for the moment. I would like to know something of the victims."

"I brought along photographs, Mr. Pons. If there is anything you would like to know, you have only to ask."

"Thank you, Sergeant. Let us just look at the photographs."

The sergeant opened a large manila envelope and offered Pons a sheaf of pictures, the majority of which had been taken of the bodies at the scene of the crime. I bent over Pons' shoulder and looked, too, as he went rapidly through the prints, which had an unpleasantly harsh reality afforded by the glaring light which had been thrown upon the brutally slain victims.

They were not inspiring to look upon. The unhappy victims of this fiendish attack were sprawled out beside rustic paths. Pictures taken at close range indicated that each had had his throat torn out, plainly, as the amount of blood revealed, while he still lived. The little girl was most pathetic, and I could hardly bear to look upon the horrible scene so mercilessly revealed by the photographer.

Pons, however, appeared to have no such qualms. "Ah," he murmured, "Stunned, then slain."

"Exactly, Mr. Pons. The marks on the neck emphatically suggest some animal. May I point out that Mr. Septimus Grayle wears his nails unusually long?"

"I observed it," replied Pons grimly.

"The tears are deep, severing the jugular in each case. Death took place in a matter of minutes; the loss of blood was very great. In no case was any sound heard, though the victims were found on bypaths away from the better-illumined thoroughfares. Only mania could explain such insensate and brutal slayings, Mr. Pons."

Pons had not lifted his eyes from the photographs. "Repeated attempts to sever the jugular, not just one gash," he said. He looked up at last. "Was this man Gilton married?"

"No, Mr. Pons. He was betrothed."

"His age?"

"Thirty-seven."

"He is financially comfortable?"

"Quite. He leaves only a sister, who inherits." Brinton paused and added, "I believe she is to be married to young Mr. Randall Grayle."

Pons closed his eyes and sat for a moment in silence. "And Mr. Alexander Grayle?" he asked presently.

"He was single, and wealthy. The four Grayles are his only heirs; they will divide his estate. But I must in duty point out to you that each of the Grayles is independently wealthy."

Pons turned this over in his mind. He did not comment on the wealth of the Grayles. "Let us return for a moment to Mr. Gilton," he said. "Is he not approximately of the same age as the youngest of the three Grayles?"

"I believe so, yes. He kept company with Miss Regina for some time. He was at that time rather indigent, but soon came into money through a series of fortunate investments."

"He was not favored by Miss Regina Grayle?"

The sergeant shrugged. "I would not say precisely that, Mr. Pons. It was only that they simply drifted apart; perhaps they had been keeping company too long. They remained close friends, though I believe the brothers did not particularly fancy him." He cleared his throat uncertainly. "But I assure you, Mr. Pons, it is Septimus Grayle who holds the key to the riddle."

"And the child," continued Pons imperturbably.

"Poor Miranda Choate! She had been at a children's party and was returning home. She had been escorted for most of the way to her door by a party of young people together with an older person who was their chaperone. There was a short distance just before her gate – by a coincidence, in the vicinity of the lane in which Gilton's body had been found; they had not walked that far, but stood at the other end until she had time to reach the gate. She was heard to call out a last goodnight. Evidence shows that she was struck down then, though her body was not found there, but down on a pasture path which led away to one side of her home."

"An only child?"

"No, sir. One of a large family. She was a pert little thing."

The sergeant stood patiently waiting on Pons' next question. He seemed somewhat puzzled by the tenor and direction of Pons' inquiry, and quite clearly could not conceive what end Pons pursued. He was no more mystified than I.

But Pons had no further inquiries. He gathered the photographs together and handed them to Brinton. "I am indebted to you, Sergeant. If I should need to send for you in some haste, I daresay you could be reached at the station?"

"Certainly, Mr. Pons, at any time. My home is in the same building."

"Capital, capital!"

After Sergeant Brinton had gone, Pons sat musing for some little time. I waited patiently on his cogitation, and presently found his eyes dwelling on me in sardonic amusement.

"Is it not remarkable, Parker, how readily the human mind is blinded by the obvious?" he asked.

"I suppose it is the obverse of being too eager to shunt aside the obvious for the obscure."

"Well spoken, Parker," rejoined Pons, smiling. "But is there not something about this curious sequence of events which gives you pause?"

"Nothing but the obvious," I replied firmly. "Here is the work of someone who is definitely unstable."

"Indeed," said Pons with heavy irony. "I submit that there is far more here than meets the eye. It does not seem to you that there is a pattern in these events?"

"None."

"Mr. Gilton was indigent; he became wealthy. His sister, who is to inherit his wealth, is engaged to marry Mr. Randall

Grayle. The little Choate girl lived in the vicinity of the scene of Gilton's death. Alexander Grayle left no other heirs but the Grayles, who are wealthy and are now destined to become more so. Either these events are totally without connection, or they are the setting of a stage, and the return of Mr. Randall Grayle or our client served as the catalytic agent to precipitate them."

I could not help smiling. "I am afraid there is such a thing as looking too far afield for the solution of any puzzle," I said.

"I am delighted to hear you say so, Parker," said Pons, his eyes twinkling michievously. "I am habitually distrustful of the obvious."

"But one need not be insistent on ignoring it. It is not beyond Septimus Grayle's malady to have led him to murder. There is an old adage that where there is smoke, there must be some fire."

"Ah, yes, but the fire may be of incendiary origin," retorted Pons. He looked at his watch and added, "I fancy we had better have a little supper, for, unless I am greatly mistaken, we shall need to return to Grayle Old Place before the night is far along."

"Why do you say so?"

"Is there not a moon tonight? I believe it is near the full. With both the moon and ourselves in Tottenham, the werewolf could scarcely resist the challenge. Moreover, it is past time for the final act of this gruesome little drama."

With this enigmatic statement, Pons led the way to the dining-room and we partook of a spare meal of beef and cabbage, Pons discoursing meanwhile on the lore of lycanthropy, with its roots in ancient beliefs of mankind, recalling many of the highly successful fictions in the genre as a parallel to references involving obscure and authenticated cases of diabolic cannibalistic acts associated with certain obscure crimes which bore at least a superficial resemblance to lycanthropic practises.

Our supper hour over, we retired to our quarters, where for sometime Pons sat deep in thought, occasionally turning to the newspaper accounts of the Tottenham murders, which he had brought along from London. From time to time he glanced at the clock, always with increasing restlessness.

"You are expecting someone?" I ventured at last.

"Now that darkness has fallen and the moon has risen, yes. I hope he will not disappoint me, or we may be too late to prevent another crime."

"Surely not!" I cried. "Who is it, then?"

"Our client. Who else? I submit that his next move must be to introduce us to Septimus by night."

He had no sooner spoken than there was a discreet, yet urgent tap on the door. Pons sprang at once to open it, disclosing Octavius Grayle.

"Mr. Pons, can you come?" he asked in a hushed voice.

"We are at your service, Mr. Grayle. I take it your brother has had a seizure?"

Our client nodded. "He has just left the house. I know the paths he will take. For the time being he will confine himself to the grounds and to the woods and byways outside the village; he seldom ventures the village itself until past midnight – and he does not always remain away from the house for more than an hour, so that he seldom invades Tottenham."

Octavius Grayle led the way rapidly to Grayle Old Place, where he entered the grounds not by the central gate, but by means of a small garden gate which opened through a hedge out of sight of the principal entrance. At once the perfumes of flowers and herbs invaded our nostrils, rising with cloying insistence in the humid evening. The moon shone high overhead, now near the full, a great luminous satellite laving all the earth in its unterrestrial radiance. Beyond the garden, the house loomed spectrally, with but little light showing in its windows, save where the moon reflected from the panes.

Our client made his way by a devious route around the house and plunged into the shadowed paths on the far side.

It was patent presently that his goal was a small eminence not far ahead and yet a considerable distance from the house. Octavius Grayle moved with an agility which was remarkable in one of his years, for soon we were mounting the slope through a glade toward an open place beyond.

At that instant there burst upon our ears a weird and horrible sound – the simulated howling of a wolf or baying of a dog in human voice. Before me, our client, who had reached the top of the knoll, turned and caught hold of Pons' arm as my companion came up.

"You hear?" he whispered harshly. "Now watch – over there."

Below, the moonlit landscape rolled gently away in grassy valleys and dark woods. Our client pointed to a valley not far distant, plainly part of the Grayle estate. Even as he spoke, a shadowy figure loped on all fours across the moonlit glade, out of one dark wood into another, and through it to emerge on the far side, once again in the moonlight, where it rose halfway and once again gave voice to that horribly suggestive ululation which so closely resembled the howling of some wild beast.

"He began it as a child," whispered Octavius Grayle. "Will he ever cease, I wonder?"

"That is in Parker's department," murmured Pons.

"If one finds the cause," I said. "There is a reason hidden deep in his subconscious for compulsions such as this."

"I hope you are right, Doctor," said our client fervently. "I do not relish living out my life to this, every moonlit night. Now mark him; he has begun to move again; he will follow the line of that valley, plunge into that wood over there, and when he emerges from it he will begin an arc which will bring him either through the copse at the foot of this knoll, or on this other slope and across part of the knoll itself. We shall watch both courses; if you, Mr. Pons, will watch the slope itself, with Dr. Parker, I will descend to the copse."

"And by what signal shall we communicate?" asked Pons.

"If his baying does not suffice, let us say the crying of a screech owl to signify that he has passed."

"Agreed," murmured Pons.

Thereupon Octavius Grayle vanished into the shadows on the far side of the slope, leaving Pons and myself in possession of the knoll. But Pons had no intention of remaining; he paused only long enough to instruct me.

"Pray hold the fort, Parker," he whispered. "I am not interested in that afflicted man. Guard yourself; we have been followed."

Then he was gone on the path taken by our client.

I looked uneasily around, but was reassured by the expanse of unbroken moonlight holding to the top of the knoll. No one could creep upon me unseen without the protection of shadows, which did not begin for some distance down the slope on all sides. I gazed once more along the route defined by our client as that customarily taken by his unfortunate brother; but Septimus Grayle was nowhere to be seen. Perhaps he had varied his route; perhaps he lingered on the edge of a wood out of range of my vision.

Suddenly his voice sounded once more, raised in that eerie crying. Small wonder that Tottenham looked upon him with fear and suspicion! Even as I thought so, even while the echoes of that fearful cry still resounded in the valleys, I heard and recognized another voice.

"Parker! Parker! Here – at once."

It was Pons. Casting discretion to the winds, I sped down the slope in the direction of his voice as fast as I could run through that unfamiliar country. Down out of the moonlight into the dense trees of the slope; through one grove and past another patch of moonlight, finding a dim, winding path; and, at the foot of the slope, into another, even denser, copse. In my headlong rush, I almost fell over Pons.

He was crouched on the ground in deep shadow. In a moment I saw that he held our client in his arms. Octavius Grayle lay ominously still.

"For God's sake!" I cried. "What has happened?"

"My flashlight is in the grass beside me, just out of my reach," said Pons. "It fell from my hand. His throat has been cut; I cannot determine how badly, but his pulse is still strong."

It was the work of but a few moments to recover Pons' flashlight, to turn it upon our client, and to ascertain that, though he was unconscious from the blow which had struck him down and bleeding profusely from his throat, his jugular vein had not been severed, no important artery had sustained any injury, and, unless the blow were more serious than it appeared, he would recover.

"What happened?" I asked again.

An exclamation of disgust escaped Pons. "I was only just too late," he said bitterly.

"I should have said you were just in time," I answered. "Was it an animal?"

"The Tottenham werewolf," murmured Pons. "It is unforgiveable; I anticipated this and was not fast enough to prevent it. Our pursuer was closer than I thought."

"The attack perhaps you did not prevent; his death you certainly did prevent. Come, let us get him to the house. I can stanch this wound here."

"We shall want Sergeant Brinton," said Pons. "There is still time for us to catch a late train back to London."

"Poor Septimus," I murmured.

"Oh, it was not Septimus," said Pons lightly. "But no less obvious, for all that."

He did not explain this cryptic announcement.

The Grayle family, with Pons and myself, were gathered about our client's bedside, when Detective-Sergeant Brinton came into the room from an examination of the house and grounds. He carried the bloodstained back-scratcher which had belonged to Miss Regina Grayle.

"Just as you thought, Mr. Pons – it was in Septimus's quarters," he said.

"Oh, no, not Septimus!" cried Miss Regina in anguish. Randall Grayle looked at Pons with distrust plain on his handsome features.

Octavius Grayle opened his eyes and regarded the tableau before him. He met Pons' steady gaze.

"You know now, Mr. Pons?" he whispered.

"Indeed, sir. I knew from the time of our initial visit here." The sergeant stepped reluctantly toward Septimus.

"But, no, Sergeant," interposed Pons. "Miss Regina is right. It is not Septimus. The charge must be placed against Miss Regina herself."

For a moment there was an arresting silence.

Then Miss Regina Grayle's placidity dropped from her; her prim face underwent an awesome transformation, glowing with a maniacal rage; with the agility and speed of a cat, she leaped forward, snatched the back-scratcher from the sergeant's hands, and struck at Pons, who caught her arm and twisted it unceremoniously behind her back. In this manner he held her.

"Your prisoner, Sergeant."

"Mr. Pons, I am afraid..." began the sergeant uncertainly, looking on with dismay.

"I think, if you will examine into the status of the family fortunes, you will find ample evidence, Sergeant," said Pons crisply. "Mr. Gilton should have repaid the money she lent him, unsecured though it was; it would have saved his life; it would have saved the life of the little girl who witnessed something which might have trapped Miss Regina; it would have saved the life of Alexander Grayle, whose bequest was necessary to conceal the loss of the money in her care she took from Septimus. Except for the bequest from Alexander Miss Regina and Septimus are both without more than the most vitally necessary funds. If Octavius had not begun to suspect something amiss, her diabolic plan might well have carried through – he would have been the fourth victim, and Septimus, as the planned and perfect suspect, the fifth."

"The problem turned on an elementary factor," said Pons out of the darkness of our compartment, as the late train sped toward London and the welcome security of our respective quarters. "There was no obvious motive, as the puzzle was presented to us, and there were too many suggestions of homicidal mania, which would rule out motive. However, of the three victims, two were possessed of means, the younger man having come by wealth somewhat recently, the older wealthy by long standing. Now, Parker, I submit that when a man of wealth is slain, the motive which at once presents itself is gain. The primary consideration at Tottenham which obscured every other was the curious behaviour of Septimus Grayle; yet to the observer untroubled by the affliction of the so-called Tottenham werewolf, the motive for gain immediately appeared."

"Ah, but it was generally believed that the Grayles were themselves wealthy," I put in.

"It is elementary that a premise is either true or not true. No one had any question but that Miss Regina Grayle was independently wealthy, and that she had therefore no need of a bequest such as her uncle left. You know my methods, Parker; I could not accept the assumption, and proceeded on the precise opposite. Though everyone stated without equivocation that the Grayles were wealthy, there was no evidence to support the premise, apart from the specious fact of their ownership of Grayle Old Place. On the hypothetical assumption that the generally accepted belief was unfounded, I could conceive of the reasonable motive and its instant application to one of the four who stood to gain by Alexander Grayle's death.

"Proceeding in this fashion, then, it followed that there was a reason for each crime. If the motive for Alexander Grayle's death were gain, then the young man and the girl might have been slain solely to confuse any investigation with the suggestion of homicidal mania. Yet a secondary motive was not inadmissible, and I had to look for it. It was perfectly plain at our meeting in the Diogenes Club that Octavius Grayle had certain apprehensions he did not reveal. Clearly, too, he was both observant and intelligent, and it was patent from the beginning even as he had hinted that the murderer was deliberately planning for the arrest and imprisonment of Septimus Grayle as the climax to the events which had taken place at Tottenham. This implied a secondary motive.

"I had to ask myself who but some member of his own family could possibly have motive for desiring Septimus to be found guilty. I confess that for a short time I was thrown off the track by the fact that both Octavius and Randall had but recently returned to England; there was thus presumptive evidence that their return was connected with the events at Tottenham, and the primary assumption, of course, was that one or the other of them was guilty. And yet I could not deny that anyone encountering the problem could be expected to reason in this manner. If neither were guilty, only Miss Regina remained. Therefore, either one of the prodigals was guilty, or the return of one or both set in motion a chain of events which culminated in the wanton crimes at Tottenham.

"Our brief visit at Grayle Old Place this afternoon confirmed my suspicion of Miss Regina. She spoke of the first victim, you will remember, with passing regret and carefully concealed animosity, which was surely nothing more than the hatred of a woman scorned – she had kept company with him, but he was now betrothed to someone else. She spoke of Miranda Choate as naughty and saucy, as if to salve her conscience. She spoke of her murdered uncle with something akin to remorse, which was as genuine as her conviction of the necessity of his death. Finally, she herself leveled at her brother Septimus by suggestion as the only possible explanation for the crimes the charge of homicidal mania.

"I had my murderer; I had then to find the motive. Sergeant Brinton supplied it. He said of Gilton, if you recall, that at the time he was keeping company with Miss Regina, he was 'rather indigent, but soon came into money with a series of fortunate investments.' Now, I submit, Parker, that in order for young Gilton to have made investments he must have received money from some source. What source more obvious than Miss Regina, who in her infatuation showered him with all the money he demanded, using not only her own funds but also those of her brother, Septimus, which were in her care? Indeed, one feels bound to ask whether Gilton's 'fortunate investments' were an actuality or whether they were simply his canny accumulation of the money he had obtained from that infatuated woman.

"Surely, then, the obvious first victim of her counterfeiting homicidal mania might as well be the young man who had spurned as well as robbed her. The selection of the child was purely happenstance; a little girl had seen her in the vicinity at the time Gilton had been slain. Miss Regina accordingly feared her, and she became the second victim. The stage was then set for Alexander Grayle's death, and he, too, died as the others – stunned by a blow from the leaded handle of her back-scratcher, and calmly dispatched while unconscious by what must certainly be regarded as one of the most unusual lethal weapons in a long roster of adventures.

"Having proceeded thus far, it was only logical to assume that if Octavius had not already arrived at the same conclusion, he must soon do so. It followed, therefore, that his death must occur with as little delay as possible, in order that Miss Regina's purpose might be accomplished. I had only to wait upon events. Our entrance on the scene would surely precipitate her violence, even as Octavius's arrival in England and his subsequent inquiry into the state of Septimus's finances set in motion the events which were the final acts in the concealed tragedy which was Miss Regina's life.

"All in all, an interesting if gruesome diversion. I am indebted to you, Parker."

X

THE ADVENTURE OF THE FIVE ROYAL COACHMEN

Returning from a professional call to the lodgings I shared with Solar Pons at 7B Praed Street, early one June morning in 192– , I was astonished to find my companion engaged in the contemplation of a fishing-rod. He stood in the centre of our sitting-room just away from the mantel and not far from his desk, flexing the rod in his long, supple fingers. At my entrance, he favored me with a glance from his keen grey eyes and the ghost of a smile on his lips.

"I note your amazement, Parker," he said, "Let me assure you that my interest in matters piscatorial is not recent. Alas! I have but lacked the opportunity to try my hand at that ancient and honorable sport of angling. Come, what do you say to a holiday on the Test?"

"My dear Pons! You are surely joking!"

"Ah, I find too little opportunity for jesting. Now that I have concluded that little matter of the lost locomotive to the satisfaction of the directors of the Great Northern Railway, a holiday would not be amiss. The Test should be beautiful at this time of year. And the trout are rising. So, at least, the papers have it."

He tossed me a copy of a newspaper from his desk. It was folded to a brief account on the front page carrying the total catch taken a day ago by an angling party under the leadership of Sir Ronald Masterman, the Undersecretary for Foreign Affairs.

"But this is a record of the catch the day before yesterday," I protested. "Trout are unpredictable. What was yesterday's creel?"

"Ah, the morning papers are remarkably silent in the matter."

I laughed. "You see! They took none. And it is now you talk of going trouting!"

Pons put down the rod and took up his calabash, which he proceeded to fill with shag. "By the way," he said presently, "I am expecting a caller at any moment. Be so good as to admit him if he should arrive while I am in my room."

"Aha! I thought there was more to this than met the eye!" I exclaimed.

"Is there not always more to everything than meets the eye?"

So saying, he vanished into his chamber, leaving me to puzzle over whatever new venture engaged his attention, for my companion's reputation for the kind of confidential inquiry work in which he specialized had now spread far beyond the boundaries of metropolitan London. The year, as I recall it, was one of those hectic years in the decade following the first World War, when most of the capitals were uneasy still, and peace seemed but a temporary illusion.

Pons was back in our sitting-room when the bell jangled to announce the visitor he had been expecting. Pons' immobile features told me nothing, but there was a restrained air of anticipation in his bearing, nevertheless, I was not prepared to greet a visitor of such distinction as the tall, broad-shouldered figure whose austere, bemonocled face was familiar to every Englishman and, indeed, to half the globe, as that of Lord Hilary Kilvert, the Secretary for Foreign Affairs, He was brisk and singularly direct. With but a flickering glance for me, he inquired, "You received my message, Mr. Pons?"

"Pray be seated, Lord Kilvert. My companion, Dr. Lyndon Parker, is a man of utmost discretion; you may speak freely before him."

"I sincerely trust so." He took off his bowler, laid it unceremoniously on Pons' desk, and mopped his brow with his handkerchief, although I should not have called the room warm. "Forgive my not sitting down, I beg you. I am too restless, far too restless to sit still. The matter is one potentially fraught with the gravest possibilities – let me repeat, Mr. Pons, the gravest possibilities."

"Dear me, Lord Kilvert," observed Pons tranquilly, "I should not have thought that a commonplace angling excursion on the Test should occasion such concern even though it involves a few foreign diplomats under the guidance of the Undersecretary for Foreign Affairs."

Lord Kilvert whirled on his feet and stared at Pons, his face ashen. "Good God! Mr. Pons," he exclaimed, "surely there has been no leak to the press?"

"Pray compose yourself," Pons hastened to assure him. "It seemed to me beyond the bounds of coincidence that your urgent call should be unrelated to the expedition duly chronicled in the papers three days ago and followed in detail daily thereafter until this morning when the expedition is conspicuous by its absence from the news columns. Surely it is not too much to suppose that some event took place which might have certain international complications?"

"Thank Heaven! I feared for a moment that some word of Spencer's disappearance had reached print."

"Ah, so it is young Rigby Spencer who has vanished! I submit, your Lordship, that this much-touted angling expedition served only to cover events of considerably more significance to His Majesty's Government and to your office particularly. The members of the party were not minor diplomats, but special envoys empowered by their governments to conduct talks on a matter close to our government. If I may venture a guess – the disarmament question?"

"You are close, Mr. Pons. The precise subject was the ratio of naval disarmament. We may assume that certain foreign countries would be most anxious to obtain advance information on this subject before our government is ready to release any public statement."

"Specifically, Japan and Russia," said Pons crisply. "Let us hear the story as you know it, Lord Kilvert. If espionage is involved, there is no time to be lost. The game is already well afoot, and we are not yet set upon it."

Without ceasing his restless pacing to and fro, the Secretary for Foreign Affairs began to talk rapidly. "You should understand, Mr. Pons, that our government had fixed upon a certain basic ratio of naval disarmament some time ago; this had been arrived at after preliminary talks by representatives of the United States government. It was committed to a formula and entrusted to Rigby Spencer, precisely because we felt that any foreign agent interested in an attempt to obtain the formula and the ratio might reasonably suppose that Sir Ronald Masterman would be carrying it. Since we will not retreat from our basic ratio, but might well be able to obtain an even better ratio, we would lose all chance to bargain if once our basic ratio were known.

"We had inaugurated the meetings officially in London. After early talks, we permitted the press to report that we had taken a brief recess, ostensibly to wait for other delegates, and some of our number went trouting on the Test from Chilbolton to Leckford, a lovely stretch of water, Mr. Pons, if you have ever had the good fortune to fish it. The party had its headquarters at an inn in Chilbolton, and journeyed from there every morning, well attended, with hampers of food and all the necessaries.

"Of course, the gentlemen enjoyed the fishing; they were meant to do so; but each evening, and occasionally at luncheons, they proceeded with the talks. They made little progress. The American delegate was quite stubborn and did not have the freedom of action which most of the others exercised; the French delegate consistently pressed for every advantage without revealing his government's demurrers in a manifest attempt to force our hand; the Japanese delegate, suspecting that his country would be asked to accept a greater ratio of disarmament, was naturally reticent and suspicious. Thus, beneath the apparent smoothness of the talks and the quite evident pleasure the gentlemen shared in the angling, there existed a definite stratum of unrest.

"However, all went well until yesterday. There had been a violent disagreement in the course of talks at the inn the previous night; the Japanese delegate had left the meeting in anger, though he rejoined the party in the morning as blandly as if nothing untoward had taken place the night before. The party went in two motorcars to that stretch of water which lies just above Leckford. The fishing, according to Masterman, was quiet at first; some trout rose, but not many. The day was grey with an overcast; rain impended. The party separated in mid-morning and did not come together again until luncheon. There was some discussion as to the advisability of returning to Chilbolton; they voted on it, but, though there were three votes for returning, the majority of the party were for continuing. Just before noon, the fish had begun to rise to the bait, and enthusiasm was growing. They went out again after luncheon. At about two o'clock rain began to fall, and, though it did not last long, the party began to come back to the cars to return to the inn. Spencer alone did not return. They waited some time for him, they scouted for him; there was no trace of him. We have not seen anything of him since.

"Of course, we threw a cordon around the entire area within an hour. Inspector Jamison of Scotland Yard has been in charge and is on the spot. We are reasonably certain that Spencer was not taken out of the region by any road or railway. What happened from the time he disappeared until Scotland Yard arrived on the scene, we cannot say; but that time was not more than two hours at maximum, and it might well have been considerably less, for we have some evidence to show that Spencer had fished his way for approximately half a mile upstream from the place at which they had lunched; he could hardly have done so in less than half an hour. His footprints, or what we assume to be his footprints, lead up to a small rise in the river bank; they do not take up beyond it."

"There was no evidence of a struggle?" asked Pons.

"None, Mr. Pons. The scene was studied with the minutest care, and it seems patent that the abduction was carried out with consummate skill. Inspector Jamison has confessed that he is baffled."

Pons smiled wintrily. "Ah, that is not a condition which could be described as exactly foreign to Inspector Jamison."

"I must impress upon you the need for the swift recovery of the memoranda," said the Foreign Secretary.

Pons sat for some time without replying, his head sunk on his chest, his eyes fixed upon the hearthrug. His elbows rested on the arms of his chair, and his fingertips touched in a Gothic arch before him.

"And the other delegates?" he asked presently.

"They have naturally returned to London," replied Lord Kilvert. "We have been delaying talks since then, because, until we know where Spencer and the memoranda he carried are, we are at a disadvantage. The Prime Minister, who has been informed of developments, is pressing us for a rapid recovery of our position."

"And the ratio? The memoranda? How were they set down? Were they documented or ciphered?"

"We do not know, Mr. Pons. The ratio and memoranda were left entirely to Spencer's discretion. The ratio need not have been set down at all; it was short enough to be remembered. But there were certain possible variations approaching the basic ratio which made it necessary to have at least some of these figures written down. We believe, therefore, that Spencer carried somewhere on his person such memoranda as were vital to the discussions."

"At whose suggestion was the expedition on the Test undertaken?"

"Why, I believe it was young Spencer's suggestion. He is an expert angler, and has also achieved some small fame as an amateur fly-tyer of no mean abilities."

"How much time does His Majesty's Government give us?" asked Pons.

"Twenty-four hours. We cannot possibly delay any longer. We can put a car at your disposal immediately."

"On the contrary, it would be more desirable that Dr. Parker and I appear on the scene as disinterested disciples of Walton. There is a train leaving Waterloo Station within the hour. We shall be on it."

I doubt that anyone would have taken us for other than what Pons intended us to represent at Chilbolton, a duo of amateur anglers. Though he had observed rather pointedly that I needed little alteration save in appropriate costume, Pons himself had undergone a considerable transformation. He looked the epitome of a countryman out for a day of piscatorial sport; he had altered his face with the addition of spectacles and sideburns, together with a small goatee, and, like myself, he was attired in typical angling clothes, save for his deerstalker cap, which was not inappropriate.

The Foreign Secretary had supplied Pons with a carefully drawn map of the region between Chilbolton and Leckford, painstakingly detailing the area in which Spencer had vanished, so that we had a very clear picture of the scene in mind. Pons had suggested that Lord Kilvert say nothing to Inspector Jamison save that Pons had been consulted and would arrive on the scene in good time and manage to reach the inspector when he needed his assistance. With this, Lord Kilvert had to be content, though he had given the impression on taking his leave of Pons that he thought him an eccentric indeed.

For most of the way to Chilbolton, Pons sat studying the map, making muttered comments from time to time.

"From Testcombe Bridge, below Chilbolton, the railway follows the Test for some distance," he said at last. "Beyond that, on the farther side, lies the road, which is not yet tarred, so that any hurried activity on the road would have thrown up a cloud of dust; it had not rained long, according to Lord Kilvert's account. Both railline and road thus follow the river at no great distance, but it is to be noted that the Test divides not far from the bridge, and it is then soon joined by the Anton. There are level marshes and reed-beds beyond, leading to the wooded hills of Longstock Park, and the high chalk downs of Salisbury look upon the scene beyond Stockbridge. The party was not fishing the main stream of the Test, but the secondary stream which runs through Leckford before again joining the main water above Stockbridge. That is a region of poplar groves and, beyond the marshes in the vicinity of Leckford, there is ample cover for any venturesome rascal. Yet it would seem a daring foreign agent, indeed, who could hope to abduct in broad daylight a member of a party as large as this one, would you not think, Parker?"

"I would," I admitted.

"Yet Spencer was either taken by someone, or he went of his own free will. He might have crossed to the road and flagged down a passing car; he might even have caught on to a train slowing down for the Leckford stop."

"He might, save that he had no motive to do so."

"At least, he had no known motive."

I looked sharply at him, but there was no hint in the head sunk on his chest and the half-closed eyes of the direction of his thoughts. "You think he may have had some such motive?" I asked finally.

"I am only considering all the possibilities. His Lordship apparently considered but one, which appeared to him as the most likely. It has too often been my experience that the most likely solution is not always the most probable, and that the most improbable solution very often emerges as the only tenable one. You know my methods, Parker."

He said nothing further until we reached Chilbolton, and then roused himself from his reverie only long enough to say that, since a study of the map indicated that the scene of the disappearance was closer to Leckford than to Chilbolton, we would ride on to that village. Then he lapsed once more into brooding silence.

The day was mild and sunny, though occasional clouds scudded across the heavens. The countryside around Leckford was indeed a lovely land. Low, wooded hills framed the valley of the Test at that place, and the face of the earth itself was a rich green, that deep summer green of mature verdure. I soon had even better opportunity to view it than I had from the windows of our compartment, for once we had left the train, Pons set out for the Test from Leckford on foot, swinging along in his long-limbed stride to the side of the old canal which carried the branch of the Test through Leckford, and followed the bank of this out of the village in the direction of Chilbolton.

We were soon out of the village and in a stretch of shaded water, where poplars rose up tall and straight, and willows and alders and osiers bent above the stream. Pons lost no time beginning to fish, casting his fly with zest and with a skill had hardly expected of him. Moreover, on his third cast, hooked a sizable trout which he played with singular ability and presently dropped into his creel.

We made our way slowly but steadily upstream, until we came within sight of the scene of Spencer's disappearance. It was Pons who first saw the rise from the low, almost boggy river's edge to a higher, more solid bank.

"If I am not mistaken, that is the site we are looking for, Parker. If I had any doubt, the presence of that fellow leaning against a tree just beyond it would have laid it; that is certainly our estimable friend, Jamison."

"Will you make yourself known to him?"

"Let us just proceed as we are. If he should be under surveillance himself, it would never occur to him to think so."

Accordingly, we went forward, Pons casting now and then, though by this time he had already taken three trout to my pair, and the foliage pressing upon the Test at this point made casting more difficult. He took care to scrutinize the shore as we went, noting footprints at the very water's edge. These might well have been the missing Spencer's for here and there the prints of others, doubtless of those searching for trace of the vanished man, were plainly in evidence, and this one line of footprints had for the most part been carefully preserved. They were lost, however, at the rising ground.

As we mounted the rise, the portly form of Inspector Jamison rose up before us, his thick moustache bristling, his sharp eyes suspicious.

"Here, here, what's all this?" he demanded truculently. "What are you doing here?"

"Ha!" snorted Pons in a disguised voice. "Here is an oaf who does not recognize an angler when he sees one. One might better ask what he is doing here. Why, the fellow looks like an imitation policeman."

Jamison flushed angrily. "Be off with you. The police are in charge."

"Fiddlesticks," Pons answered. "This water's free for the fishing, and nobody'll order us around."

"We'll see about that," said Jamison ominously. He turned and raised his voice to call, "Cort! Here, please."

Pons turned to me in mock surprise, his eyes glinting with amusement. "The oaf means what he says."

By this time, however, Jamison had had a good look at me.

"Never mind, Cort," he called out, looking indignantly at Pons. "You must have your sport, eh?"

"A man ought to combine pleasure with business whenever it is possible to do so," answered Pons. "Nothing has changed?"

"Nothing."

"Very well, then. Let us not be seen talking together."

"My men are all around the place. No one could observe us."

"Indeed! I recall at least one occasion when a similar confidence almost led to tragedy."

Pons led the way among the trees and bushes along the risen ground at right angles from the Test, in the direction of the rail-line and the road beyond it. There were no footprints to be followed, yet Pons scrutinized the ground with greater care than he had thus far looked at any portion of the area, and he had not gone far before he bent to pick up something.

He held it in the palm of his hand, and I peered at it. It was a dry-fly.

"A Royal Coachman," I said. "Dropped by some angler."

"I should hardly have thought it the badge of a police-inspector," said Pons dryly.

We moved on, and presently Pons picked up a second dry-fly, again a Royal Coachman.

"A careless angler," I said.

Then he found another, and yet two more, making a total of five, scattered throughout the grove of trees that held to the rise.

"Most careless, indeed," he commented.

He pocketed all five of the Royal Coachmen, his face thoughtful, but did not hesitate in his steady pace, walking onward until we came out into the open space along the rail-line of the London & South Western Railway. There he stood for a few moments, looking beyond the rails to the road, over which lay a mist of dust shot through with sunlight.

Perhaps a mile or more down the road lay Leckford, its roofs and gables just in sight. A little way in the other direction stood a tinker's van, and beyond it, screened by a grove of trees, a small secluded house. This seemed to catch Pons' eye; his gaze lingered thoughtfully on it for some time, as if he were anxious to scrutinize it with great care, marking its inaccessibility, though its inhabitants evidently had ready access to both rail-line and road. Then, without comment, Pons crossed the rail-line to the road, and began to walk away from Leckford. He drew up at the tinker's van; a hunchbacked old man sat cobbling shoes beside the van, and just beyond it a lone horse was tethered.

"Good afternoon," Pons greeted him. "Can you tell me who lives in that house over there?" He pointed with his rod.

"Naw, zur, that I can na. I beant long in these parts, zur."

The tinker had chosen his stand well. He and his van were shaded by the trees of the little grove along the road where the van stood; beyond, on both sides, was treeless country on which the sun doubtless shone remorsely on hot days. He had been well-guided, too, in his decision to keep sufficiently far from Leckford to avoid being taxed or troubled by the merchants or government of that village; yet he was not so far away as to enable him to obtain work from Leckford.

"You've been here for a while, though. Long enough to say whether you've noticed anything unusual going on over there."

"Naw, zur, didden notice. I beant one t' mind a body's business but m' own."

At this point, the door of the van opened, and a pretty, dark-haired girl of perhaps twenty appeared in the doorway. She looked anxiously out at the old man, with but a fleeting glance at us.

"Don't tire yourself now, Father," she admonished.

"Doan't ee worry yersel'," answered the old man.

Pons thanked him and withdrew, walking on up the road quite rapidly until he reached the vicinity of the secluded house, where he slowed his pace to a more casual saunter and took the opportunity to inspect the house and its tree-girt grounds as carefully as possible without being too obvious in his purpose. Then, inexplicably, he left the road with a murmured admonition to me, recrossed the rail-line, and plunged once more into the low country toward the blue water of the Test.

"What now?" I could not forebear asking.

"We came to fish," he answered. "Let us pursue the sport as long as we are here."

"And Spencer and his memoranda?" I asked. "What of them?"

He ignored my question and countered with one of his own. "The five Royal Coachmen told you nothing, Parker?"

"Nothing except that the fellow who was so careless could scarcely be called a true disciple of Walton."

"I submit that they were not dropped by accident."

"Indeed! And if not, for what purpose were they dropped? Certainly they marked no trail, other than to point the obvious direction Spencer must have gone."

"Now I thought that extremely significant," replied Pons. He had reached the shore of the Test now, and began gravely to cast. "I thought it so significant that it occurred to me these dry-flies offered nothing less than a complete solution to the puzzle of Spencer's disappearance."

I stared at him, I fear, agape. "Oh, come, Pons – you are reading too much into them," I protested.

"It surprises me to hear you say so. You have yourself begun to read them correctly. If the Royal Coachmen were not dropped to serve as a guide – and I daresay they were not dropped for that purpose – then they were certainly dropped for a reason which must have seemed to Spencer a sound one."

"Aren't you taking too much for granted in assuming that Spencer dropped them?" I asked.

"I fancy not. In the first place, they present themselves along the only way Spencer could have gone with the least opportunity for observation. Had he gone up, down, or across the water, he would surely have been observed by one or more members of his party. He had no alternative but to utilize the cover of the trees and retreat toward the rail-line and road; so much must have been evident not only to him, but to anyone who might seek to abduct him. I submit that he dropped the five Royal Coachmen intentionally. It follows then that he was not carried off by main force, for if he had been, he would have been unable to drop the flies; and if part of his paraphernalia were to be lost while he was being dragged away, it is beyond the bounds of coincidence that that part should be only five flies, each exactly the same as the others. No, I submit that he was not carried off by main force, as the Foreign Secretary seems to believe, but went voluntarily. I submit, further, that that is the only tenable solution, since it is hardly conceivable that he could have been forcibly abducted in broad daylight without someone at least having seen him. Remember that the tinker's van stands directly in the line of his passage, that the house beyond also commands the way he would of necessity have come from the bank of the stream."

"But if he went voluntarily," I objected, "would he not have been guilty of a breach of duty?"

"How? His duty lay in silence about the basic ratio and the accompanying memoranda. We have no reason to believe that he divulged these data."

"Then why has he not communicated with his superiors?"

"Because he is either dead or being prevented from doing so; I am inclined to believe the latter."

I was baffled and confessed my perplexity.

"My dear Parker, it is most elementary," said Pons. "I have seldom come upon such a satisfying example of the pristine effectiveness of the science of deduction as these five Royal Coachmen. One might almost say they are unique, for any variable amount of deductions might be made from them, but all must eventually reduce to a series of inevitable facts. Let us just pause for a moment and examine one of the dry-flies whose presence at the scene conveys so much information to the meticulous observer."

He laid aside his rod and I did likewise. He sat down on a fallen tree-bole, and took one of the Royal Coachmen from his pocket.

"Now these are excellently made – but they are not a commercial product, as an old hand at the rod must observe at once. Spencer is a fly-tying enthusiast; you will recall Lord Kilvert's saying so. It is perfectly reasonable to suppose that this is a product of his own hand, as doubtless are the quartet remaining in my pocket. But does it not seem to you a little more full than most?"

"There is some permissible variation."

He paused and looked under the cover of his creel, where he carried some dry-flies of his own. "Ah, here we are. Let us compare this commercial Royal Coachman of my own with this discovery."

He held the two up together.

"Well, Spencer's has a thicker body."

"Capital, Parker. In almost every other respect they seem similar. There is no variation in the wing, none in the hurl, none in hook or hackle. The quality of the red silk thread about the body appears to be the same; while Spencer has spared the shellac, certainly the thread is of the same size."

"But Spencer has used more of it. He has wound the body more thickly," I put in.

"Let us just have a closer look at it."

So saying, he drew the hurl down the hook, caught hold of the red silk thread, snapped it, and began patiently to unwind it, his eyes agleam with anticipation. What he expected to find, I had no way of knowing. What he found was a tiny slip of paper, not more than an eighth of an inch wide, and scarcely an inch long, wound carefully around the hook beneath the thread which made up the body of the dry-fly.

"I daresay this is what we want," said Pons, with satisfaction.

He unrolled the slip of paper and laid it face upward in his palm so that I could see, written in ink upon it, a series of numerals. I read them – "5-5-3, 4-4-3, 3-3-2."

"A cipher?" I ventured.

Pons shook his head impatiently. "No, no. These figures are surely understandable enough. England's five ships to America's five to Japan's three, and so on. The Japanese are quite right in suspecting that naval status inferior to that of the other maritime nations is planned at the Naval Conference. This is surely nothing else but a memorandum pertinent to the basic naval ratio. There is hardly any need to take apart the others; they will contain similar information. The question which now remains is this: did Spencer have these memoranda committed to memory, together with the basic ratio, or were these jottings his sole recourse? Let us presume for the moment that they were his sole source of information, and we find ready to hand the explanation of why he dropped them. He did so not to point a way for possible pursuit, but simply to rid himself of this information because he suspected that something was amiss, and knew that if a fellow-angler found these flies and used them, the water would soon eradicate what ink there was on the papers."

"But if he went voluntarily, I fail to follow your reasoning, Pons."

"Because you are making it a question of either-or," replied Pons. "He might have gone without duress and yet have grave doubts of his wisdom in so doing. In short, he may have been enticed away. He is a young man; he is doubtless a romantic idealist – it would take something of that to put a man into Foreign Affairs in our time, I daresay. Very well, then. Let us reconstruct the event.

"Young Rigby Spencer is fishing, with his precious cargo so adroitly concealed on his person – hooked into his hat-band or his belt or a pocket or even his creel. He is fishing off the rise when he is accosted by someone in need of help – a motorist, perhaps a young woman, whose car has come to grief along the road. Someone may have been waiting for days to accost him alone at an auspicious place and time. He cannot resist the appeal to his gallantry; but, having assented and begun to follow, he has qualms and, perhaps as surreptitiously as possible, he drops the telltale Royal Coachmen. If they were seen, no significance was likely to be attached to them; he might have reasoned that it would be so, though his place of concealment was doubtless originally planned to protect his information from foreign members of his party. By the time he realized that his suspicions were well founded, it was too late for him to turn back."

"Even a romantic idealist ought to be able to recognize a foreign agent," I protested.

"Excellent, Parker!" cried Pons. "You have hit upon my own demurrer. Let us ask ourselves whether Spencer's secret might not be as valuable to a traitorous Englishman who could offer it for sale, as to a foreign agent? I submit that the entire operation against Spencer is a little too daring and at the same time a little too crude to tempt a foreign agent. No, what seemed obvious to me from the outset was that there had been a leak from the Foreign Office itself, and someone had acted upon it. Spencer had not yet tipped his hand in conference; there was no other avenue but secret information from the source to know him the bearer of the memoranda, any more than there is now reason to suppose that there is any other tenable explanation of the five Royal Coachmen."

I admitted that Pons' deductions were cogent. "But then, where is Rigby Spencer? Are we too late to save him?"

"I rather think not. If he has admitted nothing, he may still be alive, kept so in the hope of wringing these data from him, though with each day that passes, it may be assumed that his worth diminishes. Let us set Inspector Jamison on the track."

He took up his rod and walked rapidly back along the shore of the Test.

We came upon Jamison where we had left him. At the moment he was engaged in giving directions to two young constables, but, catching sight of us, he left off what he was saying and grinned in superior fashion.

"Still empty-handed, I see. I hardly thought you'd turn him up. We entered and searched every dwelling, cordons were thrown about roads miles away, the train that passed that afternoon was thoroughly examined. We left no stone unturned, even to harassing that tinker and turning his van back there upside down."

"Spencer could hardly have slipped through your fingers, could he?" said Pons.

"I doubt it."

"Then, of course, he is still here. Perhaps you had better take him before some harm is done to him, other than that which may already have befallen him. It can hardly be comfortable to be gagged and bound."

Jamison's jaw dropped. "You know where he is, Pons?" he cried.

"You will find him in that tinker's van; it will have either a false top or a false bottom. But watch your step. That old fellow is dangerous and the girl no less so."

Jamison wavered only a moment; then he and his constables set off at a rapid trot along the rise toward the roadside where the tinker's van stood.

Pons regarded me quizzically. "You are surprised, Parker?"

"Nothing you say or do any longer surprises me," I answered. "But just the same, if I may ask..."

"It was all plainly in evidence," he replied. "The tinker's van had been in place not more than a week, possible less, as you could have seen by the condition of the grass beneath it. Rain had not fallen there; it had fallen around the van. Hence it was present yesterday. But the place where the horse was tethered indicated that animal's presence for several days, or approximately just before the coming of the angling expedition, brought there by the same source from the Foreign Office which had information about Spencer. The tinker's van was so obvious that Jamison, eager to follow the Foreign Office's directive in regard to foreign agents, hardly considered a vehicle so indigenous to the scene. And the young lady who came to the door? Was she not pretty? Young, charming? And would not her appeal for help because her old, crippled father had fallen and injured himself have moved any British gentleman, even you, Parker? Come, admit it, you have always had a soft spot for the ladies, Parker!"

I smiled ruefully.

"Besides, the entire theory was of a piece; if any part of it were wrong, then the whole could manifestly be in error. But the Royal Coachmen divulged their secret, proving that Spencer was enticed away. And in the van we found an agent who could scarcely be improved upon for her ability to be enticing to a young man like Rigby Spencer.

"As for Spencer's ingenious flies, we shall post them to Lord Kilvert and ease his mind."

Young Rigby Spencer called at 7B three days later, his alert blue eyes twinkling, his good-natured face still somewhat abashed by the ease with which he had been taken. About his head he still wore signs of maltreatment.

"I came to thank you, Mr. Pons. Though the papers tell us it was all Inspector Jamison's work, I have other facts from my superiors," he said. "We have stopped up the leak in our office, and Lord Kilvert has destroyed my Royal Coachmen."

"A clever hiding place," said Pons. "But no angler could ever lose five Royal Coachmen one after another."

"And only someone appreciative of the niceties of that royal sport would have come to that conclusion," answered Spencer immediately. "The young lady is an accomplished actress, Mr. Pons. The two of them gave me a rough time of it, though I think the worst of it was being so well trussed up as to be helpless in that false roof when the men from the Yard searched the van."

"I daresay. But in the interests of that monarch whom we both acknowledge as our sovereign, Mr. Spencer, I suggest that in matters of state, gallantry must come second," said Pons.

Watching him go off down Praed Street, Pons added, "That young man bids fair to become a valuable and trusted public servant, Parker. He has learned a lesson no amount of instruction could have conveyed to him."

"So have I," I answered. "I would never have dreamed that so much could be done with a common Royal Coachman!"

XI

THE ADVENTURE OF THE PARALYTIC MENDICANT

"All thing come to him who waits," observed my friend Solar Pons from the window where he stood. "I have waited all morning for one of those little diversions of which I am so fond and which you take such delight in recording, and now, if I am not mistaken, we shall have the offer of one."

I came to his side and looked down into Praed Street. An elderly woman stood below, peering intently up at the number above the outer door. She was tall and angular, dressed soberly in brown, and in rather old-fashioned clothes, her head crowned with one of those dreadful Queen Mary hats. She held a brochure or pamphlet in her one hand, while with the other she appeared to be marking a passage on the page she had been reading. From the wrist of her left hand hung a knitted brown reticule.

"What do you make of her, Parker?" asked Pons.

"She is certainly a study in brown," I answered. "And since a conservative in dress – no doubt also in thought."

"Ah, that does not necessarily follow. The cut of her clothes is such as to suggest her rural origin, true. And she is a stranger to London, for that is surely a street guide to the city which she carries in her hand. She is probably a spinster, for she wears no wedding ring, or else someone who has tired of wearing one, but very likely the former. She is employed in a responsible position, and her visit to Number 7B is concerned with her employment. There is a grimness about her features which suggests that she has arrived at the decision to consult someone only after prolonged consideration; but having once arrived at it, nothing will alter it. She is a determined woman, and that is a tribe, my dear fellow, which brooks no interference." He turned away from the window.

"But, come, she is on her way up the stairs behind the estimable Mrs. Johnson."

In but a few moments our landlady ushered our visitor into our quarters. The lady's sharp, black eyes fixed unerringly on Pons, and it was to him that she introduced herself as Miss Flora Jones, of Bury St. Edmunds. She extended a claw-like hand to me at Pons' introduction.

"Pray feel free to resume your knitting, Miss Jones," invited Pons. "I observe you have carried it with you to while away the hours of your journey."

"Yes, thank you, I will do so," replied our visitor, as she set down her reticule and with great deliberation removed the almost grotesque hat she wore, revealing greying hair drawn tightly about her head. As she sat down, she presented the perfect picture of solid British respectability.

"I have made up my mind to come here solely on my own responsibility," she began at once, "and I am perfectly willing to assume the consequences of that decision. But to tell the truth, Mr. Pons, I can no longer tolerate the circumstances of our existence."

"Your employer would object to this consultation?" asked Pons.

"Indeed he would. But Jabez Horton has lived for so long in retirement that he no longer has a mind of his own."

"Pray let us begin at the beginning," suggested Pons, with a faint smile on his almost ascetic features. "You are employed as a housekeeper by Jabez Horton in Bury St. Edmunds, and have for some time been so employed."

"Fourteen years, Mr. Pons. It is fourteen years to the day this week when Mr. Horton came to Bury St. Edmunds, bought my house at a handsome figure, and retained me to stay on as his housekeeper, with the assistance of my young cousin, Mrs. Ethel Hamish, who does the house today, in my absence. Mr. Horton has always been a man of very few friends. He occasionally corresponds with other gentlemen of fully as sedentary a nature, and very rarely writes letters to the *Times*. Though he has never said so, I took it for granted that he was a retired Colonial.

"He is a man of very regular habits. He rises at the same hour every day, takes his meals on the hour, spends his days reading, playing chess by post, and taking one solitary walk, customarily at dusk. He is reticent but amiable; I find it necessary to remind myself constantly that it is he who owns the house and not I who am his landlady."

She had taken her knitting from her reticule, and was now industriously knitting, the clicking of her needles making a distant obbligato to her narrative. Her fingers fairly flew at her work, which was done so automatically that she seldom removed her eyes from Pons' face even to examine her handiwork.

"It is my custom every morning to take his mail in to him. He subscribes to several newspapers and magazines, but he receives few letters. A week ago, I brought him his mail, as usual. There was one letter. I took particular notice of it because it was addressed with letters which had been cut out of a newspaper or some other printed paper, and his name had been misspelled 'Hindon'. His eye fell upon this letter the moment I handed him his mail; I saw his color change, he grew white; he gasped, and his hand when he dropped the mail to his desk was shaking. He was very greatly agitated. I have seen him so only once before, about four months ago, when he received a cablegram from South Africa. What was in the envelope, I do not know; I believe he destroyed it. I have, however, brought you the envelope itself. You will see it has been posted from Southampton."

So saying, she reached into her reticule and deposited a cheap, almost yellowed envelope in Pons' hand. I leaned over Pons' shoulder and looked at it. Its address had manifestly been painstakingly constructed from the printed page, each letter of the name having been printed separately, though the address seemed to have been clipped from a guide and pasted upon the envelope. The name was misspelled just as Miss Jones had said.

"On the following day, Mr. Horton received another such envelope, this time posted from London. When he took it from my hand, his face was the picture of dread; he could not conceal it; I was shocked. He did not open it in my presence, but I had scarcely left the room before he did so. Immediately he cried out in an anguished voice. I was on my way back to the room when the door burst open, and he ran out, hatless and without having changed his smoking-jacket, and without a word, left the house. This singular conduct distressed me exceedingly, Mr. Pons, all the more so since it was several hours before we had any communication from him. Then it was by means of a trunk call from Lowestoft, and he had called only to say that we were not to admit anyone to the house, in any circumstances. He returned home that night, and since that time he has remained virtually a prisoner in his house; he has not gone out for his customary evening walk, he has not permitted himself to be seen. I ventured to suggest that if someone had threatened him, he ought to consult the police; he forbade me to speak of the subject again.

"But now he is in such a state that he is virtually ill. Indeed, he has become so indifferent to events that I was able to abstract the contents of the final envelope and bring it along. It is a curious little thing of glass, wired to a piece of pasteboard."

This, too, came out of her reticule.

The moment Pons caught sight of it, he uttered a delighted cry. "Ah! what have we here? My dear lady, have you had it appraised?"

"I wondered," she said simply.

It was a tiny piece of glass, wrought in the shape of a miniature dagger, wired, as Miss Jones had said, to a piece of pasteboard. Below it were pasted a letter H, and the numeral 5.

"Even wrought glass has little value," I said.

"Come, come, Parker – look again," chided Pons. "This is no piece of glass. It is a diamond."

"Sent in an ordinary envelope, not even by registered post?" I asked incredulously. "Pons, you are joking."

"On the contrary, my dear fellow. It is most certainly a diamond, and cut from a stone of respectable size. Only a man of wealth would so have cut a stone of sufficient size to have brought him a princely sum at its sale."

Our visitor was already stretching out her hand for the piece of pasteboard with its precious cargo. "I must return it before he discovers its absence," she said. And, having tucked it away once more into her reticule, she asked, "Mr. Pons, will you undertake to call on him without permitting him to discover that I have visited you?"

"I shall, indeed. I shall follow you by the next train to Bury St. Edmunds," promised Pons. "I should like to keep the envelope for the time being, if you can part with it."

After she had gone, Pons placed the envelope under the table lamp and studied it. "Here," he said, "is a little object to test your powers of deduction, Parker. Come, tell me about the sender."

"Clearly, he fears to be identified through his handwriting," I ventured.

"The ragged cuttings do not appear to you significant? They are left-hand cuttings."

"He was in haste."

"On the contrary, these communications seem to me as acts of singular deliberation, very carefully planned. Certainly, they have been months in the preparation, perhaps years."

"Oh, come, Pons! You are having me!"

"No, it is not too much to suppose that the cablegram which Horton received from Capetown inaugurated the present phase of a sequence of events of which these letters are but another. Are not the largest diamond mines in the world in South Africa? I submit, Parker, that the sender of these communications is very well known to Horton, and therefore he would have no reason to attempt to conceal his identity. No, he is probably unable to write."

"An illiterate," I agreed. "He twice misspelled Horton's name."

"Twice in the same way," agreed Pons dryly. "I submit that an illiterate is not likely to make even the same error in spelling precisely the same a second time. His inability is not grown from illiteracy. And what manner of 'illiterate' would send so elaborate a notice as a diamond dagger?"

"It would seem to me that only a very ignorant fellow would send a precious jewel in a plain and insubstantial envelope."

"Or a very rich one," added Pons, "though it is seldom the common post that is stolen, only the registered. He may have known as much." He came to his feet as he spoke. "I suggest that haste is indicated. Let us not lose a moment to reach Mr. Jabez Horton in his perilous seclusion. We may already be too late."

We were fortunate enough to catch the same train Miss Jones took out of Liverpool Street Station, though we sat apart from her, Pons in contemplative silence, his deerstalker cap pulled low over his keen eyes which appeared to brood upon the passing landscape but were focussed instead upon some unknown landscape of his mind.

Despite our haste, Pons' last words were prophetic, for our arrival late that day in Bury St. Edmunds found us precipitated into the midst of great confusion at the home of Miss Jones' employer, Jabez Horton. Miss Jones herself had reached the house but five minutes before our own arrival, just as the local police-inspector, accompanied by a medical man, came upon the scene. They had been summoned by Mrs. Ethel Hamish, who had less than ten minutes previously discovered Horton dead in his study.

Miss Jones' appearance served to calm her cousin's hysteria, after which the housekeeper introduced Pons and myself to Police-Inspector Ronald Martin, and Dr. Edmund Quinn, both men in early middle-age, and both familiar enough with Pons' reputation to be affable and lenient about our presence. Pons immediately subjected the room to the customary intensive examination at which I marvelled time after time, for no details seemed to escape his eye.

The body, still in a half-upright position, sat in an easy chair beside the table. Horton was a big man, bearded, of approximately sixty years of age. In life he might have been bluff and hearty, save that Miss Jones' narrative of his reticence did not fit such a description, however much his physical person might have justified it. Horton had died, apparently, just after he had taken a drink, for two glasses still stood before him on the table, one empty, the other half-emptied. Whiskey and soda stood on a tray on one end of the table. The manner of Horton's death was plain to see; his throat had been cut from ear to ear; he made a grotesque and horrible sight. A bloody knife of some foreign manufacture lay on the floor beneath his right hand, as if he had dropped it there. Quite evident in the confining room, despite an open window, was the unmistakable smell of ammonia.

The police-inspector watched Pons' examination of the room and its effects with no attempt to conceal his interest and, when Pons at last directed his attention to the body, after Dr. Quinn had completed his examination, he inquired whether Pons might not like to hear what Mrs. Hamish had to say.

"If it will in no way incommode you, inspector," agreed Pons.

"By no means, Mr. Pons. It may well be that you will catch something I am likely to miss."

Pons smiled wryly. "I fear you, like my good friend, Dr. Parker, put too much confidence in my poor powers."

The police-inspector interviewed a still tearful Ethel Hamish in the kitchen. Miss Jones' cousin was one of those bland-faced women whose features, no matter how emotional, inevitably suggest comparison with members of the equine family. Nevertheless, despite her near-hysteria, she told a straightforward story under the watchful eyes of Miss Jones, who saw her through her story and then discreetly left the room when the inspector began to question her.

Mrs. Hamish had been about her duties all morning without other interruption than the mail, which had consisted of but one magazine and two daily papers. She had taken this in to Horton as soon as the postman had left it. Then she had prepared and taken in his lunch. He had not gone out on any occasion. Shortly after lunch, however, the Reverend Francis Birch, the local vicar, had called; he was soliciting for charity. Horton had permitted him to be shown into his study, and he had evidently given him a contribution, for the vicar thanked him profusely when Horton saw him to the door; Ethel had heard their conversation from backstairs. Half an hour later a beggar had come to the back door, but Mrs. Hamish had not opened to him. Thereupon he went around to the front, where she had had to open the door and demand that he go away, though she was filled with pity for him and at the same time intrigued by him. He was a paralytic, whose whole right side seemed to have suffered the effects of a stroke, for he dragged his right foot and got around only with the aid of a stout stick. He was accompanied by a bird, which sat on his shoulder. He refused to accept Ethel's dismissal, and demanded word with the master. Horton had overheard the altercation and came out of his study, calling out, "Here, Ethel, what's all this?"

Then he had caught sight of the beggar. "It's this beggar, Mr. Horton," Mrs. Hamish had explained. "He won't be off, though I've told him." Horton had come up to the door and looked at the beggar. He had muttered something. It sounded like "MacKaugh," but Mrs. Hamish could not now be certain. To her surprise, Horton had dismissed her and invited the beggar into his study. Soon thereafter he had come to the kitchen for whiskey and soda. What he and the beggar had talked about, she did not know. But Horton had sounded genial when he saw the beggar to the door; Mrs. Hamish had heard them speaking from upstairs. She had watched the beggar go off down the street, while Horton returned to the study. Then she heard Horton call to her, to tell her to take the whiskey and soda away when she found time. She did not think she had to hurry; he had not sounded urgent. She took her time. She had not heard him call again, but the beggar was still in sight far down the road with that bird of his flying after him, when at last she went downstairs and discovered Horton as they saw him.

The study had not seemed to her altered in any respect, since her last visit to it, save that a window stood wide open. She did not know whether Horton had opened it, or whether one of his visitors had done so.

"There is one important question, Mrs. Hamish," said the inspector, who had carefully refrained from interrupting her statement. "You are quite certain you saw the beggar you describe going off down the street when your employer called to you?"

"Yes, sir."

"And how long a time would you say passed between the moment he called you and the time you discovered Mr. Horton dead?"

"P'raps a quarter of an hour."

"And the beggar was still in sight at this time?"

She nodded. "You see, sir, he walked very slow-like. A real cripple he was. And there's no houses on this side of the street; you can see for quite a way."

"Well, it would seem probable that Mr. Horton took his own life, but in case the finding should be otherwise, it would then be possible that someone entered the study through the open window during that interval and took his life."

"I suppose so. There was no one come through the doors, that I'll swear."

"You heard nothing in the study to suggest a struggle?"

"Nothing, sir."

The inspector turned to my companion, who had preserved a reflective silence. "Would you like to ask anything, Mr. Pons?"

"I submit that the mendicant's feathered companion does not seem to have been adequately described," said Pons. "I daresay Mrs. Hamish must have noticed it. How big was it, Mrs. Hamish? As big as a rook, a raven, a kestrel?"

"As big as a kestrel, sir."

"It was not a familiar bird?"

"No, sir."

"Ah, the bird of ill omen or ill passage, most likely," said Pons dryly. "And the beggar, Mrs. Hamish. How old would you say he was?"

"Real old." She was hesitant; then she added, "More than sixty. Being like he was, crippled and all, it was hard to tell."

"And Mr. Horton – did he appear to be upset at the sight of his visitor?"

"He was surprised. I could see it by the way he looked. But I thought it was the seeing of that bird on his shoulder."

"Did Mr. Horton seem in any way disturbed when he came to the kitchen for whiskey and soda?"

"No, sir. He was more like his old self than he had been for weeks – months, you might say. Almost cheerful, he was."

"Mrs. Hamish, there is in the study a mild smell of ammonia. Did you at any time in the course of the morning have occasion to use ammonia in that room?"

"I did not enter the study until I brought Mr. Horton his mail," said Mrs. Hamish with prim severity, quite as if Pons had suggested that she had been guilty of a misdemeanor. "We never use ammonia in the house."

"And in a partially open drawer of the table, there is a revolver. It was Mr. Horton's?"

"Yes, sir."

"Thank you, Mrs. Hamish. Come, Parker, I would like a word with Miss Jones."

The inspector interposed, firmly but respectfully, his watchful eyes fixed on Pons' face. "Is there anything you especially noticed, Mr. Pons?" he asked.

"I would commend to your attention particularly the mendicant's curious companion," said Pons, and passed by, as if unaware of the bafflement that shone forth in Police-Inspector Martin's ruddy face.

Miss Jones received us with a face devoid of emotion, though there was stony regret in her voice when she said briefly, "I waited too long, I fear, Mr. Pons. I cannot believe Mr. Horton took his own life."

"We shall discover that in good time," answered Pons. "Can you now suggest any source for the smell of ammonia which still lingers in the study?"

"No, Mr. Pons, I cannot."

Pons deliberated for a moment. "You mentioned that your late employer was in the habit of corresponding sparely. Can you give me the names of his regular correspondents? Particularly, I suggest, someone in Lowestoft?"

"I believe I could find them for you, Mr. Pons."

"You mentioned Mr. Horton's receipt of a cablegram some months ago. Did Mr. Horton retain it?"

"Yes, I know just where it is. Excuse me."

She left the room at once, with purpose in her step. I sought to catch Pons' eye, for certain of his questions and the recommendations he had made to the accommodating police-inspector mystified me; but he did not glance in my direction, and sat lost in thought, toying with the lobe of his left ear, a habit in his preoccupation.

Miss Jones returned and handed Pons the cablegram she had mentioned. Pons read it and passed it on to me without comment. It, too, was addressed to Jabez Hindon, and bore this cryptic message:

> MATTER OF BURKE'S ESTATE ALL SETTLED. THE OLD MAN IS FREE AS FAR AS KNOWN. ALL MY BEST WISHES. FAREWELL.

It was signed simply H.

"And here," added Miss Jones, "are the names and addresses of his regular correspondents. There were but two, and these envelopes are representative of many among his papers."

"Douglas Harrigan, Lowestoft," read Pons. "And Zaharias Heggett, of Norwich. They are almost in the immediate vicinity; certainly neither place is very far from Bury St. Edmunds, either by road or by rail. I shall just take these envelopes with me, Miss Jones. What of their contents?"

"Unless they have been impounded by the police, they are in the study. Mr. Horton's body has been removed."

"Let us just see, if you please, Miss Jones."

The three of us descended to the study, where the inspector was in charge. Miss Jones went straight to the desk, opened a side drawer, and drew forth a packet of letters which she offered to Pons.

"With your leave, Inspector," said Pons.

"Certainly, Mr. Pons. I shall be grateful for any assistance you may be able to give me."

"Very well, then, let us just examine these letters, which have come to Mr. Horton from friends in Lowestoft and Norwich. There are not many; neither man appears to have been a verbose correspondent. What we are looking for, Inspector, is certain information which we may find in these letters from a day approximately four months ago when Mr. Horton received this cablegram."

Pons handed the cablegram to Inspector Martin, and while the inspector puzzled over it, he busied himself with the letters, sorting rapidly through the pile.

"Now here we are," he said. "Last winter. The letters appear to be but the usual round of trivial events, set forth from one man to an old friend. They are written in fortnightly intervals. Now, then," he went on, riffling through the pile, "the date of the cablegram is April twenty-seventh, and here is a letter postmarked the twenty-eighth at Lowestoft." He opened the envelope in his hand, took out the letter, unfolded it, and read "'A cable from H. You have probably also had one. What are we to do?' Admirably succinict, our Mr. Harrigan."

He turned the letter over to Inspector Martin and picked up another. "Ah, here is one from Mr. Heggett in the same vein. How commendably reticent these gentlemen are! And here is Mr. Harrigan, evidently in answer to Horton's reply. 'Sit tight, indeed! We have done nothing else for these last twelve years.

Let us not wait, but go out to meet him. H. would know where to reach him. I am cabling him today.' Our Mr. Harrigan, at least, is forehanded. Here is yet another, dated the following day."

As Pons opened the letter, a clipping dropped out. He caught it deftly, but gave his attention first to the covering letter. "Ah, this is most terse of all. 'Too late'." He turned to the clipping, read it silently to himself, and placed it without comment on the desk for all to see. It was clearly a clipping from a metropolitan paper, the typeface of which suggested the *News of the World*. It was headed *Guymon Director Dies*, and was concise.

> Capetown (Reuters): – Alastair Higby, late of Guymon Diamonds, Ltd., was found dead in bed early this morning by his manservant at his home of Boerwal Road, Capetown. A preliminary report indicated that Mr. Higby took his own life. He had been in ill health for some time, and had been despondent and melancholy for the past few days. Mr. Higby retired from the directorate of Guymon Diamonds, Ltd., eight years ago.

We had hardly finished reading this before Pons placed beside it a once-crumpled rectangle of paper, upon which were pasted five letters, clipped from printed headlines. All were the same letter, and across one had been placed a large X, in a shaky hand.

"That is all," said Pons. "We hardly need more."

"I'm afraid this is all very puzzling, Mr. Pons," said the inspector.

But Pons was looking at his watch with an air of absorption. "I fear there is not much time to be lost, Inspector. Dr. Parker and I are off to Lowestoft to call on Mr. Douglas Harrigan. I shall be happy to communicate any little discoveries I may make. Good evening, Miss Jones."

When we were seated once more in a train on the way to Lowestoft, fortunately in a compartment empty of other passengers, I observed that the problem presented by Miss Jones was a mystifying one, indeed, and added, "Not the least part of it, I should point out, was your own conduct of it, Pons."

"On the contrary," answered my companion, "the whole thing is as plain as a pikestaff, and my conduct would surely have been completely explicable to anyone but that good young police-inspector, who was, alas!, too much impressed with our presence to use his wits. I have come to expect this obstinacy in the face of the elementary from you, Parker, but I am always distressed by it in our constabulary."

"Obstinacy, indeed!" I protested. "I am certainly not thickheaded enough to believe for an instant that Horton killed himself. He was clearly murdered, but by whom, I would not at this point presume to say. I may say, however, that I suspect the man MacKaugh."

At this my companion burst into laughter which was nothing short of uproarious. Noticing my stolid refusal to join in his laughter at whatever had touched him, he controlled himself.

"Pray forgive me, Parker, but you have an uncanny faculty for rousing what must surely seem a too often dormant sense of humor," he said. "It had not occurred to me that you had so misunderstood. There is no man named MacKaugh involved in the matter, I assure you. There is only a native South American bird known as a macaw, the companion of that curious figure, the paralytic mendicant. But come, Parker, you have all the facts; you need only reconstruct them properly."

"It could not have been the vicar," I began slowly.

"Dear me! Why are we always so willing and ready to exculpate the clergy, who have certainly as much opportunity to commit crimes as other professional men?"

"And the beggar, by all accounts, would hardly be a match for a man as strong as Horton must have been."

"Ah, that leaves us with the macaw," said Pons with impish sobriety. Then he smiled and raised one eyebrow, lending his aquiline features an expression that was almost Mephistophelian. "The smell of ammonia suggests nothing to you? Let me elucidate a little. You may have noticed on the floor around the body small fragments of glass, varying in thickness."

I confessed I had not noticed them, though I had been aware of Pons' scrutiny of the floor about the bloodstained dagger.

"What does this added fact convey to you, in the light of events?"

"That something was broken."

Pons closed his eyes. He sighed. "Let us go back to the beginning. Mr. Hindon arrives here fourteen years ago..."

"The name is Horton, Pons."

"Is it, indeed? I wonder. Let us just postulate that Horton is the assumed name, Hindon the correct one. At least, it is safe to assume that Hindon was the name he used up to fourteen years ago. I submit that his anonymous correspondent deliberately used his old name as an added factor in inspiring fear, for he was the only one who had no reason to fear anyone. Hindon's South African correspondent used his alias, and his cablegram began this sequence of events. You will recall its wording: 'Matter of Burke's estate all settled. The old man is free as far as known. All my best wishes. Farewell.' Now this is plain as a pikestaff; one of the most elementary ciphers is involved. Taking every fifth word we have a clear warning: 'All is known. Farewell.'"

"But how do you arrive at every fifth word, Pons."

"Why, it is elementary, Parker. It would be the natural figure to suggest itself because there were five men involved in the problem."

"What five men?" I asked in bewilderment.

Pons clucked his disapproval. "Dear me, Parker, this is child's play. It is all clear enough. There were originally five men whose names began with H. They were banded together in some form of association or unified by some common deed. They were thus the five H's. Now, if you were one of them, and you wished to communicate with another without signing your name but only your initial, how would you identify yourself to your correspondent? Surely you would assume a number. Thus there could have been H, H 2, H 3, H 4 and H 5."

"Ah, the diamond dagger!"

"Precisely, Parker. It was signed 'H 5', as you saw. And Mr. Higby, surely, was H. Mr. Hindon or Horton, if you prefer, could have been one of three – H 2, H 3 or H 4. His friends Harrigan and Heggett bore the remaining numbers. Thus you will plainly understand the significance of the printed communication which our late friend received from Southampton and which Miss Jones thought he had destroyed, though he had saved it from oblivion after crumpling it up. The crossed-out H represented Mr. Higby; the score was one to three. Hindon understood very well. And he was not unaware of the significance of the progressively nearing places of mailing – first Capetown, then the port of Southampton, finally London; someone was coming steadily closer. The diamond dagger came from London; this could have been nothing more or less than a warning of death; this, too, Hindon understood; he rushed off at once to take council with Mr. Harrigan of

Lowestoft, and perhaps the two of them telephoned through to Heggett of Norwich. If they held a council of war, they must have decided to stand pat."

"You are suggesting that the beggar is H 5?" I inquired incredulously.

"Surely it is obvious? You will recall the manner of his communication, the ragged cutting of the letters? He is not left-handed; his right side is very largely paralyzed; he cannot write."

"And a man of but a quarter of Horton's strength would have been able to toss him from the room like a paperweight,"

I retorted.

"That is only too true, in any ordinary circumstance."

"And you will recall that the maid's testimony was not shaken – the beggar was well down the street the last time she spoke to her employer. She is his best witness."

"You are a stubborn man, Parker," said Pons, nodding. "I fear I cannot cope with such stubbornness."

"We are left with the open window, and I am afraid, Pons, that it is too much to expect me to believe that the beggar came back and crawled into the room through the window when even the door must have been enough for him to manage. Someone, then, went through the window. It was not the Reverend Birch, and it was most certainly not the beggar, since that would have been simply beyond his ability to do, always assuming that his paralysis was genuine."

"I think we may be certain of that."

"Very well, then. The window was obviously the place of entrance and escape."

"Certainly someone escaped by it. I concede so much. But I am afraid that the only person who did get through that open window was Horton."

"Or Hindon, since you prefer it so."

Pons shook his head, with a little smile about his lips. "This time, no, my dear Parker. Horton, not Hindon."

With this exhibition of sheer contentiousness, Pons lapsed into thoughtful silence, from which I was disinclined to rouse him. He sat unmoving, save for the lighting of his calabash, until the train drew into Lowestoft at dusk. For my own part, I could not very well contain my feeling of triumph, even though I had learned from experience it might be short-lived.

Our quarry, Douglas Harrigan, proved to be a tall, thin-faced man past middle age. He was not unlike Pons in appearance, and I saw at a professional glance that he was a sick man who had not very many more months to live. We did not succeed in getting in to see him until Pons sent in a note; then Harrigan, who lived alone with one manservant, sent for us. We found him bundled up in a dressing-gown in a small sitting-room.

"So it has come to this," he murmured at our entrance. "I know you by reputation, Mr. Pons." He turned to his servant. "Leave us, William." After he had gone, Harrigan asked, "Which one of them called you in, sir?"

"The late Mr. Hindon's housekeeper," answered Pons. Harrigan's eyes narrowed, and his jaw jutted briefly forth. "So, Hindon is gone, too!"

"And Heggett?"

"Only a day ago, Mr. Pons. Suicide!" He laughed bitterly. "Higby, Heggett – now Hindon. Only I am left; it is between us two now. It will be either Hrenville or me. Well, I am ready for him."

"But not, I fancy, as ready as I am. He will surprise you, Mr. Harrigan. He is a paralytic; his right side is virtually useless; he has difficulty in walking. He has not the strength of a rabbit."

"And yet three men have died after he threatened them?" asked Harrigan in manifest disbelief.

"And you will be the fourth, unless I can prevail upon you to permit me to take your place when he calls. We are not unlike in appearance. A little grease paint, and I may be able to deceive him."

"I can fight my battles alone."

"Pray overlook my insistence. His methods are strange."

"Sir, I will permit your concealment in the room. And your companion's. But I will stand against him myself."

Pons looked about for convenient hiding places, his eyes lingering on a doorway to an adjoining room, on a cabinet against one wall. "Very well, Mr. Harrigan. I daresay he will call on you either tonight or tomorrow morning. He will hardly dare to let much more time elapse, or the coincidence of his presence on the scene of death in Bury St. Edmunds and Norwich will arouse a hue and cry for him. Now, then, we have not much time. I am in some doubt only about what happened in Capetown fourteen years ago."

Harrigan hesitated for some time, staring straight ahead of him. Clearly, he was struggling against the habit of the long silence under which he had lived with his secret. But at last he sighed and spoke.

"I suppose it will all come out in good time, anyway. And it cannot matter now to anyone but myself. The five of us were banded together in a plan to loot Guymon Diamonds, Ltd. Higby was the brains; he planned and the rest of us carried out his plans. We looted the firm both in the mines and at the office; it was systematic, and we knew we were bound to be discovered. But Higby had plans for that moment of discovery; the four of us were to take the blame, but before our arrest, we were to dynamite one of the least productive of the mines and be 'caught' in the cave-in."

"But it did not go according to plan, I take it?"

"No, Mr. Pons, it did not. Almost, but not quite. We went down into the mine, we set the time fuses, and we slipped out without being seen. Higby's car was waiting for us. But Hrenville didn't get out in time, and there were others in the mine; there weren't supposed to be. Two other men were killed, and Hrenville was badly mangled, which is undoubtedly the reason for his paralysis. Hrenville was the only one recovered, and because it was assumed that the rest of us had been buried in the cave-in, it was Hrenville who had to bear the prosecution for the looting. Higby, of course, was in the clear, and though Hrenville blamed us for his capture, and for letting him take thirteen years in prison, which was what they gave him, there was nothing we could do. Higby slipped us out of South Africa, and we came back to England under assumed names. We made very few changes, but settled in parts of the country which were far enough away from our native places to avoid any chance of meeting anyone we knew. Higby faithfully divided the loot, and held Hrenville's share for him when he turned up. It was considerable, Mr. Pons.

"Well, when Hrenville got out, he demanded more than his share. Higby balked. So Hrenville got nasty. I looked for that to happen, all along. I wanted to deal with Hrenville, but before I got through to Higby, he was gone. Whether it was Hrenville's work or not, I don't know. It might be that Higby took his own life; he had lived for so long as a solid, respectable citizen, that he could hardly have faced life without that respectability. He may have done it. But not Hindon, and not Heggett. My own name was originally Harrison; Heggett's was Haggerty. You see, we made but slight changes, just enough to avoid identification. Hrenville and Higby had no need to alter their names." He shrugged. "I don't know that it matters now, except as a principle. Hrenville lives only for his vengeance. I, like all the others, have received my warning."

"The diamond dagger."

He nodded. "Hrenville follows such rules as we had. Oh, we were clever thieves, Mr. Pons! But that was long ago, now. It seems hardly to be believed."

At this point in Harrigan's reminiscence, the doorbell pealed.

A momentary silence fell in the room. Outside sounded the footsteps of Harrigan's manservant on his way to answer the door.

"William!" Harrigan called sharply.

His man appeared on the threshold. "You called?"

"William, if that is a cripple at the door, show him in here. I will see him. I expect him."

William withdrew, and Harrigan waved us away. "It could be no one else, gentlemen. Conceal yourselves."

"I will take the cabinet, Parker; you take the adjoining room. Follow my signal, but keep your nostrils protected."

We took our places, myself with my eye to the keyhole of the door behind which I was concealed. In but a little while, William ushered into the room we had just quitted a wisp of a man, a pathetic figure in reality, who dragged himself along with the aid of a stick, and was seemingly unable to walk except by dint of lurching hideously from side to side. To one shoulder clung a silent bird with a hooked beak and a long, sweeping tail. It was brightly colored, and wore white patches of feathers around each eye.

Hrenville lurched to a position directly before Harrigan. "Ye were expectin' me, Mr. Harrigan?"

"I was, Mr. Hrenville." He turned to his man. "You may go, William. I will call when I am ready for you."

"I'm not much of a man, Harrigan," said Hrenville in a thin, whining voice.

"Half man, half bird," said Harrigan, contemptuously. "What are you here for? A half-man like you sending threats!"

"I wanted to see ye before ye died, Harrigan," said Hrenville slowly, with an almost benign expression on his twisted face.

"Old times. Old crimes, eh? And new, too!" He cackled with laughter. Then suddenly, leering at Harrigan, he swayed on his stick and asked, "What do ye think o' my bird, Harrigan?"

"Parrot, is it?"

"Macaw. The most remarkable macaw you ever did see." He turned to the bird, fawning upon it. "Ye've heard the man, Mac. Talk to him."

"'Parrot, is it?'" mimicked the parrot in a perfect reproduction of Harrigan's voice.

"Say some more, pet," whispered Hrenville.

"'Half-man, half-bird. What are you here for? A half-man like you sending threats! You may go, William. Parrot, is it?'"

The macaw preened his feathers, chuckled, and was still.

"And if I was to say to you, 'Good night, Mr. Harrigan?" Hrenville went on, his eyes fixed on the bird. "What would you be saying'?"

"Good night, Mr. Hrenville." The parrot reconsidered. "Good night, my friend."

"We've had a good little talk, Mr. Harrigan."

"We have, indeed," said the macaw.

"And then, afterward," said Hrenville in a horrible voice, "I would whistle and he would come to me. See – " he turned once more to his feathered companion. "Go to the door now, Mac."

Obediently the bird flew to the door by way of which Hrenville had entered the room. There it perched high on top of the frame, waiting.

"Do ye mind if I show you what a remarkable bird that is?" asked Hrenville.

"Go ahead," said Harrigan.

"I'll need to open a window."

"Right over there," said Harrigan.

Hrenville dragged himself to a window and opened it. He came back to where Harrigan sat. Harrigan watched him intently, puzzled and off his guard. Hrenville came close to the chair, fumbling with some baubles in his hand. Two of them rolled from his fingers. He bent to retrieve them.

"Ye'll have to forgive me, Harrigan. I'm not the man I was. We're gettin' old, the both of us."

But when he looked up again, pulling himself up along his stick, he had something wadded in his nostrils. At the same moment, Harrigan began to claw at his throat, choking and gasping. The thing in Hrenville's left hand was a dagger.

With a bound and a flying leap, Pons was out of the cabinet and upon Hrenville. It took but a moment to push Hrenville aside, knock the weapon from his hand, and drag the chair with Harrigan in it away. By that time, I too, was in the room, my nostrils covered with my handkerchief, for I had recognized the gas fumes which were choking Harrigan, and which had been released when Hrenville had stepped upon the ampules containing the concentrated fumes of ammonia, strong enough to have put Harrigan into a stupor for sufficient time to permit Hrenville to cut his throat.

Hearing the commotion, William, too, came into the room, armed with a small but serviceable revolver.

"This man," said Pons, "is to be delivered to Police-Inspector Martin of Bury St. Edmunds, charged with the murder of Jabez Hindon, alias Horton." He turned to Harrigan. "As for you, Mr. Harrigan, I am afraid that our report will of necessity include the affair of the looting of Guymon Diamonds, Ltd."

Harrigan smiled a bitter smile. "I will never stand trial, Mr. Pons."

On the train back to London, we were accompanied by the remarkable macaw which belonged to the paralytic Hrenville. The bird sat decorously on Pons' shoulder, preening itself, as if aware of the role it had played and the role it might yet need to play at Hrenville's trial.

"I trust that the matter has now been solved to your satisfaction, Parker," said my companion, not without a glint of humor in his eyes.

"Yes, yes, I see it all," I said testily. "The ammonia fumes stupified Hindon, and the parrot spoke in his voice after Hindon was dead. Hrenville left him in the room, and at his whistle, the parrot spoke his last line, which was coached him by his owner, and then the bird flew out of the window."

"Elementary, my dear fellow," said Pons. "It was really obvious from the beginning, when Mrs. Hamish testified to seeing the bird 'flying after' Hrenville. So it was indeed the 'Horton' she had heard who escaped by means of the open window, just as the bird would have made off tonight. And how ingenious of Hrenville to send the macaw far enough away from the fumes, high on the door frame! What a time and patience of training he must have put in on this remarkable bird! As a matter of fact, I know just the place for him once the trial is over. You will recall that little service Her Majesty performed for us as a reward for some trifling errand we did for her? She caused my brother to be knighted. I believe she would appreciate the gift of this bird."

He turned to the macaw, imitating Hrenville's voice.

"What do you say, Pet?"

The macaw cocked its head at Pons and said gravely, "Elementary, my dear fellow." He swayed on Pons' shoulders and peered at me, adding, "What a time and patience of training he must have put in on this remarkable bird!"

For more details and a full list of titles:

visit https://www.hachetteindia.com/home/yellowbacks

WELCOME BACK TO THE GOLDEN AGE

Edgar
Wallace
THE COMPLETE J. G.
REEDER STORIES

E.W.
HORNUNG
THE COMPLETE RAFFLES

Edgar
Wallace
THE COMPLETE JUST MEN
VOLUME 2

Arthur
Morrison
THE COMPLETE MARTIN
HEWITT COLLECTION
VOLUME 1

E. Phillips
Oppenheim
THE GREAT
IMPERSONATION

Allan
Pinkerton
THE EXPRESSMAN AND
THE DETECTIVE

H. Rider Haggard
MR. MEESON'S WILL

Melville Davisson Post
MASTER OF MYSTERIES
THE COMPLETE UNCLE ABNER COLLECTION

Jack London
THE ASSASSINATION BUREAU LTD.

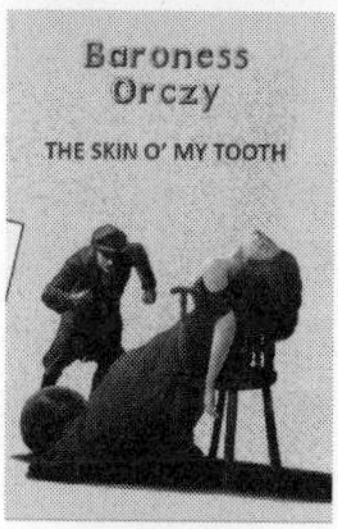
Baroness Orczy
THE SKIN O' MY TOOTH

Earl Derr Biggers
SEVEN KEYS TO BALDPATE

Horace Walpole
THE CASTLE OF OTRANTO

Sexton Blake
THE SEXTON BLAKE COLLECTION
VOLUME 1

Francis Beeding
THE HOUSE OF DR. EDWARDES

A. E. W. Mason
AT THE VILLA ROSE

Fergus Hume
THE MILLIONAIRE MYSTERY

Donald Henderson
A VOICE LIKE VELVET

Richard Hallas
YOU PLAY THE BLACK AND THE RED COMES UP